WOUNDS

Also available by Sara Blædel

Louise Rick/Camilla Lind Series
The Midnight Witness
The Silent Women
The Drowned Girl
The Night Women
The Running Girl
The Stolen Angel
The Forgotten Girls
The Killing Forest
The Lost Woman
A Harmless Lie
The Silent Widow
The Death of Elin
The Woman in the Hotel (short story)

Family Secrets Series
The Undertaker's Daughter
Her Father's Secret
The Third Sister

Also available by Mads Peder Nordbo

Matthew Cave Series
The Girl Without Skin
Cold Fear

WOUNDS

A NOVEL

**SARA BLÆDEL AND
MADS PEDER NORDBO**

NEW YORK

Books should be disposed of and recycled according to local requirements.
All paper materials used are FSC compliant.

This is a work of fiction. All of the names, characters, organizations, places, and events portrayed in this novel are either products of the author's imagination or are used fictitiously. Any resemblance to real or actual events, locales, or persons, living or dead, is entirely coincidental.

Copyright © 2025 by Sara Blædel and Mads Peder Nordbo

All rights reserved.

Published in the United States by Crooked Lane Books, an imprint of The Quick Brown Fox & Company LLC.

Crooked Lane Books and its logo are trademarks of The Quick Brown Fox & Company LLC.

Library of Congress Catalog-in-Publication data available upon request.

ISBN (hardcover): 979-8-89242-167-6
ISBN (paperback): 979-8-89242-272-7
ISBN (ebook): 979-8-89242-168-3

Cover design by Meghan Deist

Printed in the United States.

www.crookedlanebooks.com

Crooked Lane Books
34 West 27th St., 10th Floor
New York, NY 10001

First Edition: August 2025

The authorized representative in the EU for product safety and compliance is eucomply OÜ Pärnu mnt 139b-14, 11317 Tallinn, Estonia, hello@eucompliancepartner.com, +33757690241

10 9 8 7 6 5 4 3 2 1

CHAPTER

1

THE BODY WAS lying on moss-covered flagstones close to the gable end of the disused inn. The forensic team's powerful floodlights illuminated the peeling, whitewashed limestone wall. Even from a distance, Liam Stark could see the outline of a body under the tarpaulin in the white pavilion they had erected to protect the site and keep prying eyes away.

On his way there, he had received a short briefing that a dead body had been found behind the abandoned building. The report was quickly supported by the first officers on the scene, who reported to dispatch that the deceased was an unidentified middle-aged man. The officer had told Liam that they'd presumed he was probably destitute, judging by his disheveled appearance.

"A couple of kids found him," Frank announced as he made his way toward Liam, pulling down his hood and removing his hairnet. The pathologist, along with a crime technician, had completed the site investigation. Frank nodded toward the tarpaulin, adding that Liam was welcome to look at the body now.

It had stopped raining, but the atmosphere was still damp, and occasional drops of rain still fell from the surroundings. The square behind the old building was muddy, and in front of what had once been the kitchen entrance to the inn, weeds grew in abundance. Liam leaned forward to lift a corner of the green tarpaulin. He caught a glimpse of a furrowed face and registered how dark wisps of hair lay across the man's forehead before instinctively taking a step back when the pungent smell rising from the corpse hit him.

"Has he been here long?" he asked, turning to the crime technician who had participated in the site investigation. The technician had been on his way across the courtyard to join his colleagues from the National Forensic Service but instead had come back to help Liam. He looked down at the body, shrugging his shoulders.

Liam pulled the plastic cover completely aside, and together they looked at the dead man.

"You'd think so looking at the condition of the body," the crime technician began, but then shook his head. "But it doesn't look like the tarpaulin has been on the ground for very long. If he had been here for longer, we would see that photosynthesis had stopped under the covered area."

"Photosynthesis?" Liam squatted down next to the body. The man reeked of urine and dirt. And blood.

"Any vegetation under the tarpaulin would wither without light. And that's not the case here. Also, the relatively warm and sunny weather we've been having lately would have started the process of decay as the temperature under the tarpaulin rose. That doesn't seem to have happened either, but it's too early to say for sure. I could be wrong, and we will continue our investigation once the body has

WOUNDS

been taken away. But if you ask me right now, which in essence is what you're doing, I'd say that the preliminary investigations indicate that he was placed here under the tarpaulin after the onset of death, and that he hasn't been here that long." The crime technician turned to Frank. "But Master here can probably make a more educated guess on the time of death and how long he's been here."

The pathologist had an expression of concentration on his face, signaling that now was not the time for jokes or idle chitchat. "I need more time before we move the body," he said.

"Do you think we're dealing with a homicide?" Liam asked, even though he sensed it was too early to start pushing for answers and knew the pathologist might shut down and get angry as a result.

But Frank nodded and added dryly that it would be hard as hell to imagine that the man had rolled himself up in the tarpaulin to take a nap outside when he could have gone inside. "The door is broken open, you can just walk in. But there's also something else . . ."

He carefully put the hairnet and hood back on and squatted down next to Liam but with his back to him, bent over the dead man on the ground.

Liam looked expectantly at Frank's back, but nothing more came. The pathologist was apparently thinking hard and didn't seem to be bothered by the fact that they were waiting for him to go on. Liam felt the cold of the ground penetrate his clothes. He had left in a hurry and had only brought his fleece sweater for warmth.

The call from Dybbøl was the lifeline he had been waiting for all day. During two days off work while still on call, he hadn't received a single message from work. In the past, this would have been a dream come true, but now it was just the opposite. The phone had been glued to his hand from the moment he got out of bed, and it had been on the table on top of his napkin when he ate dinner with his parents. Actually, it was Dea Torp that the chief constable wanted to send to the dead man behind the inn, but before Dybbøl could speak, Liam, with a deep sense of relief washing over him, had hurriedly announced that he would go there straightaway.

He had felt his mother's gaze on him but ignored it and promptly got up from the dinner table, and before the pot was placed on the trivet, he was out the door.

He had felt disgusted with himself. An embarrassment that he knew his parents saw through. He couldn't stand his situation. Liam Stark, fifty-one years old, deputy chief inspector in the Reactive Criminal Investigations Department, Odense Police. Address: mother and father's house in South Funen. It was fucking pathetic. And now he was cold and regretted leaving the house so abruptly. And to top it all off, he was starving too.

After he separated from Helene, every day had felt like a new day in prison. They had been together for twenty years, and now he was back to square one. It was pitiful, pathetic, and embarrassing that he had moved back to his old room in his parents' organic, self-sufficient farmhouse with the two elderly people milling around all day at a snail's pace, fixing things and wanting him to be happy. So any opportunity to work instead of being there to help his father in the garden was so welcome that he had immediately refused to disturb Dea, even though it was undoubtedly her turn if the score were to be evened out.

He put his hands in his pockets and looked at Frank expectantly, but knew it wouldn't pay to push any further until Frank was ready. Then he shrugged and walked toward Thorbjørn. His colleague was standing with a small group of locals who had gathered in the cobbled parking lot. On the worn end wall of the inn stood the name *Verninge Inn* in rusty iron letters that clearly showed signs of decay and lack of maintenance. The building stared blankly at the small crowd from its row of black windows.

"These two young men found him," Thorbjørn said, pointing to two teenage boys in hoodies and skater pants.

Liam introduced himself and held out his hand. As he got closer, he could see their pale, tense faces in the streetlight. They couldn't be much older than thirteen or fourteen. "Do you usually hang out here behind the inn?"

One nodded while the other shook his head vigorously. Liam concentrated on the one who had nodded. "When was the last time you were here?"

The two boys exchanged quick glances, but neither of them had time to say anything before Thorbjørn told them the technicians had found joint roaches not far from where the deceased lay.

"Do you know anything about that?" Liam asked instead. Now they both stood silent, staring straight down at the ground.

Thorbjørn took over—there was something about his height and stature that had a special effect on young people in particular. As if some of the investigator's brute strength had already cracked their defenses. The two boys stirred uneasily as he calmly began to explain that the abandoned roaches had just been collected by the Forensics Department and that they would soon have the DNA of the people who had smoked those joints. "This means that you might as well have left your name and address. If it's you who's been smoking weed, we'll know soon enough. And then we'll have to have a serious talk with your parents." Thorbjørn paused and smiled at the boys. "There is, of course, another option, which is that you admit you're the ones who usually hang out here behind the inn and can therefore tell us if this man was here on Friday. Then maybe we don't have to talk about joints anymore."

"He definitely wasn't there on Friday," the taller of the two blurted out.

"When were you here on Friday?" Liam asked.

"After school. We were here until we had to go home to eat," the tall one said, before continuing frantically, "Now you won't need to say anything about this to anyone, right?"

Liam was about to say that they might have to, but he didn't have time before Thorbjørn promised the boys that at least they didn't have to worry about that anymore.

"And you're absolutely sure?" he asked instead.

Now they both nodded.

"Definitely, because of where he's located, so you have to pass him if you want to go into the inn, and we usually go in there and sit when we meet after school. We would totally have seen him."

"And what time did you head home?"

"I have to be home at six, so it was probably quarter past when we set off," the tall one explained. His friend nodded in agreement.

"And you definitely weren't back over the weekend?" Liam asked.

WOUNDS

They both shook their heads. "No, we were only here on Friday."

"Have you noticed anything over the past few days that isn't usually here? Anything at all? A car? Voices? Headlights?"

They both shook their heads almost imperceptibly.

"Do you know of anyone else who comes here?" Thorbjørn asked. "I mean others who illegally enter and . . ."

"It's not illegal to be here; there's no one here," interrupted the otherwise quiet boy.

"It's illegal to trespass on private property, but we'll overlook that if you help us out here."

Liam found himself smiling at his younger colleague's cowboy tricks. He was playing at making the two boys feel like they were in a TV thriller. But fair enough if it got them talking, Liam thought, and left the boys to Thorbjørn, while he himself went back toward the back of the inn to ask the technicians if he could have a look inside.

* * *

On the way back, he leaned against the window to look into the inn itself, but he could only see so much in the glow of the streetlight. He formed a funnel with his hands and stuck his head right up to the window, but then he instantly retreated. All he could see was himself. His hair was unkempt and his auburn beard needed a trim.

Darkness was closing in around the inn, with just the white light from the floodlights illuminating small, sharply defined areas. Liam bumped into a couple of old trash cans and a pile of discarded plastic chairs stacked in a rickety tower and tucked away in a small nook. He took out his flashlight and continued toward the back door. It seemed that Frank had finished with the body and the thinking, and when he spotted Liam, he waved him over and announced that the deceased would be taken to Forensic Medicine within ten minutes.

"I'm planning on doing the autopsy as early as tonight."

Liam looked at him, his eyebrows raised in surprise. Normally, at least a couple of days would go by before they could expect an autopsy report. The body was again covered by the tarp, but Frank signaled with a toss of his head for Liam to follow.

They both squatted down again before Frank carefully lifted the plastic cover to reveal the upper half of the man's body. He pulled a latex glove onto his right hand in a practiced manner before lifting up the corpse's dirty shirt and exposing the man's torso. With his other hand, he pulled a small Maglite from his pocket and aimed the beam at the man's chest.

"Look at these wounds. He has them all over his body," he said, shining his light over several uneven scars that looked like flaps cut into the skin and pulled together with rough stitches. "That's probably not the cause of death. But I'd like to know what the hell this is."

CHAPTER

2

"NO COMMENT," CHIEF Constable Margrethe Dybbøl said briefly. "As we have already announced, a press conference on the Amalie Vedel case will be held tomorrow at nine o'clock." She disconnected the phone call and looked again at the case spread across her kitchen table.

She tried hard to push away the possibility of another murder that would require manpower. Manpower that would have to be taken from the ongoing investigation, and she had none to give. The familiar tightness in her chest made her reach for the White Russian her husband had made for her after the evening coffee they had enjoyed at opposite ends of the house. She in the kitchen with her laptop and police reports, he in the office down the hall. They worked too much. That was a fact, she thought, straining to hear if any music was being played in Zenia's room but not hearing anything. Maybe her daughter had left without her realizing it. She picked up her cell phone to see if Zenia had sent a message.

But all that had arrived was a text message from Liam Stark briefly stating that the autopsy would begin as soon as the deceased male was brought to the forensic medicine institute. This did not bode well, she thought.

Dybbøl had called him several times, but each time his phone went straight to voicemail, and to be honest, she had her hands full with the press conference tomorrow anyway. She drained the glass and licked the cream off her upper lip as she enjoyed the effects of the alcohol, which soothed the anxiety that the heavy workload stirred in her. She won't get much sleep tonight either.

Fourteen days had passed since seventeen-year-old Amalie Vedel disappeared from her home where she lived with her parents. The case was already being touted as a new Emilie Meng case, and she felt that after the first week of getting nowhere, they were doomed by the public to fail. But that couldn't happen, she had told her husband when he'd pulled out a chair and sat down next to her earlier that evening.

"Did you screw up?" he had asked. The overweight Labrador that had been lying at Dybbøl's feet had stood up and put its snout on his thigh, as if it needed to point out that it had been ignored all evening.

"No, we just haven't found the slightest thing that points to a crime, but the media, as you know, is convinced that one took place."

The fact was, they didn't have many clues to go on. The girl had left home somewhere between four fifteen PM, when her mother had left to go shopping and pick up her little brother from soccer practice, and five PM, when her father came home from work. She hadn't left a message, as the family usually did on the blackboard hanging in the kitchen. Instead, she had left her cell phone in her room. Something she would never normally do, both her parents claimed. Whether she had taken money with her, neither parent could say for sure. She had an afternoon job in a shoe store, and the money she earned there was her own. They didn't know how much money she had. What the police had been able to provide so far was that the girl had withdrawn DKK 5,300 from her account, leaving a balance of just DKK 14.75.

Dybbøl started making notes of the information she could release during the next day's press conference. They hadn't mentioned the bank account yet. She knew she would be flayed over that information because it made it look like the young girl had planned to leave as she emptied her account, which clashed with the fact that she had left her cell phone in her room and had apparently not taken anything with her. But this was again a sticking point, because her parents didn't actually know if there were any clothes missing from her closet. They also had difficulty identifying their daughter's circle of friends. They were sure she still saw a couple of old school friends, but new friends had been made since she started high school, and they didn't know any of them.

* * *

Margrethe Dybbøl looked up as her daughter strode past the door to the hallway. "Zenia?"

The tall girl came back, pulling an anorak over her head. "What?"

"Are you on your way out?" Dybbøl looked at the clock. It was late, almost ten PM.

"Why?"

"Because we were going to talk about your birthday." She could tell right away that it sounded wrong. Almost reproachful, as though it was her daughter who hadn't had the time. When they cleaned up after dinner, they had agreed they would discuss the celebration. Her eighteenth birthday was in two weeks, and the only thing that was certain was that her daughter had asked that her aunt and uncle not be invited. Lis wore real fur and Lars went hunting, neither of which matched her daughter's values.

It had almost triggered one of their endless discussions. But Søren had managed to turn their attention to the spinach lasagna he had quickly placed on the table. Her husband was so much better at dealing with the fact that their daughter had become an animal activist than she was.

Now the evening was almost over. She had been so immersed in her work that she had forgotten all about birthday preparations.

"Come on, sit down," she offered, gathering the police reports to clear some space. "Let's talk about what you want."

"Buns, cake, REMA's hazelnut spread . . . family."

"There's a bit more to it than that," Dybbøl said, feeling a bit offended. "It's a big day! We could have it in a restaurant, or order catering from outside and have long tables down the hall?"

"No, I'd prefer it if we just did what we normally do." Zenia reiterated that she didn't want Lis and Lars there.

"I can't not invite them just because you have something against fur. They've been here for your seventeen other birthdays."

"Yes, but it's different now, and they know how I feel about fur!"

"Yes, thank you!" Dybbøl replied, barely holding back a sigh.

"I guess it's my day," said Zenia. She stood in the doorway, clearly eager to get going.

"Yes, but it would be nice if you didn't have to be such an activist about everything all the time."

"Activist! It's not being a fucking activist to be against animal abuse! It's common sense, and you could learn something from it."

"Why don't we just . . ." Dybbøl tried.

"You and Dad aren't much better," her daughter continued, reaching into her backpack. "Invite them if it's so important, but don't buy regular Nutella; it's full of palm oil."

"I'll remember that," said Dybbøl. "Zenia, I just want you to have a good day!"

"I know . . . thanks . . . I just can't stand them. They won't even try to understand or just so much as listen when I try to explain. It's like he thinks it's hilarious to talk about hunting and dead animals with Dad when he's sure I'm within earshot. It's not. It's fucking provocative."

Dybbøl knew she was in over her head, but she also felt a responsibility to help her daughter adjust her social compass.

"You could also try to accept that not everyone thinks exactly like you."

"So I should accept that people exploit and kill animals. Nice one, Mom!"

"That's exactly what I mean, Zenia. You can't be mad at the whole world because it doesn't think like you."

"So if a majority is in favor of rape, it's just something we have to accept?"

"Stop! You can't compare rape to hunting pheasants!"

"That wasn't the point anyway."

Dybbøl realized that she was tired and that she needed to pull herself together so that the conversation didn't go completely off the rails. "You will make life easier for yourself if you try to accept that others sometimes have different views to yours."

"Accept that the rest of you think it's okay to breed solely for killing and eating? No thanks!"

"You're going to have to tone down that attitude, Zenia, otherwise life will always be an uphill struggle," she tried again.

"Tone it down yourself!" Zenia sneered and turned around.

"With whom?" Dybbøl shouted after her. She got up quickly and hurried out into the hallway, but only just in time to see her daughter slam the front door behind her.

She stood for a moment looking out toward the garden path, feeling the simmering irritation she was struggling to contain. This was not how she had raised her daughter. Not even close. Inclusiveness and understanding had always been high on the list, but they had obviously failed. She decided that she needed to talk to her husband about it. Søren was better at dealing with Zenia when she was being so stubborn. But it had to be on the other side of the Amalie Vedel case.

She went back to the kitchen table, sat down at her laptop, and looked at the screen in resignation. "All of us in the old house on Morelvej would be happy to see you at ZENIA's 18th birthday party on—"

WOUNDS   15

That was as far as she got.

* * *

"Can't Liam take some of this stuff off your hands? Isn't that what a deputy chief inspector is supposed to do? It shouldn't be the chief constable herself sitting up late into the night," her husband said as he came into the kitchen with his empty glass and asked if she needed anything. "A cup of chamomile tea to help you sleep?"

Dybbøl shrugged.

"I try to spare him a little; he's under pressure at home. He's going through a divorce and has just moved. Plus he just took the case that came in tonight."

"You have to take care of yourself once in a while," Søren said calmly. "Maybe you and Zenia could go on a weekend trip, go to a spa or something? Or all three of us could go to the boathouse where we used to fish. It's been a long time since we've been there."

Dybbøl nodded, wondering if their daughter would be more at ease and less in opposition to everything if she had a mother who didn't work all the time. A mother who went on weekend trips and suggested they do something together. She accepted the cup her husband held out to her and shook her head when he asked if she wanted to go to bed.

"I have to write this godforsaken report!"

"Have you not had any news at all?" he asked, pulling out the chair in front of her.

"We have nothing, that's the problem. They're coming for me tomorrow." She shook her head. "I don't have a grip on the situation. I can't even control my own daughter!"

Her voice became husky due to how tired she was. Søren stood up and gave her shoulder a squeeze through her thick, beige shawl.

"I'm going to take Lady for a walk, and when I come back, I'll take my wife to bed." The dog excitedly got to her feet and scampered out into the hallway.

"Yes, you do that." She reached for his hand and gave it a squeeze. "I'm going to invite a couple of Zenia's friends for lunch soon so we can talk about her birthday. Maybe we should organize some kind of surprise; don't you think she'd enjoy that?"

He smiled at her and said that it probably shouldn't be a barbecue.

"I was a little rough on her before she left."

"I heard that."

"She's going to have a hard time in life with that attitude, and I know deep down she's not like that. She's the sweetest and most caring person. I really want her to understand how hard it is for those around her when she acts like this."

Her husband had put on his coat when he came back into the kitchen.

"Maybe she just needs some space," he suggested. "Maybe we should try to go with it. All young people need to rebel. They need something to care about, something to fight for. They need a place to feel at home and to feel like they can make a difference. That they have a voice that is heard. We shouldn't be so upset about that. I think we should be happy that our daughter has values that she feels strongly about. Would you rather have a daughter who knows about all the beautifying filters on TikTok and

Instagram, someone whose values are about looking perfect in her selfies? Because there are a lot of young girls like that, and I know what I'd rather have."

Dybbøl was exhausted. She knew he had a point and didn't really have the energy to go on with this conversation.

"Where was she going?" she asked instead of answering.

"She didn't say anything to me," he replied, and clicked the leash on Lady's collar.

"What about when she's coming home?"

"No, I just heard you guys talking before she left."

Dybbøl reached for her cell phone and texted Zenia, asking her to let her know where she was and when she would be back.

"It's fall break," Søren reminded her.

"Yes, but still. She knows I'm working on the Amalie case, and all parents are naturally a little more concerned about their teenage daughters at the moment," she said.

"So you think there's been a crime?" her husband asked her from the doorway.

"When a seventeen-year-old girl disappears and is still missing after fifteen days, we definitely consider it a probability that a crime has taken place."

CHAPTER

3

LIAM PULLED OVER, stopped the car, and stepped out into the cool of the fall night. For a moment he closed his eyes and took a breath deep into his lungs. His mother stubbornly insisted that if you went outside once a day and took ten deep breaths, you would never get sick, and that it worked best in freezing weather.

He looked at the house and saw no lights on. Helene and the children were probably fast asleep. It was past midnight, and he still had an hour before he had to report to the forensic pathologist's office. He had considered driving to work and taking a power nap but instead had driven to the house that had been his home until a month and a half ago.

He found it hard to come to terms with the fact that he wasn't in there himself. In the bed they had bought together shortly after they had their first child. In general, it was hard to understand what had happened. When and why it had gone so wrong. He hadn't felt it happening, but of course he knew that his work was too much. Far too much. And he had let it happen . . . until Helene had had enough.

It wasn't just now, she had said. It was year after year after year, when she and the children always came last. "There are always dead people. Always victims and causes. And they are always just that little bit more important than the rest of us. I don't want to do this anymore. I can't do it anymore."

He wanted to go in and crawl into bed with her. But his wife had made it very clear that she knew what she was doing. There was no going back. It was her choice, not his. He missed her. God, how he missed her. Missed lying there at night, listening to her breathing, which he knew like the back of his hand after their twenty years of communal life.

Above him and the house, the stars shone brightly in the night sky. It was the high season for shooting stars. When Andreas and Laura were little, they had often stayed out in the garden with deck chairs and blankets and stared into the infinite depths to catch the tiny lines gliding brightly across the sky. The children were big now, but not so big that he couldn't easily tell where they placed the blame for the divorce.

He sat back down in his car. He resigned himself to the fact that it wasn't going to be a night with much sleep, and that was fine. He was beginning to appreciate steering clear of dreams and too many thoughts. A short nap on the office couch when he was done at Forensics would have to do.

He switched on the seat heater, turned the radio on, and rubbed his tired face before heading toward Odense. Helene was right again. It was almost one o'clock, and for the rest of the night he would focus on a dead person instead of crawling under the covers to lie next to his wife's warm body.

* * *

Liam rang the bell at the large glass doors to the Institute of Forensic Medicine at Odense University Hospital. The institute was a bit secluded but within walking distance of the hospital itself, and during the day, it was nigh on impossible to find somewhere to park.

After a short wait, forensic technician Robin appeared. He showed little sign of fatigue as he let him through the glass doors.

"You're up late," Liam said.

"My girlfriend is at a cactus conference in Saint Louis, so I might as well take the shift."

They followed each other down the hallway.

"Cactus? Is she as nerdy as you, then?"

Robin laughed. "She works at Plantorama; she's away on business . . . It's actually a cactus and succulent conference."

When they reached the autopsy room, they parted ways.

"I'm going back to my desk," Robin said, "but of course you can call me if you need me."

The young man hurried back to his lair, which, when Liam had last looked in, looked more like a cartoon geek's playground, with tables, chairs, and shelves crammed with figurines, masks, wigs, replica weapons, books, loose sheets, LEGOs, cacti, and all manner of boxes and cans. He pushed open the swinging door to the high-ceilinged autopsy room. He'd never quite gotten used to the medicinal smell and the clinical feeling of entering the sterile rooms. The long steel table with a drain at one end. The many meters

WOUNDS 21

of square white tiles from floor to ceiling. He pulled a gown over his shirt and donned a hairnet before walking toward Frank, who was standing in the autopsy booth at the end of the hall.

The pathologist looked up briefly from the body and saluted, and Liam squinted at the small chalkboard on the wall by the autopsy table. Frank had already filled in some of the victim's data. Height and weight. Brain. Lungs. Liver. Spleen. Thymus. Everything looked normal, except perhaps for the height-to-weight ratio.

"I made us some coffee," Frank said, pointing to a metal table on wheels near the door. "You can help yourself."

Liam nodded and studied the naked body on the steel table. The man was lean and sinewy, as expected. "What can you tell me about him?"

"Unidentified white male, Danish in appearance, very slim, or lean, I should say. Tall and with a fine set of teeth. About sixty years old. Well groomed."

"So not homeless?" Liam asked, looking at the clothes folded in a pile ready to be taken to his colleagues at Forensics.

"It doesn't look like it. Or at least not over a long period of time. He's taken good care of his teeth, and his clothes are actually in really good condition; they're just filthy."

The skin shone bluish and pale in the cold light emitted by the large lamps. The chest had been cut open and closed again. But that wasn't what caught Liam's eye; the many scars on his torso did. They differed in size and weren't identical. They looked like the doors on an advent calendar cut into the skin. Around the incisions, the skin appeared red and irritated, and between the incisions, it was white, like skin that had not yet healed and grown back.

"What the hell is that?" Liam looked at the patchwork that had been sloppily sewn together to cover the man's body. The freshness of the wounds and scars varied. Some seemed completely fresh, while others looked almost healed. He looked at Frank.

"I have no idea. I haven't seen anything like this before, but I can say that it happened before the man passed away."

"Could he have done it himself?"

"It's possible, but I doubt it." He was silent for a moment, as if searching for an explanation. "The flaps of skin have been cut free from the subcutaneous tissue. A scalpel was probably used. It's been incredibly painful. But yes, it could theoretically be him; I just find it very hard to imagine that you would subject yourself to that kind of self-torture, but anything is possible, I guess, and bizarre acts have happened before—"

"Does he have scars like that on his back?" Liam interrupted.

"No, there are no scars on the back of the body, but there are traces of fixation around the wrists and ankles. And as you'll see in a moment when I turn him over, there are bedsores in several places on the back of the body."

"So you're saying he's been restrained for an extended period of time?" Liam asked, leaning forward as the pathologist lifted the lean body to let him see his back.

"I'm not saying anything; I'm just stating that the man has been lying on his back a lot in recent weeks. And that his hands and legs have been restrained for an extended period of time."

"That would also explain the urine," Liam added. The pungent odor had been so strong that it couldn't have come from just a single urination, but rather old urine that had dried into the clothes, and now that the man lay undressed in front of them, it was clear to see that the urine had left a large red rash.

"Perineal dermatitis," Frank nodded, adding that it was also common on the back of the body. "Occurs when the skin has too much contact with moisture and substances found in urine and feces over a long period of time." He spoke into his Dictaphone.

"Cause of death?" Liam dared to ask. He knew Frank didn't like to be interrupted.

"Asphyxiation," the pathologist quickly replied. "Crushed larynx. It was a little hard to spot at the scene because there were no obvious bruises on the neck, but I found pinpoint bleeding in both eyes. And our scan confirmed that there is damage to the throat. So, yes, the man was definitely strangled. But it's more the rest of the abuse that's of interest to me."

Frank examined the pale body of the deceased. "The oldest scars are two weeks old, they're all in various stages of healing, so he was alive when some of these were inflicted on him."

He pointed down to one of the man's wrists. "If we compare the time perspective of the healing process with the assumption that the man has been restrained, I think there is good reason to believe that he has been injured. That it was done against his will, and that he has been locked up for a long period of time or at least prevented from moving freely. This is also consistent with the emaciated body."

He was silent for a moment before continuing, "If so, this is one of the most brutal cases I've come across. As I said, it must have been incredibly painful, but it is also

24   SARA BLÆDEL AND MADS PEDER NORDBO

absolutely devastating for the victim's psyche . . . This abuse has resulted in both physical and psychological torture."

Frank looked back at the victim. "The skin has been loosened and then put back on so it can heal. It's been like being skinned alive bit by bit."

"When you say loosened, how deep is the cut? Is it professionally done? A surgeon, a doctor?"

"The skin is a much tougher organ than people normally think, and we can do several different transplants. In this case, most of the scars are cut deep, but not into the muscle tissue. The incisions are mainly in the dermis and subcutaneous tissue, and because there has been one side of each square that hasn't been touched, there has been a good blood flow, so the skin has grown back, but new scars have been added all the time, so the pain has also been increasing." Frank nodded to himself. "I don't want to believe it's a doctor who has cut these patches of skin free, but I simply can't say for sure."

"Okay." Liam nodded thoughtfully. "So he's been lying there cut up for a few weeks, but how long do you estimate he's been dead?"

"Not long. He was dead for four hours at most before you found him, so you can do the math."

"So around five PM yesterday?" Liam said. Frank nodded.

"It was cold out there yesterday, so there may be a slight inaccuracy. But it was around that time, and that will also be the time that will be in the autopsy report."

"The technicians don't think he died at the inn but that he was placed there under the tarpaulin. What do you think about that?"

"I agree. He didn't die exactly where he was lying, but based on the site report and the preliminary autopsy alone, I can't say for sure whether he was killed out there. We've done nail scrapings, and as you can see, the deceased has superficial abrasions on his hands, and there were also marks on his trouser knees. This could indicate that he tried to get away, to flee the scene, and was then suffocated. But it's more up to Forensics to uncover that part when they know if the soil under his fingernails came from the place where we found him."

Liam looked again at the pile of clothes on the table. "So we just have to find out who he is?"

Frank nodded. "I'll do my best to push for a quick DNA analysis, and tomorrow morning, I'll initiate the dental identification process. We'll get the whole package going so we can get a name for him."

"Thanks," Liam quickly replied. It was two o'clock, and by eight o'clock they should be able to identify the man.

"There's something else you need to see. Something that might also help us identify the man."

Frank had sat down in front of his PC, which stood on a high table, and pushed the mouse. "This X-ray was taken when he was brought in, and as you can see, the deceased has an injury to his back, which I believe has restricted his mobility, and"—he clicked on a new image—"he has also suffered a fracture of the right femur."

"Is the damage old or more recent?"

"They're not new injuries," Frank replied. "I think it's reasonably likely that the two injuries combined have incapacitated him for some time and perhaps even disabled him to the extent that he hasn't been able to work since the accident, but of course it depends very much on the nature of the job."

"Can you say anything about how he could have gotten those injuries? A traffic accident? A fall?"

"No, not now, but we can be more precise about how old the injuries are and what caused them; it just requires more specific studies of fractures and healing, which we will of course do." Frank looked intently at the lit screen with the X-ray photos on it. "But . . . yes. The femur and back look like they date back to the same time." He hesitated. "A fall would be my early guess . . . from at least a few meters. It takes a lot to break the femur." He pointed to the last image. "The femur hasn't healed very well, which might indicate that it happened in a country with a less stable healthcare system; alternatively, the man wasn't in a cast long enough." He looked at Liam. "But that's conjecture. However, I would say with a little more conviction that you're looking for a man who limped or perhaps couldn't walk at all."

"But . . ." Liam looked searchingly from the image to the dead man's body.

"If you're thinking of asking if there's a connection between the scars and the bone damage," Frank said, "I'll have to disappoint you; you'll probably find out before we do."

Liam gave Frank a crooked smile. "You know me too well. When would it make sense to come by again?"

"We're going to take a break for a couple of hours, and then we'll continue with further examinations tomorrow. I'll let you know."

"I'm busy myself tomorrow morning, we have a press conference, but I can come over afterwards?"

WOUNDS   27

"Is that the Vedel case? I thought you weren't on it?"

"I'm still head of the Reactive Department, so I have to go down and show my face to the media."

"Any news about the girl?"

"Nada, she's vanished into thin air, and now Dybbøl is doing her best to keep us on good terms with the press so they don't despise us and hinder the investigation too much. She's hoping for some peace and quiet so we can concentrate on actually finding the girl . . . ideally alive and well."

CHAPTER

4

D EA TORP STRETCHED sleepily and felt warmth pulsating through her body. She felt lulled into a sense of security she had not felt for a long time. It hadn't featured in her life at all since she lost her husband. A part of her died with him, or at least it had felt like that for many years. She hadn't thought much about carnal pleasures in the years that had passed. In fact, she loathed the expression. She had repressed anything resembling intimacy, had pushed it away, preferring to keep her distance and hide away. Cold, Liam had called her when they talked about it. But now the heat was present in every cell of her body, her skin was sweaty, she was relaxed and . . . well, almost happy, she thought, reaching out to the other side of the double bed. But it was empty.

Dazed by sex and the previous evening's wine, she propped herself up using her elbows. It was nice to be able to stay in bed and come to slowly on a Tuesday. She reached for her cell phone on the bedside table. It was almost eight o'clock, and there were five missed calls from Liam and two from Dybbøl.

WOUNDS   29

She threw the phone onto the duvet and let herself fall back into the pillows. She was off duty and wasn't even on call.

She heard him in the kitchen and smelled coffee. She pulled the duvet up to her chin and closed her eyes. "What have you done to deserve this fortune?" her grandmother would have said. Now she repeated the words to herself. He was thirteen years younger than her. The first time they were naked together, she had been ashamed, but she forgot all about giving a shit the moment she felt the desire, both his and her own. Now she didn't give what she looked like a second thought. On the other hand, she thought a lot about how messy it was that they worked together.

They had flirted. Or rather, he had flirted so overtly that everyone noticed when he came in in the afternoon and sat down on her desk. In uniform, completely irresistible. But they hadn't officially announced that they had become a couple. Liam knew, and maybe a few others, but otherwise they tried to keep a lid on it.

Her cell phone rang again. She didn't bother looking at who it was. She had "Do Not Disturb" turned on, so only calls from Liam and her daughter were getting through. And it wasn't her daughter. They weren't really talking at the moment. It was as if her daughter saw it as a personal insult that Dea had found happiness and was infatuated again. Dea couldn't take it.

The door to the bedroom opened, and Rolf came in with a breakfast tray. Not once in her seventeen years of marriage had she been served breakfast in bed. Now she had it several times a week.

Her cell phone rang again.

Her colleague from the canine patrol unit nodded toward the nightstand. "Go ahead and take it."

"I'm off duty," she reminded him.

He smiled and poured coffee from the coffeepot into the mug they had bought together in Ebeltoft. They had stayed at the Molskroen Hotel on their first real date. She was the one who invited him, and it had gotten off to an awkward start because he didn't appreciate gourmet menus quite as much as she did. In fact, he had just wanted a steak, but there wasn't one to be had. She had ordered more wine and a shot with their post-meal coffee, and the evening had ended well.

Her cell phone rang again, and she finally surrendered.

"We'll need you in today," Liam announced without so much as a hello. He seemed tense and not in the mood for any objections to be raised.

"I'm off," she tried anyway.

"Days off are suspended until further notice," he stated, telling her to get to the police station as soon as she could.

"Fuck you," she muttered. It wasn't directed at him. Nor was it directed at her being ordered to work; such were the rules of the game in Reactive—the criminal investigations department. It was directed at herself. Like a little girl, she had ignored her calls while she floated around in this love bubble that sometimes made her feel like she was suffering from monumental madness. She was unable to control the desire and lust she experienced and felt far too old for it.

"Important?" Rolf asked, handing her a cup topped with warm milk. He ran a finger down her cheek, and his eyes locked on hers. That was all it took for a shiver to run through her again.

WOUNDS

"A dead body. I think they're just under pressure because the Amalie case is going nowhere fast. Have you finished searching the last areas north of Odense?"

He nodded.

"We're going to search areas down around Nyborg today; we'll meet there at ten o'clock. Right now it seems like Dybbøl is flying blind. There is no system in where she sends the search teams. We've already searched a radius of twenty kilometers from the girl's home."

Dea nodded. Rolf came from the North Zealand Police force and had only been on Funen since spring, yet he and his German shepherd Ask, with their vast experience and skill set, were the first to be called out when the canine patrol unit was needed.

"I agree with Lene that everything indicates the girl was picked up by a car. Either she was forced into one or she went in of her own free will. If she had moved on foot, the dogs would have picked up a scent we could go after," he continued.

Inspector Lene Eriksen, head of investigation in the Amalie Vedel case, was Dea's direct competitor in the investigation hierarchy. She nodded, having thought the same thing herself. They had found no witnesses. There simply wasn't a single person who had seen the young woman that afternoon or since. She hadn't been caught on any of the surveillance footage they had access to. She wasn't seen at gas stations or ATMs, nor at the train station. Right now, a small group of investigators were reviewing the highway department's security footage from the highway, and Dea considered herself lucky that it wasn't her job to do so.

They were also conducting surveillance from the Great Belt. Dea thought for a moment about her young colleague Nassrin. She would have hated the job; she would have grumbled and complained that it was always the young police trainees who were assigned this kind of routine work. Dea was struck by the familiar grief she often felt when she thought about her and the fact that they had lost her. She'd died in the line of duty, and it would have been better in every way if she had sat through boring routine work instead.

"Hello," Rolf whispered, and she realized he was pulling the straps of her camisole down over her shoulders.

She shook off her thoughts and shooed him away before she threw the comforter aside and headed for the bathroom. She made it halfway across the living room before regretting it and running back to throw herself at him again.

* * *

"Do you want to ride with me, or are you driving yourself?" he asked as they stood in the courtyard. He had already let Ask into the back of his large station wagon and was heading toward the door to the boiler room. Rolf lived on a four-acre farm in Nårup that had belonged to his family since 1882, but he'd only recently moved in himself. He had inherited the farm from a childless uncle, and the first six months had been spent fixing up the farmhouse. It had all worked out well. After he took over the farm, the position on Funen was advertised, and he left North Zealand. He had big plans for the place, and Dea couldn't help but get swept up in his enthusiasm when he talked about all his ideas. His commitment was

WOUNDS   33

based on the joy he felt for the place and its surroundings, which wasn't hard to understand.

She felt a sense of joy herself, waking up to the view of the surrounding landscape. She took a deep breath and inhaled the scent of autumn, being reminded of the many Morten Korch stories she has read depicting rural Denmark. It was as if a calming hand had been placed on her shoulder, as if she'd entered a pocket of time that she could sink into for a moment and find rest. An old walnut tree stood in the middle of the courtyard, and fallen green-and-black orbs full of nuts were scattered around the yard, ready to be picked up and dried. Rolf's uncle had made schnapps from them, and there was still an impressive collection of bottles of the cognac-like schnapps in the house's utility room.

Dea followed Rolf to the boiler room. She hadn't even had time to explore the other buildings that had once housed a reputable plastics factory but had long since closed down. The last time the machines had been running was sometime in the late nineties. She hadn't explored the fields around the property either, although she had planned to go for a run in the area on a few occasions. It just never materialized, as they had spent their time together instead. But she had been out in the barn; during her first visit to the farm, Rolf had insisted on taking her for a ride along the edge of the forest in the big Massey Ferguson. She had also been instructed to keep an eye on the pellet stove because it was the only source of heat in the house, so it had to be kept going.

"Rolf?"

He wasn't in the boiler room. She slid a door open and came through the old cloakroom. It wasn't very big, but big enough for the employees to hang their coats up back in the day. Curious, she continued to the old workshop floor and got the feeling that everything was as it had been when it was abandoned all those years ago. Large machines, boxes, tables and conveyor belts. All around were small stable windows in the long outer walls, while the gable wall at the end of the room consisted of three colossally high gable windows in rusty iron with beautifully rounded arches at the top, and only now did she notice the beamed ceiling, displaying exposed beams all the way to the top.

"Imagine if you could do this room up," she said, turning to Rolf, who had come in and stood behind her.

She went to turn on the lights, but the switches didn't work. "You can," he said. "I'm having some plans drawn up. I want to have the whole length of it converted into living space, then maybe I can rent the farmhouse out."

There was a view of the fields and forest beyond, and even though dawn was just breaking, the light was almost magical.

"What's in those rooms over there?" she asked, pointing to a pair of mahogany-brown doors.

"Offices. It was originally stables until 1892, when my great-grandfather converted the farm into a dairy farm, and then in 1977 my grandfather converted it into the plastics factory."

"Did you come here as a child?"

"No, not really. I probably only inherited it because there was no one else."

Dea picked up a thin, dusty plastic spoon. "Did they make these?"

"Among other things," Rolf said, taking the spoon and brushing the dust off it.

WOUNDS   35

Dea walked over to an orange box on the wall. The box read *MAIN SWITCH* in black lettering. "Does it all still work?"

"Are you going to start molding spoons, or should we get to work?" he asked with a laugh.

"I guess we should probably get to work."

He waved his hand around. "It all works: the furnace, the molds, the sanding belt, the packaging machine. It can all run, even though it's been sitting there for all these years. It wasn't that long ago that I tested it."

She grabbed the main switch with both hands and pressed it down. The system kicked in, and the lights came on in a few places. Several of the old machines began to whir. The large, dusty spiderwebs that crisscrossed the huge room glittered in the bright artificial light. She could feel his hand caressing her arm and then his lips against her neck. As much as she was enjoying the moment, she wriggled free and said they really had better get going.

CHAPTER

5

Margrethe Dybbøl briefly greeted Dea Torp as she made her way to the press conference. Her colleague of the same age looked refreshed and happy as she walked down the corridor with a coffee cup in her hand. In fact, she exuded everything Dybbøl herself felt drained of. Most of all, job satisfaction.

Dybbøl smoothed down her jacket and glanced at her notes one last time before joining Liam and signaling that she was ready. She perceived his scrutinizing gaze and knew she looked like hell. She'd hardly slept a wink. After she and Søren went to bed, she had gotten up again to run through the case and her notes one last time. At three AM, Zenia still hadn't come home, nor had she responded to the messages she had sent her. Dybbøl had stayed up until half past four to wait, but her daughter didn't appear. She'd decided she wanted to apologize. She had been too harsh, and Søren was right. There were so many things their daughter could have developed into, and an activist was certainly not the worst. She shouldn't be reprimanded for taking responsibility for the world she grew up in. As Dybbøl sat there in the kitchen waiting, she had also concluded that she and Søren would be fine if they introduced a few more meat-free days in their weekly meal plans.

It was now ten AM. Zenia still hadn't given any sign of life, and a renewed irritation shot through Dybbøl's body. Here she was, having to perform, being held accountable for failing to find a young girl who had disappeared, and all the while, her own daughter hadn't even bothered to send a short message to put her mind at ease. *That's what you might call having your head up your own ass,* she thought.

With irritation quivering just under the surface, she opened the door and stepped out into the waiting crowd of journalists. It was the first time they had held a major press conference on the case, and many had gathered in the police station's rear courtyard. Normally she wasn't a fan of large press conferences, especially in cases where they were in such a tight spot, but there was so much guesswork in the press that they had to try to take some kind of control, if only to be able to refer to their own statements from the press conference going forward. This made the job a lot easier for those in charge of the media when calls came in on the matter.

She gathered herself and painted a smile on her face before nodding around in a friendly manner. "Thank you for coming . . ." She cleared her throat. "I'm Chief Constable Margrethe Dybbøl," she began, before introducing Liam and the lead investigator on the case, Lene Eriksen. She turned briefly to the two to signal that they were in this together. Then she started.

"As you all know, seventeen-year-old Amalie Vedel has now been missing for fifteen days. She went home after classes at the Odense Cathedral School. We know that Amalie cycled home from school as usual, as several witnesses saw her on the paths through the city and in Dalum, where she lives with her parents. We would like to ask anyone who saw Amalie on this route to contact the police. We are very interested to know whether she was seen in the company of anyone.

"Photos of her route will be sent to the editorial offices. We know that she made it home after school and that she then disappeared between four fifteen PM and five PM, a period of forty-five minutes after her mother left home and before her father came back from work."

Dybbøl paused for a moment before disclosing the new information they had. "Her cell phone was left in her room with her school bag when her parents came back. However, I hasten to add that we have not yet found any signs of foul play. I say this because shortly before she disappeared, the young girl emptied her savings account and withdrew fifty-three hundred kroner."

Dybbøl looked out over the group of journalists with a firm and determined gaze before continuing. "We are investigating the case as a possible crime, but it is important to emphasize that we still consider it likely that there is another explanation for her disappearance."

She hoped they understood that it was too early to rule out that the girl could still turn up safe and sound. She nodded to Lene. "I now give the floor to the head of investigation, Lene Eriksen. She will answer any questions about the case, but as you can understand, we don't have much to

WOUNDS 39

work with, so this is very much an appeal to citizens to contact us with information that may lead to new knowledge about Amalie Vedel's whereabouts from the time she disappeared up to now."

Lene came and stood next to Dybbøl with a stiff smile. Hands flew up. Lene pointed to a young woman from *Stiftstidende*.

"Amalie has been missing without a trace for fifteen days. And even though you say it's still possible that she'll turn up safe and sound, doesn't that suggest that a crime has been committed? Shouldn't you already be doing everything you can to find her?"

"We've done everything we can. Right now there are dog patrols out across parts of Funen. And"—she spoke with extra emphasis—"this is the second time they are searching these areas. The matter has our full attention."

"It wasn't many months ago that several citizens were killed in the case from Tommerup. Could the same person be behind Amalie Vedel's disappearance?" the woman continued, ignoring the others who were ready with their questions. "Are you sure you caught the right culprit then so that it won't happen again now?"

Dybbøl quickly looked at Liam and wondered if he should be the one to answer, as it had been his case, but she let Lene continue.

"There's no doubt that we found the right culprit this summer, and we can say with certainty that the case is solved." Lene pointed to another journalist.

"Morten, *Ekstra Bladet*. Why is the investigation in the doldrums after just two weeks? Don't we live in a society where we can see what everyone is doing if we want to? Are you covering up your team's sloppiness at the beginning of your investigation?"

Lene didn't flinch as she turned to the journalist. "As you know, a victimless case is a bit special, but I want to make it clear that we have gone through Amalie's home with a fine-tooth comb. We've searched her high school and interviewed her friends. We've been through her cell phone data. We have combed through all relevant security footage from the area around her home. And we've expanded the investigation into surveillance. We've interviewed potential witnesses at key locations. We have followed up on one citizen report after another. We are in constant contact with her parents. I can't say it any clearer than that. There are no clues. There is no sign of where she is or what has happened since she left her home."

"Isn't it very unusual for a seventeen-year-old to leave their cell phone in their room?" Morten followed up.

"Yes, and it's partly because of that phone that Amalie's parents have contacted us. But the vast majority of people who disappear want to be left alone until they choose to reappear."

Good answer, Dybbøl thought, nodding approvingly to her investigation leader.

"Mogens from *Politiken,*" a man broke in without being invited to speak. "Has Amalie disappeared like this before?"

"Amalie has previously been out of contact on weekends when she went on trips with friends to other parts of the country, but we have of course questioned all those friends, without it leading to anything in this specific case." Lene Eriksen looked around at the many hands that were raised with a steady gaze before selecting a journalist and pointing toward her. "Last question."

WOUNDS 41

"Mette, *Dagbladenes Bureau*. If someone abducted Amalie, wouldn't you know about it by now?"

"Unfortunately, it's not that simple, but when you look at Amalie's family, who are ordinary wage earners, it's unlikely that she was kidnapped for ransom."

"What I mean," Mette continued, "is that if someone has abducted her and they haven't made themselves known for the past two weeks, the chances of them letting Amalie turn up alive again are pretty slim, right? Aren't you thinking rape and murder?"

"That's very specific, and I can't answer that based on our knowledge and preliminary investigation," Lene said.

"But you don't hold a young girl captive for no reason, and if no one has heard anything, then . . ."

"There's no indication that she's being held captive." Liam took over before the speculation got too out of hand. "We have nothing to indicate that this is an abduction, so let's call it a day for now."

"Yes," agreed Dybbøl. "Thank you very much for your attendance and support. The essence of this meeting is that we're asking for your help in requesting information that can lead us in the direction of Amalie Vedel." She hesitated. "And of course, as always, you are welcome to contact us."

Hands flew up again, and a chorus of questions were shouted out simultaneously. Dybbøl nodded to Liam and Lene to indicate that they were ready to leave.

* * *

Liam had rushed off to the Institute of Forensic Medicine as soon as the press conference was over. Frank had stationed himself by the entrance and was ready to greet him. Liam quickly marched up the last few steps, and as the sliding door slid open, he asked if they had managed to identify the man.

"Unfortunately, not yet." Frank led him down a hallway with a row of offices and pointed to some orange chairs around a table. "But I have an autopsy report for you, which I've also sent you by email. But there's something we need to consider."

He sat down in one of the orange chairs and laid the report on the table. "I contacted a good friend at the Trauma Center to see if they had encountered injuries like the ones we have on the victim, and the answer is yes."

"The broken bones or the scars?" Liam looked at him inquisitively and felt some energy build up in his body. He could have done without the Dybbøl press conference. He would never get used to the feeling of standing there like a prop while the chief constable held court. But she didn't fail to remind him that it was part of the job when you were the head of a department. He had barely paid attention while it was going on; it was none of his business and his mind had been elsewhere. He'd slept for four hours on the couch in the corner of the office, and after splashing a little water on his face, he'd put yesterday's clothes back on. But now the tiredness was gone and he was listening to Frank intently.

"The scars . . . There's something called blood kink or blood play, and it's basically a form of fetishism."

"And it looks like this?"

"I can't say whether the injuries look exactly like blood play, but my point is that although the deceased's torso looks dramatic, these are superficial wounds that might well be a fetish of some kind."

Frank pulled out some prints from under the autopsy report and pushed them over to Liam. "This is something that's on the internet for everyone to see, but it's not very nice to look at. Bloody bodies. Cuts and bruises. A bizarre fascination, if you ask me," said the forensic scientist, who didn't usually come across as squeamish. "You can google blood fetish or blood play yourself if you need to see more. I'm not saying this is the explanation, but I think it's worth looking into."

Liam looked at the sheets. "When I hear words like *kink* and think about the fact that the man has apparently been restrained for a long time, I think about BDSM."

Frank stroked his chin thoughtfully and seemed to agree.

Liam read a section in the autopsy report. "Did you find any evidence of a sexual nature?"

"We can tell if there has been ejaculation or if it's been close by looking at sperm formation and the amount of semen in the scrotum, and in this case there was no ejaculation, but there was a thick fluid at the bottom of the urethra."

"What does that mean?"

Frank made a doubtful face. "I've sent the fluid for testing, because it's possible that the man died under conditions where so much blood flowed to his penis at the time of death that it looked like he had an erection. And the fluids in the urethra could just as easily be from his prostate gland, so it's simply a leak and not an incipient ejaculation."

"Will I get an answer to that in the autopsy report?"

The pathologist nodded. "Yes, but Liam, either way, none of that has anything to do with the cause of death, as he died of asphyxiation with one hundred percent certainty, and this way of dying can actually cause an erection . . . It is most often seen in men who die as a result of hanging."

Frank looked up. "It's called rigor erectus or angel lust, to be more contemporary."

"But if he had been hanged, you would have seen it, right?"

"Well, he definitely hasn't been hanged, but choking after a strong pressure on the larynx I guess feels the same way to the dying person. But blood play doesn't really have much to do with sexual intercourse either, as it's more about teasing and ejaculation."

Liam cracked a smile.

"I read up on it!" the pathologist said, and smiled back.

"It's something," Liam admitted, "and I think it's worthwhile looking at the fetish angle. If only to see if anyone recognizes the man. How's the identification going? It would be damn nice to know who he is so we can move on."

"The coroner is on his way, and we've sent DNA samples for examination . . . There was no match on the fingerprints. You'll have the DNA results tomorrow at the earliest."

"When can forensic dentistry get back to us?"

"Normally I would promise you an answer later today or tomorrow, but it's fall break. It's like the whole country has shut down and everyone's gone away. You'll hear from me as soon as there's any news. I've attached a picture of the man's face in case you need to put out an APB. And there are pictures of the scars."

Liam thanked him and decided that once he had circulated photos of the scars to the other police districts in the hope that someone might have come across something similar, the first thing to do was to find out who in Odense knew about blood fetishes and blood play. After a quick

WOUNDS

mental check, he realized there was no one in his own network he could question. "Neat teeth, well groomed, decent clothes . . . Would that be atypical in a fetish environment?"

Now it was Frank who broke into a smile. "I don't think you can judge like that."

Liam took the autopsy report and papers from the table.

"We're heading out into the fetish community to see if anyone recognizes the scars. Thank you for your input, and call us as soon as you have identified the man."

The pathologist stood up to escort him out, but Liam fended him off and said he could see himself out.

CHAPTER

6

LIAM THREW THE keys to Dea, who had offered to drive. He'd filled her in on the case from the Verninge Inn, and while he was on his way back from his meeting with Frank at the Institute of Forensic Medicine, she'd found two tattoo-and-piercing parlors that both had fetish as part of their branding. "Scar fetish," she'd said when he came back. "I didn't know it was a thing. I'm guessing they probably don't mean my C-section."

He had informed Thorbjørn that they were heading out and that there was still no ID on the man. Thorbjørn had promised to keep in touch with forensics and call if they managed to ID him. Liam had left the picture of the deceased Frank had given him and agreed with his colleague that they would wait to see if the police found a name for him. If not, they would put out a media alert the next day. Thorbjørn was on the case.

"Should I just sell my racket or what?" he asked as they drove out of the police garage.

Dea looked at him, clearly confused.

"It's been three weeks since we've played, and we can't keep booking the court if you're going to keep canceling."

It was her who had suggested they start playing paddle tennis together shortly after his breakup with Helene. He was well aware that it was her nurturing gene that had triggered her: an attempt to show that she was there for him. Much to his surprise, they had had a great time, but it had been short-lived, as she had started seeing Rolf all the time, and that trumped their training Wednesday after Wednesday.

"We'll do it next week," she said, giving him a quick glance. "How are you feeling?"

He shrugged his shoulders.

"I don't know, I can't really feel anything. Maybe it's a good sign." He and Dea had talked for hours after Helene made it clear that she couldn't stay in a relationship with him and wanted a divorce. In fact, Dea had been the only person he felt he could confide in because she was open-minded and knew everything about spending every waking hour working in the police force, but he couldn't keep crying on her shoulder now. He found it hard to keep bringing up his misery when Dea was obviously in love, happy, and basking in the joy of having morning sex.

* * *

The small tattoo shop was located in the basement of a run-down building opposite the old sugar factories in Odense. A few empty energy drink cans littered the sidewalk along with withered leaves, candy wrappers, and greasy pizza boxes. Just above the basement was an apartment where all the windows were covered with dusty, dark-purple velvet. On the velour hung a small, bright neon sign that indicated in yellow lettering that the store was open. Liam's shoulder pulsed and ached as he walked down the stairs.

"What's up?" Dea said. "Are you in pain?"

"I must have slept in a funny position last night."

"You were sleeping in the office, I gather?" She didn't say anything about all the calls she had ignored before he finally got hold of her.

He opened the door, which set off a bell that shrilly echoed a series of notes reminiscent of something from *Close Encounters of the Third Kind*. The room was almost as dark as it appeared to be from the outside.

"Hey," a young woman exclaimed as she peered out from a curtain behind an old-fashioned glass counter. The shelves were covered in the same dark-purple velvet as the windows, showcasing a large array of silver jewelry. Liam couldn't immediately figure out what it was all for. "What can we do for you?"

"Hey," Liam replied, showing his badge before introducing them both.

"Do you have an appointment with my boss?"

"No." Liam looked at her inquisitively as she dropped the curtain and came to meet them. She had large black plates in her earlobes, and her lips and eye contours were also painted black. She had a series of furrows cut into her skin down her forehead. Like vertical wrinkles. "We need your help," he said, explaining that it was regarding a specific type of scar.

"Scars?" the young girl said tentatively.

"Yes." Liam did his best to avoid looking at her forehead. "We're dealing with something, and we simply don't know what it is." He held a picture toward her so she could see some of the scars. "Have you ever come across anything in this store that looks like this?"

"What's going on, Miriam?" A shaven-headed, muscular man emerged from behind the curtain. His arms and neck were covered in tattoos, and his T-shirt looked like it was painted on his skin.

"They're from the police," Miriam said, turning to him. "They're asking about some scars."

"Deputy Chief Inspector Liam Stark." Liam took over as he held the picture toward the man. "We're here to ask if you recognize this type of scar."

"Should we?" the man grumbled. He snatched the picture out of Liam's hand, studied it closely, and then shook his head. "I don't recall seeing this type before . . . unfortunately. And we don't do that here at all. In fact, I don't know if there are any places that do. I certainly don't know of any."

"Sorry," Dea broke in, looking at Miriam's forehead. "You might know more about this kind of thing. Where were your own scars made?"

Miriam looked down at the table with a shy smile. "I had it done in Poland, and it was supposed to look like a Klingon forehead, but it isn't dented enough."

"Klingon?" Liam said.

"From *Star Trek*," Dea said quickly, looking at Miriam. "I can see it now that you mention it."

"Thank you."

"But it's not something you can get done here?" Liam continued addressing the man.

"No, with us it's mostly tattoos and piercings of all kinds . . . We're not allowed to tattoo or cut people on their faces. We can't help you."

Liam pulled out a new photo. "The reason we're asking is because the scars are on this man who was found dead last night."

"Okay," said the big man, raising his eyebrows as if trying to figure out what it had to do with them.

"Do you recognize him?"

Miriam looked at the picture with an uncertain expression and shook her head.

"Me neither," the man said. "I've never seen him before." Liam folded up the picture and put it back in his inside pocket. "We've come across the term *blood fetish*. Does that mean anything to you?"

"I can see why you're asking," the man said, "but I would say that you might want to try the BDSM community if you think that might have been done as a form of play, if I may say so."

"Scars like mine," Miriam said, "would be more like a scar fetish."

"Could it be as severe as in our photo?" Dea asked.

"Yes, it can, but it's not normal," said Miriam. "It might be more of a cutter . . . I mean, self-mutilation, and my scars aren't like that at all."

"And it's not my thing anyway," the man said.

* * *

Dea shook her head as they stood outside again. "Self-mutilation. That doesn't sound too pleasant."

Liam grabbed his shoulder again. "Nope. Fortunately, it doesn't look like that's what we're dealing with in this case."

"Shall we move on to the next one right away, or do you need to sit down? I could really do with a sandwich. I've only had coffee."

"Let's just move on and get the next one over and done with." He couldn't bear her concern and consideration. Couldn't bear to be made a victim. He ran his hands through his red hair and decided to stop by the barber's to fix his beard so he wouldn't look as divorced and miserable as he felt.

"You should have that shoulder looked at," said Dea.

"It just needs to be worked out, so if you could find the time to keep our paddle arrangements, it'll be fine in no time."

"So no coffee break?"

"Nope. Let's get on with it. I'd like the man identified today, and I'd like to know how the hell he ended up behind the inn."

"Is Piil going through the surveillance footage from the area?" Dea quickly added in her usual confident manner.

"There are hardly any surveillance cameras; it's just a small patch of land. There's a trucking company, they have several cameras pointing toward the square, and they could throw up something interesting. She's on it."

* * *

"Shouldn't it be called Fetish Ink?" Liam asked, studying the sign above the door that read Tattoo 5000. Below it, in uncertain letters, a series of words were painted directly on the wall in red paint: *Tattoos—Piercings—Body Adornment.*

"It's here, but I guess they changed their name."

They had just stepped through the door when Liam felt his phone vibrating in his pocket. He quickly excused himself and walked back out onto the sidewalk. "We've identified the man," Frank announced, explaining that it was the dentist who had pushed everything else aside to concentrate on this task. "It's Jørgen Andersen, an early retiree with an address at Skibhusvej 36."

Liam thanked him and hurried to call Thorbjørn to ask him to check if there were any relatives who needed to be notified.

He reentered Tattoo 5000 to join Dea, who was introducing herself to the man sitting on a chair in the middle of the room. "Dea Torp, inspector with the police here in Odense." She held her badge toward him. The man was tattooing a younger woman, but the small machine in his hand had stopped buzzing.

"Can we talk to you for a minute?" Dea continued.

"Now?" the tattoo artist asked, looking at his customer.

"It shouldn't take long," Dea continued, staring down at the woman's arm, where black ink and reddish skin merged in a gothic pattern. "Nice!"

"Thank you." The young woman smiled proudly at Dea and began to carefully examine her new body art.

"Can we take a little break?" the tattoo artist asked, and the young woman nodded obligingly as he used a clean, dry cloth to gently dab some color off the woman's arm. "There's coffee and vanilla wafers out back."

"Have you worked here long?" Liam asked.

"Thirteen years, so yes, I guess you could call that a long time. It doesn't feel like it." The man smiled and looked proudly around his store.

"We have some questions about scars," Liam said, explaining that they had already spoken to another tattoo artist who couldn't help. "But maybe you can?"

"I can try." The man thoroughly wiped his fingers with a new cloth. "What are you looking for?"

Liam pulled out the picture of the murdered man they now knew to be Jørgen Andersen. "Have you seen scars like these before?"

"Ouch . . ." The tattoo artist looked carefully at the image and then shook his head. "It's not something I recognize, no. Means nothing to me."

"We thought it might be related to blood play or some kind of scar fetish."

The man made a doubtful face. "It's not something I've heard of here in Odense at least, but I know it's done in other places . . . lumps under the skin to look like horns, sharpened teeth, and yes, also pretty wild scars . . . you name it."

Liam looked around the room. It was large and a little gloomy. The walls were full of photos of large tattoos, piercings, and other body adornments.

The man cleared his throat, his forehead creased in thought. "Can I see the photo of the scars again?"

Liam handed him the picture. He stood looking at it for a long time. "Okay," the tattoo artist said quietly. "This does remind me of something, actually . . . I think this looks more like Monika le Fevre's artwork. Have you thought about that?"

"Monika le Fevre?" Liam repeated, looking questioningly at Dea, who shook her head.

"She had an exhibition a few years ago," the tattoo artist continued. "Fall 2017, I think . . . But these were animals

54   SARA BLÆDEL AND MADS PEDER NORDBO

that had been cut up while they were alive . . . and then later stuffed. She's a pretty well-known taxidermist."

"Animals with scars?" Dea broke in. "You mean like this?"

The man nodded. "Yes. Dogs, cats, mink. Probably bigger animals too." Dea and Liam looked at each other briefly.

"Do you know Monika le Fevre personally?" Liam asked.

"No, I just saw the exhibition. It caused quite a stir. Like when they'd put goldfish in blenders in Kolding, or when they slaughtered the giraffe in Copenhagen Zoo."

"And the scars from le Fevre's exhibition looked exactly like this?" Liam asked, pointing to the photo of Jørgen's torso.

"Not quite, because the animals were stuffed, so the scars were dry and white, whereas these look fresh." The man looked at the picture intently.

Dea's cell phone buzzed, and she left the store.

Liam googled le Fevre and nodded to himself. Then he held his cell phone up to the man. "Is this what you were thinking about?"

"Exactly! They're not identical, but can't you see that they look pretty damn similar?"

Liam nodded; they did look alike. He thanked the tattoo artist, said goodbye, and joined Dea on the street. Dea was still on the phone, so Liam walked along the sidewalk and called Frank. "I think we might have something," he said, and asked if the pathologist would take Jørgen Andersen's body out again and compare his scars with those on Monika le Fevre's animals. "I'll send you some photos right away. We need to know if he's been used as a human work of art."

CHAPTER

7

A HUMAN WORK OF art. The man was abused, emaciated, and had been restrained for a long time. It was simply not what she needed right now on top of the Amalie Vedel case. Margrethe Dybbøl closed her eyes and leaned back in her office chair.

She still hadn't heard anything from Zenia. Søren had canceled all his morning appointments and had stayed home when his daughter hadn't come back yet, but she could tell it was probably mostly for her sake. He hadn't seemed seriously worried when they spoke after the press conference this morning, and he didn't mince his words when he reminded her that she had been harsh with their daughter. Too harsh, in his opinion, it seemed. He clearly thought she had just made Zenia really angry, which was why she'd decided to stay out. But now that it was almost four o'clock, he had just called, and this time Dybbøl sensed her husband's growing concern. He had been in contact with all her friends. Talked to the young man their daughter had dated until recently. But no one had heard from her.

Dybbøl had called and texted Zenia at least twenty times, but her cell phone remained unconnected.

"Chief?"

Standing in the doorway was lead investigator Lene Eriksen. "The canine patrol units have returned. Nothing in the whole area." There was something sharp in the investigating officer's voice that made Dybbøl sit up straight. For a moment, the two women stared at each other. Then Lene took a step forward and closed the door behind her.

"I had no time to prepare for the briefing on the Vedel case," she said. "I think I have enough on my plate."

"You know that I need to be one hundred percent up-to-date when we have a case with this kind of attention. I need to be one step ahead of what the press find out for themselves. I've just been made aware that BT had a drone hovering over the canine unit you refer to. It would have been nice if I had been informed that we were searching down by Nyborg. Now the speculation is that she may have thrown herself off the bridge. I need to know that kind of stuff so I can prevent it from becoming headline news. It's too late for that now. How do you think her parents will feel when they read about it?"

Before the head of the investigation could say more, Dybbøl added, "By the way, you can join the conversation I'm having with them tonight. They've insisted on coming in here. Because of the damn headlines. We all have enough on our plates."

"I understand that," Lene replied in a tight voice. "But maybe we could just do it over the phone or in private. Another briefing will eat up the time I could otherwise spend out in the field."

WOUNDS   57

"Yes, okay," said Dybbøl in a more subdued tone. "But I don't want the Vedel case to end up as a TV 2 program that we all have to deal with for years to come."

"None of this is helping the investigation!"

"We have no actual leads, dear Lene. That's the problem!"

"We're doing everything we can!" the investigator exclaimed angrily. "And if it's that bad, put Liam on it instead!"

Dybbøl didn't have time to retaliate before Lene was out the door. They needed to talk about her way of communicating, but not right now. Dybbøl was well aware that it would serve no purpose. There wasn't much in this world that could irritate an investigator more than a case with no leads.

* * *

Liam called Thorbjørn from the doorway and announced that he was ready to leave.

"A locksmith will meet us out there in twenty minutes," his young colleague announced, saying that he had advised Forensics that they might need to get a team out.

"Have you managed to locate any relatives?" Liam asked.

"No other persons are registered at the address. The deceased was neither married nor had children, and no close relations are listed in his health records."

Right now, Liam was mostly interested in finding out who Jørgen Andersen was, what circles he had moved in, and who had left him as a patchwork quilt behind the abandoned inn, but it was of course important that any relatives be informed of Jørgen's death.

* * *

The locksmith was waiting for them as they climbed the stairs of the well-maintained three-story redbrick building where Jørgen Andersen's first-floor apartment was located. There was a dusty smell in the hallway, and just below the small spy hole in the doors were uniform nameplates on a narrow metal rail, indicating rental apartments that could quickly be turned over to a new tenant. But Jørgen Andersen had lived in the unit to the right for thirteen years, so people had to know about him.

Liam followed Thorbjørn into the small two-room apartment. Several jackets hung on hangers in the hallway, and there was a small shoe rack filled with both indoor and outdoor shoes beneath. The men continued into the living room, where a folded newspaper on the coffee table sat next to a coffee cup, but apart from the abandoned cup, the place was immaculate.

Thorbjørn went into the bedroom. "All the clothes look like they've been ironed," he said from inside. "It's neatly arranged and looks like an army recruit's closet."

Liam looked around and realized that even books and magazines seemed to be arranged in alphabetical order. He remembered an old detective who had once lectured him that the neater things looked on the surface, the more dirt and grime was likely to be found underneath. The kitchen was spotless. There was a plate and a set of cutlery in the dish rack, and a knitted dishcloth hung over the faucet.

"You could almost wonder if anyone ever lived here," Thorbjørn said from the living room.

"I think he just had a lot of spare time," Liam said. "He was on early retirement. Have you come across anything that connects him to Monika le Fevre?"

Thorbjørn shook his head. "We have to take his PC in to examine its contents." He was already unplugging the charger from the wall.

"I'll go down and check if there's any mail." He took the small key dangling from a hook next to the hallway mirror and took a few steps down to the row of mailboxes hanging on the wall next to the front door. The mailbox was overflowing with leaflets and flyers, ranging from ads for window-cleaning services to animal protection appeals. At the top were a few letters that looked like they were from the government. Liam quickly flipped through it all. The oldest post was from nineteen days ago.

When he returned to the apartment, Thorbjørn was standing by the window looking out over the parking lot with his phone to his ear. Liam squatted in front of the cabinets integrated into the wall bookcase opposite the sofa, hoping to find an address book or something that could help them work out who Jørgen Andersen had been in touch with.

When Thorbjørn turned and ended the conversation, he told Liam that Piil from their IT department had just announced that Jørgen Andersen had a mobile subscription with CBB. "There has been no activity for the past thirteen days."

"It's sad if no one has missed him or looked for him. Two weeks is a long time." He thought of Amalie Vedel, who had been missing for sixteen days and for whom heaven and earth had been moved to try to find her. But, of course, she was also a young woman with parents who'd immediately feared something was wrong.

"We'll continue looking for relatives," Thorbjørn said. "I've put Piil on the case, but she hasn't found anyone yet. She'll call me back as soon as she has something."

"Have her check previous jobs and colleagues too," Liam asked as he got to his feet. It wasn't just his shoulder that hurt; it was actually his whole body. He decided that he would drive home to his parents' house to sleep. The couch wasn't going to work in the long run. "Let's talk to a few of the neighbors before we head back to the farm."

Thorbjørn had packed up the computer and found that there was no cell phone or iPad in the apartment.

"We'll come back if we need to collect personal papers," Liam decided, and while Thorbjørn went out to the car with Jørgen Andersen's PC, he knocked on the door of the apartment opposite. He knocked three times before giving up and continuing upstairs.

On the second floor to the left, a sleep-deprived young man opened the door. He scratched his wild hair and squinted his eyes. "I'm from the police," Liam said, thinking about his own son.

The young man's gaze changed significantly, and he looked behind him nervously.

"I just need to know about your downstairs neighbor," Liam continued. "Jørgen Andersen. Do you know who he is, and when did you last see him?"

"I don't know," said the youngster. "We don't talk to him much, but he's okay."

WOUNDS 61

"Have you seen him in the last few days?" Liam pressed.

"I don't think so, actually."

"The last couple of weeks, then?"

He shook his head. "I haven't seen him for a while," he said. "But I don't go around watching him either."

"Do you live alone in the apartment?"

"No, my girlfriend lives here too, but she's sleeping. She's pregnant."

At the same time, Thorbjørn called from the stairwell. Liam thanked the young man and walked with quick steps down to his colleague.

"Piil just called," he said. "Jørgen Andersen worked for a number of years with a tomato grower between Bellinge and Brylle, but his last job was at the terrarium in Vissenbjerg, where he was a sort of handyman."

"Did she also say anything about where Monika le Fevre lives?" Liam interrupted.

"Yes," the colleague nodded. "In Vissenbjerg. Just below the Vissenbjerg forest."

"Do we know when he stopped working at the terrarium?"

"Yes, in March 2018."

"So it was after the Monika le Fevre exhibition. That took place in October 2017." He hadn't had time to read up on the exhibition in question but relied on the tattoo artist's memory.

"It's about five hundred meters as the crow flies between Monika le Fevre's address and the terrarium in Vissenbjerg," Thorbjørn continued, holding out his mobile.

* * *

Dea had driven through Blommenslyst and Skallebølle. It was no more than half an hour's drive from the police station in Odense, yet she felt like she was in a completely different world. Exactly the same as at Rolf's old plastic factory. There was a calmness to the landscape, which she saw as a haven of tranquility. She always felt at peace when surrounded by nature.

The farm was at the end of a field road, and tall trees rose majestically along the driveway. She slowly rolled her black Passat into Monika le Fevre's empty courtyard. The red farmhouse with black woodwork and white windows was located in a valley between Vissenbjerg and Skalbjerg. The house was fairly old, but everything was well maintained and freshly painted. Maybe being neat came with the job, she thought as she turned the engine off.

Monika le Fevre was the only person associated with the address, although in several of the pictures Dea had seen, she had been standing with a man who was described as the artist's partner. Before she left, Dea had had time to read up on the artist of the macabre stuffed animals. According to the articles she had found, Monika was recognized for her taxidermy skills. A skill she must have inherited from her father, Holger le Fevre, who turned out to be a world-renowned taxidermist too.

Dea had read in a report in *Børsen Pleasure* that the farm had been her parents', but in 2012 Monika had taken over, and according to Virk.dk, her company was also registered at this address. She was forty-nine years old and had no children.

Dea got out of the car and walked toward a front door painted green. She grabbed a heavy door knocker shaped

WOUNDS 63

like a lion's head and let it fall against the door. The impact made a resounding noise, but nothing happened. She looked around for a bell, but found none, and instead went to look in the nearest window. The interior was deserted and dark. She turned and looked out over the courtyard. There were hardly any weeds between the cobblestones, and against the red-washed walls grew well-groomed perennials of various sizes. She knocked again and checked her watch. It was almost eight o'clock. People should be home by now. If they weren't, they would either be out late or not come at all.

A faint light seemed to emanate from one of the wings, where she thought a workshop might be. She started walking across the courtyard toward a large gate, which was also painted green. She thought about texting Liam to see if she could look around inside if it was open, but decided against it and put her phone back in her pocket. She'd been in the game too long to ask for permission. Right now she was just here to ask a few questions. Besides, she had already pushed the gate open.

She stood for a moment in the semidarkness, taking in the smell of the barn. She shouted hello and called Monika's name before turning on her cell phone torch and walking in the direction the light was coming from. She entered a large room that was divided into several smaller rooms by glazed walls. The floor was paved with large cobblestones, worn smooth over hundreds of years. Just like the outside, the barn was well maintained down to the last detail. If you were one of the best taxidermists in the world, you probably had to have a great eye for detail and visual aesthetics, Dea thought, walking over to the part of the building that appeared to be the workshop. This was where the light came from. An architect's lamp shone over a workbench, but Monika le Fevre was not there.

Dea stopped for a moment and looked around. Stuffed animals were scattered around in cupboards and on shelves. There was a pungent smell in the room—formaldehyde perhaps, she thought, heading toward the end wall, where there were three tall, old cabinets. Two of them were filled with smaller stuffed animals, while the third contained a number of thick glass jars with various small animals and body parts floating in alcohol. The labels on the jars were yellowed and showed signs of age.

In front of the display cases was an elongated steel table that reminded her of the ones they worked on at Forensic Medicine. Dea thought of Monika's father. Maybe he and Monika shared the workshop space, as her parents still lived near the farm in Vissenbjerg.

Fascinated, she craned her neck back and observed a large owl hanging from the ceiling on an invisible string, looking quite alive. The whole bird—from its fluffy plumage to its bright, almost-pale green eyes and the way it hovered in the air—had so much life in it. She had read that there were world championships in taxidermy. And that there was big money in it. Holger le Fevre had once won with a stuffed elephant, which, according to Børsen, had earned him the equivalent of just under a million kroner. She had tried to google him, but it was as though he had stepped out of the limelight in recent years and barely existed on the internet. Perhaps it was a natural consequence of the furor that had arisen in the wake of his daughter's spectacular exhibition that her father had retreated a little and scaled

WOUNDS 65

back his activities, she wondered. A fact box about the exhibition had stated that Monika le Fevre had cut into the animals while they were still alive, and it was this that had triggered a huge outcry.

Dea looked around one last time and was again captivated by the owl hanging from the ceiling. She turned her phone so that its torch shone on the floor while she googled owls and Denmark. Yes, she was right. Owls were protected, she thought. She walked over to the worktable. In addition to the architect's lamp, there was a lamp with a built-in magnifier, felt mats, beaker tongs, scalpels, and cotton wool. She hesitantly lifted a felt mat and sniffed it. It smelled strongly of the pungent odor that hung in the rest of the room. She went to the closet and lifted a rabbit from a shelf. The skin was cut across its back. The incisions looked like small square doors, or little windows into the body itself. She took a picture of it and a few of the other animals. She hadn't seen Jørgen Andersen herself, only the pictures Liam had gotten from Frank, but the scars looked similar. She sent the pictures to Liam and was turning to leave when she spotted a woman in her late forties striding purposefully across the courtyard.

"Monika?" Dea tried as she stepped awkwardly through the green gate and closed it behind her.

The woman quickly shook her head. "Jane. I live in the house right over there." She pointed to the road and said she had come because she had seen the car.

"Dea Torp," Dea continued. "I'm from the police in Odense. Do you know where I can find Monika le Fevre?"

"No, we've been wondering too," Jane said. "The lights haven't been on since Sunday, and she doesn't usually go for days without telling us, because we're the ones who look after the cats when she's not home."

"Are you worried about her?" Dea asked with interest.

"There's just been so much going on, and it hasn't been very easy for her."

"Are you referring to the period following the exhibition?"

The woman nodded. "Sometimes she came to us because she didn't like being alone. But that subsided after she got a restraining order against the man."

"A restraining order?" Dea repeated. "On what man?"

"The older man who showed up out here and threatened Monika. He was both abusive and violent and harassed her for a long period of time, until the police issued a restraining order prohibiting him from being near Monika's property."

"Do you know the man's name?"

Jane shook her head and said she had never spoken to him. "But I've seen him out here several times."

Dea hurriedly messaged Piil, and when the answer Dea was expecting came a little later, she called Liam.

"Monika le Fevre had a restraining order against Jørgen Andersen. He behaved very aggressively and offensively toward her on several occasions. Piil is in the process of finding the police reports."

CHAPTER

8

AMALIE VEDEL'S PARENTS entered Dybbøl's office holding hands. They were pale, and their faces were lined with grief and despair. "You think she's dead," her father exclaimed.

Troels and Cecilie Vedel were both in their late thirties. He was a lawyer, and she worked as an independent communications consultant. It wasn't their first visit to the police station, but it was the first time they had insisted on coming.

Dybbøl started to shake her head, but he cut in before she had a chance to speak.

"You think she took her own life, that she threw herself into the Great Belt from the bridge. Our daughter would never do that. But if that's your assumption, why aren't there divers out? We just came from down there; we've been walking along the water's edge all afternoon after we were told that you were looking for her body on the shore."

Now Margrethe Dybbøl raised a hand to stop him. She'd had enough of all this. She and Søren still hadn't heard from Zenia; in fact, no one had heard from her. And now Amalie Vedel's parents were suddenly talking about dead bodies at the water's edge. Hunger gnawed at her stomach, and she looked at the empty coffee cup on the table. The day had slipped away in a haze. A busy haze that she didn't yet feel she had fully grasped. So now she stopped him.

"We have no reason to believe that your daughter took her own life," she said brusquely. "As I told you on the phone when you called, it's the media that has cobbled this story together. We haven't searched the Great Belt Bridge or searched the water. We have only expanded the search I told you about. We take this very seriously, and we have launched a major police operation to search for your daughter. This search involves, among other things, having our dog patrols out to search larger areas. We also have IT investigators continuously getting access to relevant surveillance in an attempt to find clues that we can work from. A search as extensive as the one we have launched here investigates the case from every conceivable angle. It involves witnesses—there are people on a dedicated phone line right now to take the calls we hope will come in following our latest alert that went out in the wake of today's press conference. As you know, we've updated her description after you came forward and told us she may have borrowed your red sports jacket."

Dybbøl nodded toward Troels Vedel but failed to say that the fact that they had only just discovered this now didn't exactly help the police's work or increase their chances of finding the girl. A vintage red bomber jacket with the legendary Alfa Romeo logo on the chest. Until today, Amalie

WOUNDS   69

Vedel had been wanted in a short black leather jacket, which
turned out to be hanging in her room. "We have circulated
an international alert, which means that she is not only being
looked for in Denmark but also abroad. We have checked if
she has traveled anywhere from one of our airports."

"Well, her passport is at home," Amalie's mother
interjected.

"Yes, but you can travel from one borderless Schengen
country to another without a passport. We are on it. We're
looking for your daughter with everything we have. Everywhere we can. And we would also launch a water search if
it was deemed necessary."

It wouldn't be solely for the parents' sake, but Dybbøl
didn't say that either. It would be just as much for the sake
of silencing the journalists who were now looking that way.
She had already inquired about the possibility of getting
assistance from the water search dogs. Whether she should
have started earlier was one of the questions that could be
raised later. Dybbøl rubbed her forehead.

Cecilie Vedel had started to cry, and her husband put
his arm around her.

"I understand your despair, I really do." Dybbøl spoke
calmly, making an effort to keep her voice low. "It's an
unbearable situation you're in." Just then, her phone rang.

Instead of rushing to switch it off, she stood up and
apologized as she quickly left the office—it must be Søren
calling so late because he'd heard from Zenia. "Have you
spoken to her?" she asked without looking at the display.

"Margrethe, the minister of justice wants to talk to you
tomorrow morning." Her secretary's voice was measured.
Everyone was measured when it came to updates on the

Amalie Vedel case, as if no one knew how to broach the topic without putting their foot in it. "The press is after him. I spoke to someone from his front office who told me that they've been pushing all day for him to go on TV 2 Nyhederne to comment on the case and the lack of progress. It sounds like the media is ready to judge us incompetent and wants the minister to pressure the National Police to set up a special task force to take over the case. He won't be on TV tonight, but he will talk to you tomorrow morning."

Margrethe Dybbøl sighed and stood with her cell phone in her hand for a moment before going back to Amalie's parents. When she entered the office, they had both stood up and were putting their jackets on.

CHAPTER

9

"I'D BETTER GET going," Liam said, looking out into the Wednesday morning darkness that hung over the well-kept farmhouse garden. It had done his whole body good to get a decent night's sleep, and he hadn't been able to bring himself to get up and drive without first having some breakfast with his parents. He felt he owed them that much anyway, even though he was impatient to hit the road. It was just after seven o'clock, so it wasn't like anyone was waiting for him. Yet. And actually, it was very nice to sit here in the warm kitchen smelling the coffee gurgling through the old machine on the kitchen counter, where it had been for as long as he could remember.

"What are you thinking about?" his mother asked.

Liam was hurtled back into the here and now and looked at her. "Work."

"Work?" She placed a bread basket a little too hard on the table and went to fetch the soft-boiled eggs. "It's because of work that you're sitting here now and not at home with your family. Maybe you should think about that."

"I thought you didn't like Helene very much," he retorted. It was the same old conversation, precisely the one he couldn't stand. But he had needed a bed, a bath, and to feel like he belonged.

"I never said that, and that wasn't the point, you know that!"

Liam looked out into the garden again. It was getting light out there; he could see his father walking around with his headlamp. "I'll find somewhere else to live."

"No, you can stay here, you know that. We have the space for it."

There was silence for a moment.

"I've been thinking about inviting Andreas and Laura down here next weekend," she continued. "They can stay the night. Wouldn't that be good for all three of you?"

"Yeah, that's a good idea, Mom," he said with a nod, although he wasn't really keen on the idea of his older children seeing him living in a room under his old parents' roof. Liam's cell phone rang. He picked it up, stood up, and walked to the window with his coffee mug in hand. "I have to go," he said when he had finished the call.

"That sounded like work?"

"Yes." He nodded and put the mug down.

"You should find a more normal job, Liam. One where you also have time off once in a while."

He nodded and grabbed his jacket from the back of a chair by the wall. "Don't wait up for me tonight."

* * *

Liam pulled up a chair next to Piil.

"Sorry for calling so early, but I thought you might want to see this," she said.

"Don't worry," he hastened to say. "I was on my way in anyway."

Piil looked up from Jørgen's somewhat clunky PC, which was plugged in on her desk. "Are you in?" Liam asked, and leaned forward.

"I'm in." Piil opened a folder. "And I can tell you right away that Jørgen Andersen didn't exactly go out of his way to secure his computer." She paused to click around on Jørgen's computer and then continued. "Well, he has an anti-virus protection program that's active, but it's on the cheap side, and he hasn't bothered to delete files on his hard drive or in his mailbox."

"Should he have?" Liam said, thinking about his own laptop. He never deleted anything, just let it grow as long as there was enough space.

Piil shrugged. "When you spend so much time online, you normally protect yourself, but on the other hand, he probably didn't feel he had anything to hide."

"Did he?" Liam's interest was piqued.

"Well, as we know, Monika le Fevre got a five-year restraining order against him on April 9, 2018, and when I look at his emails, they confirm that the restraining order was appropriate, to say the least." She looked at him with raised eyebrows.

"So there has been contact between them?" He turned to the screen and tried to figure out what Piil was talking about.

She nodded. "There's a lot of material to go through, so I can't give you the full overview yet. But he has a folder in his mailbox called 'le Fevre,' so yes, there has been contact. At first, she tried to counter his rather crude attacks in connection with the exhibition, but as he became more and more abusive in his language, she tried to shut him down. When he continued his attacks, she threatened to report him to the police. She followed through, and the last of the many emails he sent were returned when there was no longer a recipient. But then, after a couple of years, he seems to have tracked down her new email address. She has apparently kept a very low profile online in the intervening period. But when he returns, she once again reports him to the police without responding to him."

"So he'll get a fine?"

"Yes, he was actually fined three times for violating the restraining order. It appears that he was fined twice as a result of the emails he sent to her after the restraining order was issued, while the most recent violation took place at her home earlier this year. She was able to produce a photo that she took with her phone back in June showing him at her house. According to the police report, he claimed it was an old photo, but this was rejected because in the photo he was pouring red paint over her car, which she only bought this year."

"So they had a confrontation a few months ago," Liam noted. He thought for a moment before asking Piil to locate some of Jørgen Andersen's former colleagues, from both his last job at the terrarium and his employment at the tomato nursery. "I want to know what they know about his intrusive and unpleasant behavior."

"The tomato nursery closed down as a business," said Piil, "but the woman who lives there has lived there for forty-three years, so I wonder if she knows Jørgen."

WOUNDS 75

"Let's start with her. Has anything else come up?"

Piil nodded. "I logged in to Facebook as Jørgen—again, no security! He was quite active in animal protection and animal rights groups and got annoyed by a ton of things. For example, the way mink, caged hens, and dairy calves are treated."

"That makes sense." Liam's cell phone rang, and after checking the caller ID, he apologized to Piil for having to take the call.

"I found le Fevre!" Dea said. "She crashed on Sunday not far from the Verninge Inn, and she's been in a coma ever since."

CHAPTER

10

"COULD LE FEVRE have done this to Jørgen?" Dea asked as Liam pulled a chair over to her desk. She held out her cell phone and showed him the pictures of the scars on the animals she had seen in Monika le Fevre's workshop.

He flipped through the pictures, looked at them for a moment before slowly shrugging and handing the phone back. "I doubt we'll get a search warrant based solely on this. I can see that the scars look like Jørgen Andersen's, but we need something more. If she was behind the abuse of Jørgen's body and left him under the tarpaulin behind the inn, it would mean he has been there since Sunday, before she crashed the car. According to the autopsy report, he died late Monday afternoon. He was strangled and had a crushed larynx."

"But it's still a strange coincidence that she was near the inn when she crashed. The accident happened just outside Verninge," Dea pointed out, clicking on a map on her computer. "It was a single-vehicle accident; there were no witnesses. She crashed head-on into a tree and had to be cut

WOUNDS

free by the rescue team. A young man called the emergency services. I have his number here."

"Did we have people at the scene?"

Dea nodded. She pulled up the twenty-four-hour report on her screen and skimmed it quickly. "The call to report the accident came in at six thirty-seven PM. It's described as a violent one-person accident. The report estimates that she was traveling at least a hundred ten kilometers per hour, and as I recall, the road between Knarreborg and Verninge has several bends that are not conducive to high speeds."

"Braking?" Liam asked. "Could she have been trying to avoid an animal?"

Dea shook her head. "No, there was no sign that she had braked or tried to swerve."

"Suicide?"

Dea hadn't seen Rolf coming, and she gasped when he put a gentle hand on the back of her neck and gave it a little squeeze before leaning down to kiss the top of her head. Liam greeted him briefly. The fact that he had seen this intimate moment between her and Rolf seemed to make him feel awkward.

"Hi!" She gathered herself and smiled at Rolf as he put a bag from Emmerys and a coffee next to her computer. He pulled off his jacket and said there were tea biscuits if Liam wanted one. "We need to get the technicians out to that farm," Dea said, turning her attention back to Liam as Rolf sat down on the corner of her desk, as had been his habit before they started dating.

"Not without a search warrant," Liam repeated. "We can't. If we end up having to press charges, then we're shooting ourselves in the foot by going in there."

"I've already been there," she reminded him. "But of course it was just to talk to her; I didn't search anything. And I wasn't looking for signs that Jørgen Andersen had been there."

Liam ran a hand through his hair and sat staring ahead for a moment. "We need to get something more on her before we can go in. I buy that she could be behind the assault, but I can't imagine the circumstances under which she would have killed him." He drummed his fingers on the desk, lost in thought. "First of all, it would be interesting to find out if Jørgen Andersen was on her farm just before he ended up behind the inn."

He looked pleadingly at Rolf, who hurriedly nodded. "Ask and I don't start until noon; I'm only here because I drove Dea in this morning. He's lying down in the car. I was going to do some training with him, but we can easily drive out there. Was it Vissenbjerg?" He looked at Dea. She had told him about the workshop and the stuffed animals when she got home, and Rolf had agreed that the owl thing could not be legal.

Liam had gotten up and returned a little later with the shirt Jørgen Andersen had been wearing when he was found. It must have just come back from forensics, Dea thought. She had seen Thorbjørn walking with the characteristic brown paper wrapping.

"It would help us get a warrant if we could say that the deceased was at le Fevre's address before he was left behind the inn. But then she wouldn't have acted alone." He handed the shirt to Rolf.

"No problem. Ask and I will head out there right away. Is there anything else you want me to be aware of when I'm at the address?"

WOUNDS

Liam shook his head slowly. "First of all, we're trying to get an overview of what the hell could have happened. All indications are that there was a violent conflict between the deceased and Monika le Fevre, and in that light, the bizarre scars may not seem so unmotivated after all."

He turned to Dea and told her to go to the hospital.

Dea nodded quickly. "I'm going there now." She gave Rolf a kiss and took a tea biscuit from the bag before pulling on her jacket and swinging her bag over her shoulder. "I'll let you know when I know what her condition is and when we can expect to be allowed to question her."

Liam nodded, and she struggled to decipher if her relationship with Rolf bothered him or if he didn't really care and was just so hurt from his divorce that falling in love in general made him uncomfortable.

They were interrupted when Thorbjørn appeared in the doorway and announced that there was news in the Amalie Vedel case.

CHAPTER

11

DYBBØL HAD BEEN on her way out the door to meet with two of Zenia's friends when Lene Eriksen stormed into her office to tell her that the red bomber jacket Amalie Vedel had been wearing when she disappeared had just been found.

They had quickly summoned the others from Eriksen's investigation team, and Dybbøl had sent for Liam. Now that everyone was gathered, Lene stood by the large whiteboard, and Dybbøl stepped away to send a message to Nanna, her daughter's best friend, who had contacted Zenia's other friend to arrange for them all to have lunch. She apologized profusely for being late and asked them to order at her expense, adding that she would join them as soon as she could.

There was an intensity in the room that was like an electric charge in the air, and no one reacted when Dybbøl's secretary stuck her head in to ask if anyone wanted coffee. "Just bring some water, please," Dybbøl asked before she went and sat on the windowsill facing Hans Mules Gade. She greeted Liam and immediately saw the irritation in his eyes at being pulled away from his own investigation.

WOUNDS 81

But as head of the Reactive Criminal Investigations Department, he had to be present when there were breakthroughs or new, important clues in important cases. He knew that very well, she thought, becoming a little annoyed herself.

Lene Eriksen pinned a photo of a red jacket to the board. On the left breast of the jacket, the white Alfa Romeo logo gleamed, and above the right pocket was the small tear that Troels Vedel had pointed out to them.

"This jacket was found this morning at a rest stop not too far from Malmö. It was a Danish couple living in Malmö who found it, and they recognized it from the new photos we sent out after the press conference. Amalie's parents have confirmed that this is the jacket she was wearing when she disappeared. Inside the jacket we found a pack of chewing gum and a lip balm. Both items have been sent to forensics." Lene now pinned a map on the board. "The jacket was found here." She marked the location with a red marker. "Unfortunately, it's a rest area without a gas station, so there's no surveillance on-site, but we have established cooperation with the police in Malmö and are in the process of making arrangements to review surveillance from the Øresund Bridge and a number of gas stations between the bridge and the location where the jacket was found."

Dybbøl felt Lene's watchful gaze on her and tried to concentrate, but she found it hard not to think about Zenia. Could she remember anything at all from the night she last saw Zenia? Had it been raining? Was it cold? All she could remember was that it was dark when Zenia left the house in anger. Would she be able to give a description? Had Zenia been wearing her new sneakers? Or were they still at home? Søren thought their daughter might be with some of the other animal activists. They were a group that hung out together, but that group was an abstract concept because Dybbøl and her husband didn't really know any of them. Most of all, she wanted to leave the briefing and go down to see Piil to get her to track her daughter's cell phone.

"The rest area is currently being investigated by the Swedish technicians," Lene continued, standing by the board. "But for now, we have nothing more." Again, her gaze landed on Dybbøl, who pushed away her own worries and stood up resolutely from the windowsill.

"Thank you," said Dybbøl, looking at the board with the modest clues. "This morning I had the pleasure of meeting the minister of justice. I'll spare you the details, but I think I explained that we need peace and quiet, and I promised that we would try to avoid more headlines that cast doubt on whether we are carrying out our search well enough or whether we as a police unit are up to the task."

Several of the police officers shook their heads, not only because everyone knew you couldn't make promises like that but also because of the deeply unfair accusations.

"So let's get something positive out there. Inform the media about the breakthrough and tell them we are working closely with the Swedish police force and are currently looking for Amalie Vedel in southern Sweden."

The press coordinator in the corner nodded.

"What else do we think about the jacket?" someone asked.

"She could have run away and forgotten the jacket," Lene said. "Or she could have deliberately left it behind to leave a clue for us."

"Agreed," said Dybbøl, and closed her eyes for a moment. "We can't rule out the possibility that she was abducted either. But if that's the case, and the perpetrators wanted us to stumble upon a clue, we would have heard from them long ago. So if someone has abducted the girl, they are not going to let her go voluntarily. So it's up to us to find her."

"Sweden is a huge country," Liam said, looking at the map. "The rest area where the jacket was found is close to both the E6 and E65. They could have gone anywhere."

"Let's see what the Swedish technicians say about what they find on-site," Lene said quickly. "All things being equal, it must be better that we now have something concrete to go on!"

"Definitely," Liam said. Dybbøl sensed that he was scrutinizing her, as if he could sense that she was only half present. She walked over and sat down behind her desk.

"The jacket is definitely a breakthrough," she said again. "We all know how much the chances of finding a missing person are reduced when so much time has elapsed. If she had been out on an adventure, she would most likely have come back now that the money has run out and she needs clean clothes and a good bed to sleep in. And honestly, she's been wanted for days; wouldn't she have reacted to seeing herself in the media? So I think we need to continue to work on the basis that Amalie has not voluntarily disappeared."

* * *

Dea pushed open the double door to N2 in the Neurology Department. The hospital corridor was quiet. For a moment she stood waiting and looking around before she walked over and knocked on the doorframe to the nurses' station. "Dea Torp," she introduced herself, discreetly showing her badge before explaining that she was the one who had called about Monika le Fevre.

"Just a moment," said a young woman dressed in blue. "I'll find the doctor; he's on his way up."

"I'm right here," a middle-aged man behind her stated. He held out his hand. "Carstensen. We can talk in my office."

Dea nodded and followed him down the hall. He pointed to an office and let her go first. "I'm a consultant here at Neurology. I understood from our ward nurse that you wanted to speak to Monika le Fevre. I'm afraid that's not possible."

Dea was about to say something, but he hurried to continue. "Monika le Fevre has not been conscious since she was brought into our Trauma Center on Sunday. As you are of course already aware, she was hospitalized after a violent traffic accident. For the first twenty-four hours she hovered between life and death, but thankfully we seem to have managed to stabilize her. We are still keeping her in a coma until the pressure in her brain subsides."

"How bad is it?" Dea asked, surprised that no one had informed her of the severity of her condition when she spoke to the department earlier. "Is there any telling when you expect it will be possible to talk to her?"

The chief physician leaned back slightly in his chair and shook his head.

"I don't dare make so much as an educated guess. She has suffered severe blows to the head, and right now it's not even possible to say what her condition will be when she wakes up."

He paused briefly and looked at some papers on his desk. "But she's waking up?" Dea dared to ask.

"We very much hope so," he said, explaining that a new scan had been ordered that would give a better overview of the damage she had sustained to her brain. "When we have the results from that, I'll be better able to predict the possibility of an interrogation."

Dea nodded and asked if Monika le Fevre had anything on her when she was brought in. "A coat, bag?"

The consultant shrugged and said that if she had anything, it would be placed in the patient's locker in the ward.

"Can I see her before I go?"

He told Dea that le Fevre was in room eight. "I think her mother is still in there, so we can ask her if Monika had any belongings with her when she arrived. I assume it's in connection with the police investigation into the accident," he said, and stood up.

"Exactly," Dea replied quickly, and followed him out into the hallway.

* * *

The room had a single bed and was almost in total darkness. It took a moment before Dea saw the outline of a person in an armchair next to the hospital bed's headboard. The small lamp on the bedside table was aimed at the floor.

"Can we come in?" the consultant asked, and waited a moment before the woman in the chair moved.

"Sorry, I must have fallen asleep," she said, straightening up in a jerk and turning to face her daughter in bed. "Has something happened?"

"No," Carstensen quickly replied. "But the police are here. Would you be able to speak to them now?"

Le Fevre's mother adjusted the bedside lamp and said they could turn on the ceiling light. Dea watched as Monika's mother squinted her eyes to get used to the bright light—she must have been sitting in the dark for quite some time.

The woman in the bed seemed frail. Her hair was red and her skin pale except for the blue-black marks from the traffic accident. Her face was obviously badly bruised and swollen around one eye. Dea started to walk into the room. As she drew closer, she could see that Monika's hair had been shaved away in a circle just above her left temple.

Dea greeted Monika's mother kindly. She had to be somewhere in her seventies, but sadness and worry covered her face like a tight mask, making it hard to judge her age.

"My name is Dea Torp," she said, and stood by the wall so that her presence didn't seem too overbearing. "I'm from the police in Odense."

The mother nodded silently, but then she straightened up a little in the chair and told Dea that her name was Irene. "Just come closer. I can't hear very well." She pointed to a chair at the end of the high hospital bed. "I was expecting you might come. I haven't been home much since the accident, and I guess we need to make a decision about what to do with the car," she said, looking at Dea with a little uncertainty. "I'm sure my daughter is insured, and of course we'll pay to have it taken away. Or has it already

WOUNDS

been removed?" She shifted uneasily, as if it was hard for her to come to terms with the fact that the world outside was still spinning.

"Don't worry about that now," Dea said quickly. "We've arranged for it to be picked up and taken away. But I would like to ask you if your daughter had any belongings on her when she was brought to the hospital?"

Dea looked expectantly at the older woman. She had black circles under her eyes and seemed fragile.

"Belongings?" she repeated. "Well, she wasn't conscious at all. She hasn't been for all this time." Her eyes glazed over and she wrung her hands.

"Sorry, I didn't make myself clear," Dea said quickly, and clarified. "Was she wearing a coat? Did her bag come in with her, or is it still in the car?"

"Her bag?" Irene seemed confused and obviously hadn't considered whether her daughter had a bag with her.

Dea moved her chair a little closer to Irene. She had gotten off to a bad start; the older woman looked ill at ease. They sat in silence for a while before Dea changed tack. "Do you know where your daughter was going when she crashed?" Then she asked instead, "Did you talk to her on Sunday?"

"We were supposed to have dinner together, but she canceled," Irene said a little hesitantly, as if it was something she was just remembering now. "We had a bit of an argument because I'd already prepared the food, but then something suddenly came up."

"How did she sound when she canceled?" Dea asked.

"So are you implying that she had been drinking? She hadn't. Monika very rarely does that."

"No," Dea hastened to interrupt. "I mean, did she sound like her usual self? Did anything unusual happen on Sunday or in the days leading up to it?"

Now there was something wary in the mother's eyes. "Tell me, what is this about?" she asked sharply. For a moment, it felt as if the sound of the ventilator became louder and made Monika le Fevre's presence in the room very clear.

"Do you know of a person named Jørgen Andersen? And do you know anything about the restraining order your daughter had placed on him?"

The disorientation in Irene's eyes was clear. "Yes." It came hesitantly. "That man has been harassing us for years. Why are you asking about him? Is he responsible for my daughter's accident?" The woman had turned even paler, if possible, but the sharpness in her voice had disappeared and she slumped slightly, as if a new fear had struck her. "Was it him, the despicable human, who led Monika to have this terrible accident? Is he the one who tried to kill her?"

"No!" Dea said automatically as her mind raced. The accident had happened about twenty-four hours before Jørgen Andersen's body was found, and she reminded herself that according to the autopsy report, he only died late Monday afternoon, so he was alive when Monika crashed the car. But was it likely that it was him—emaciated and injured—who had tried to drive Monika le Fevre to her death? "Jørgen Andersen is dead."

Irene put her hand up to her mouth in horror and shook her head. "He's dead, that's awful."

"It's very unlikely that he could have hurt your daughter," Dea said, not mentioning that she was more interested in finding out if it was the other way around.

WOUNDS   89

"But if he has nothing to do with the accident and my daughter, I don't understand why he has to be brought up now?" Irene had straightened up in her chair again.

Dea jumped into it.

"On Monday, Jørgen Andersen was found beaten and killed with a number of wounds on his body. Wounds very similar to the ones your daughter once inflicted on the animals that were part of her exhibition."

Silence fell. The monotonous sound of the ventilator sounded unnaturally loud in the hospital room once again. Irene opened her mouth and drew in air, as if she wanted to say something, but stopped. She took a deep breath. "Are you saying Monika has something to do with this?"

"We don't know," Dea answered honestly, "but all things considered, it's a possibility we need to explore."

The mother hid her face in her hands. Her upper body trembled. Dea reached out to place a comforting hand on her arm, but Irene raised her hand in defense. "Don't you touch me!" She wiped her eyes. "I want you to leave now."

"I'm not saying that's what happened," Dea tried. "Jørgen Andersen only died on Monday, when your daughter was already here, so she couldn't have killed him, but we have a murder case where there are some similarities that point toward your daughter's exhibition, and we need to follow up on that."

"Okay," Irene said shakily. "It just seems completely . . ." She paused. "I understand that."

Dea hesitated. "Can you tell me why Jørgen was given a restraining order the first time?"

"Yes," Irene said quickly. "Besides sending horrible messages threatening our lives, he showed up at Monika's farm and threw red paint on her property. It took us days to get it off!"

Dea thought for a moment. "Did your daughter have support from people who backed her exhibition? I wonder if someone might have carved animals in the same way as your daughter to show their sympathy?"

Irene le Fevre thought for a moment before shaking her head. "No, that doesn't mean anything to me. Of course there were people who supported her, because not everyone deliberately misunderstood the message, but she was very, very alone and it made us very unhappy as parents to see our daughter so lonely. My husband is also an artist and can of course stuff animals; he's the one who taught Monika the technique. But cutting wounds into the animals while they were alive to allow them to grow into scars was something Monika did solely to highlight human exploitation and disrespect for animals. It's ironic that it was animal activists like Jørgen who went into a rage over the exhibition because they saw Monika's work as animal cruelty, when Monika's message with the artworks was to make people think about whether we have the right to behave as badly as we do toward animals in our industries."

Dea nodded. "Did she change after the exhibition?"

The mother nodded vigorously. "She changed a lot . . . Everything changed. First the outcry that arose in the wake of the exhibition. She was prepared, of course; she created it to start a debate. But she wasn't at all prepared for the vile attacks that came, and she felt very misunderstood and unfairly treated. At first, things went very well. It was exactly the debate she had hoped for. Factual and nuanced. But then the crazies came on the scene." She quickly covered her mouth. "Sorry, now I have to watch what I say. But the whole message was distorted, and a completely unreasonable and horrible hate campaign against our daughter arose."

Her eyes became shiny again.

"How did the anger toward you manifest itself?"

"I've never experienced anything like it. People can be so vile and rude. Like their behavior doesn't mean anything; they just don't care what they do to others. You wouldn't believe how disgusting it was, and it just went on and on. Monika still gets threats from time to time, even though it's been four years since the exhibition was taken down. It never stops." Irene's voice trembled.

"It would be useful to see those threats," said Dea.

"I haven't saved them, but it's possible my daughter has," Irene said, shaking her head. "I'm sorry, but it was a very difficult time for us. Especially for Monika, of course. Her partner, Peter, left her a few months later. He simply put his tail between his legs and ran away. I'll never forgive him for that."

She put a hand on her daughter's sheet. "So yes, it's safe to say that everything changed. She withdrew from society, became shy, and in recent years, she hasn't really had the courage to take on new projects, even though both my husband and I have tried to encourage her to get going again."

"It must be painful to witness," said Dea.

Irene le Fevre nodded. Her gaze was distant. "She's all we have."

Dea stood up and thanked her for her time. "What happened to the animals that were once on display?"

Her mother looked at her in surprise. "I don't know, actually. I don't think she ever brought them home, so they're probably still at Brandts Klædefabrik, if they haven't gotten rid of them."

CHAPTER

12

SOMETHING HAD HAPPENED to Zenia during the year, and it had picked up in the spring, Dybbøl thought as she walked across the cobblestones past Lørups Vinstue and across Claus Bergs Gade to Grønttorvet. Her daughter had become so obsessed with her colossal urge to save all the animals of the world. For just over two years she had been living a plant-based lifestyle, and Dybbøl thought she and Søren were going to great lengths to accommodate their daughter's way of life, but on the evenings when meat was served, she would leave the table, offended, and make numerous pointed comments about her parents apparently supporting animal cruelty.

Søren had tried several times to calm her down. Most recently, their daughter's trump card had been to accuse them of condoning rabbits being skinned alive in China so that their skins could be used for junk in Western countries, because in her world, that was the same as occasionally eating meat. Dybbøl was so tired of the constant arguing. Right now, however, her irritation had faded and was overshadowed by her increasing concern, which only grew now that she could tell Søren had also run out of explanations for where their daughter might be. And why she was nowhere to be found. He was still leaning toward her having run off with the other animal activists. And right now, Dybbøl actually wished she were getting a call from colleagues from one of the other police districts saying they had gotten their hands on Zenia and arrested her after an act of defiance somewhere. Again, she was struck by the feeling that she should have prevented their relationship from getting so far off track. She should have been more understanding, and she should have been more careful to maintain the closeness she had had with Zenia when she was little and told her mother about even the smallest things.

She waved through the window when she spotted her daughter's friends sitting at a corner table.

"I'd like some sparkling water," she said to the waiter in the small restaurant as she took her seat. She looked at the two girls on the other side of the table. "More Coke?"

Zenia's friend Nanna shook her head. "Water is fine."

"With lemon," Dybbøl continued, addressing the waiter, and then she asked if the girls had eaten. They hadn't, and after a quick look at the menu, they ordered Caesar salads and Dybbøl requested a chicken salad.

The waiter disappeared down the narrow dining area, and Dybbøl looked at the two girls. Nanna had been best friends with Zenia since they were very young, while the other, June, had joined in second grade. "Have you heard from Zenia?" Dybbøl asked, trying to make it sound breezy.

Nanna shook her head and looked at her cell phone. "Not since Monday . . . I'll send her a snap of the menu."

"It's nice of you to meet me here during your fall break." Dybbøl smiled, but everything about the meeting felt unnatural. It was Zenia's birthday they were supposed to talk about, but her worry felt like a punch to her stomach. She tried to pull herself together. "It means a lot to Søren and me that Zenia has a good day!"

"Of course," said Nanna. "I'd like to make a giant raspberry shortcake; I'm pretty good at it, and Zen loved raspberry shortcakes when she was little."

Zen. Dybbøl savored the word. "What do you think she'd be most excited about if she could choose anything? A big party without parents, or maybe something where we do something to support Greenpeace?" She actually didn't know if Zenia had anything to do with Greenpeace. "Or WWF?" she added tentatively.

"I think she just wants to have a big family party with everyone she knows."

"Have you talked about it?"

"No, but she's a real family person," said Nanna. *Is she?* Dybbøl was about to exclaim, but thought better of it. "She said a few months ago that she wanted to entice you to have a big birthday party where everyone she's ever known in her life would come."

"It's almost too simple," said Dybbøl, feeling moved. "I thought activism and partying were the most important things to her now."

"She's a real homebody," June said, smiling at the waiter who put a plate in front of her.

Nanna's cell phone buzzed, and Dybbøl stared at it, paralyzed. "Sorry, that was just my sister. We're going to IKEA later."

Dybbøl looked down at her food. "Can you see if your message to Zenia has been read? I'm a bit sad that we haven't heard from her. It's not like her."

"It hasn't. But that's how it is every time I think Zen is out on a mission. She forgets about the world around her and doesn't think about much else. She'll text; she always does."

"And is she out on a mission now, do you think?" Dybbøl heard how desperate she sounded.

Nanna shrugged. "There were definitely plans for it. Last week she talked about a chicken farm somewhere in Jutland, but I don't know when they were leaving; I didn't actually ask. I'm sorry to say it, but it can be a bit much when it's not something you're interested in."

"Chickens . . ." Dybbøl looked up guiltily from her chicken salad.

"I don't know where they were going," Nanna said quickly, as if she regretted spilling the beans.

"Have you found out anything about Amalie Vedel?" June asked. "If you don't mind me asking?"

"You can, but unfortunately the answer is no." Dybbøl took a sip of her water. "There are indications that she's in Sweden. Do you know her?"

"We've played volleyball together for a number of years."

Dybbøl put the glass down with interest. "Is she the kind of person who shows up for training?"

"Yes, she usually does, and her mom usually drives her to and from practice."

Dybbøl could see that the girl was curious about her friend's whereabouts.

"It's just our impression that she can be gone for a few days without us being able to get hold of her," Dybbøl

WOUNDS

continued, and hastened to add, "Just like Zenia right now." She felt confused. Unable to gather her thoughts, she pushed the uneaten food away irritably. "Do you know if Amalie and Zenia know each other?" she asked instead.

"I don't think so," June said, shaking her head slowly. "I only know Amalie because we were in first grade together before I changed schools."

"Zen has never talked about Amalie," said Nanna, "and I don't know her either."

"She was at that party, you know . . . at Bob's!"

"I don't remember," said Nanna, looking down at the table with red cheeks.

Dybbøl gave up trying to keep up. She couldn't make sense of their conversation and tried to concentrate on the birthday again. "I also need to remember to ask Zenia to update her wish list so it's ready when we invite guests."

"She's already done that," Nanna said. "I was sitting with her when she updated it on Saturday."

Dybbøl emptied her glass of water. "Good, then we'll go for a big traditional birthday gathering at our house, and it will be with buns, cake, raspberry slices, flags, cocoa, cousins, and the whole shebang." She felt a twinge in her heart. Why didn't she know that this was how Zenia wanted to spend her birthday? "I was wondering . . . if you hear anything from Zenia, could you let me know? Just so I know she's okay?"

CHAPTER

13

THE BASEMENT OF Brandts Klædefabrik stood in stark contrast to the bright, high-ceilinged exhibition rooms aboveground. The young girl who followed Dea down the stairs looked searchingly down the hallway. "He should be in the workshop down here."

Dea followed her toward a wide double door. The girl knocked but didn't wait for an answer before opening the door and leading Dea into a cluttered workshop bathed in an artificial yellowish light.

"Is someone there?" a man said, looking up from a structure he was either building or taking apart.

The young girl nodded kindly to Dea and disappeared again without saying anything more. The automatic closing arm slowly pulled the door closed behind her.

"Dea Torp," Dea introduced herself to the man. "Odense Police."

The man stood up. He was wearing a blue canvas suit, and his bright-green eyes looked at her with interest. His hair and beard were unkempt and completely gray. He had combed his hair back with some kind of wax, which in no way managed to tame the wild locks, and his beard was gathered with a small red elastic band under his chin. He held out his hand in greeting. "Kenneth!" He squeezed his green eyes shut and took a few steps toward her. "What the hell? Diksen? Is that you?"

"Uh . . ." Dea stopped and scrutinized him. "It's been a long time since I've heard that name. Hi, Kenneth!" She smiled crookedly at him.

"It is you!" Kenneth exclaimed. "Damn, it's been a long time, huh?"

"A lifetime," she admitted. "At least that's what it feels like."

"And you're a sheriff now?" Kenneth laughed. "Who would have thought it?" He stepped closer and opened his arms invitingly. "Can you hug sheriffs on the job?"

Dea accepted the hug. "I didn't recognize you with that big beard."

"Isn't it cool?" Kenneth took a few steps back and fiddled with the red elastic band. "What brings you into my inner sanctum?"

"I'm actually here in connection with an exhibition you hosted four years ago. Were you also head of the workshops back then?"

He looked at her inquisitively and said that they weren't so hung up on titles now. "Was it the one with the animals?"

She nodded.

"Yeah, that one kicked up quite the fuss." He broke into a wide grin. "We still have some of the animals here in the basement. It was like everyone was suddenly afraid to touch them. There's probably fifteen of them down there."

"Do you think I could take a look at them?" Dea asked, but he was already heading for the door.

"Come with me." He let her go first and pointed to a staircase.

"Did you follow what it was all about back then?" She asked as they walked down the semidark hallway that led deeper into the basement.

"Hell yeah, it was hard not to . . . what a shitstorm . . . people were after us for a long time afterwards." Kenneth opened the door into a dark room, and a dusty smell greeted them. He turned on the lights. It was a large room full of shelves, boxes, and large picture frames with their backs facing outward.

"What exactly was she trying to say with her exhibition?" Dea asked, and stopped.

He studied her for a moment, but whether it was still the unexpected reunion or because he was surprised that she hadn't understood the purpose of Monika le Fevre's exhibition, Dea couldn't tell.

"Monika's point was to highlight how humans exploit animals. That we keep them captive in often miserable conditions and breed them only to kill them so we can eat them."

"And that's what she wanted to show by subjecting them to abuse?" Dea asked.

"Yes, think of all the millions of pigs and chickens that are born in this country to be fattened up quickly while living in small cages, then off to the slaughterhouse and onto the dinner table they go."

"But Monika le Fevre didn't use pigs and chickens, did she?"

WOUNDS   101

"No, she used domestic animals. That was the whole essence of it. She wanted to shock people. That's why she chose to use the kind of animals that people have a personal and emotional relationship with. For example, cats and dogs. So people could really react to the cruelty."

"You seem pretty committed to the cause," Dea noted.

He nodded, and the smile from before was gone. "Nowadays, I have nothing to do with what we exhibit; I'm only responsible for the practicalities. But yes, I was definitely involved in that exhibition. It was supposed to run for two months, but we took it down after about four weeks."

"Because of the pressure?"

"We've never received so many angry calls, and I was out washing paint off the facades at least ten times." He shrugged. "Again, it's not my place, but I think they felt it could damage us permanently if we didn't back down and do something about it."

Kenneth counted shelves with a finger poking the air. "They should be here at the end," he said, and walked purposefully to one of the shelves. He kept his eyes on Dea as he pulled a box from the shelf. "Are you in contact with anyone else from back then?"

"Not at all," she said. "But the first few years I saw a lot of Henriette and Gitte."

"Ha, Charlie's angels."

Dea smiled; she had forgotten they were called that.

"Here's at least one," Kenneth said as he handed her a box.

She put it on the floor and opened the lid. It was a cat, shaved smooth of fur on the side of its body, where it had a large, angular wound that had healed completely. "As I understand it, she made the wounds on the animals while they were alive, let them heal like this, then the animals were euthanized to be stuffed and put on display."

"That's pretty much what triggered the violent hatred," Kenneth said. "But the animals were old, and many people euthanize their pets before it's time, and that was part of the message: Man exploits all other living things. But from what I understand, Monika's animals were always anesthetized, so it was completely painless for them."

"Can I take a few of these boxes in to the police station?"

He pulled out two more and said that for his sake, she had to take them all. He could use the space.

"What do you need them for, if I may ask?"

She had been expecting that question and quickly replied that they would be used in the investigation into the harassment that continued to target le Fevre.

"Give me five minutes and they'll be packed and ready to go . . . and then you can drop by for a cup of mocha and a chat another day."

* * *

Liam screwed the cap on his mineral water and slipped it into the compartment in his car door. He looked at the old red house at the end of the dirt road they had driven down. Jørgen Andersen had worked at the nursery before he switched to the terrarium and then stopped working.

The house seemed worn down. On one side of the driveway was a greenhouse about thirty meters long. The greenhouse windows were dark, and several of them were covered in algae. The whole place had a distant feel of a bygone era. Behind it all was a barnlike building with a tall, old stone chimney in the middle. "Are you sure this is it?"

"That's the address we have, so yes, and an elderly woman named Edna Clausen should live here," Thorbjørn replied, and got out of the car.

Liam followed, although he was skeptical. The house looked abandoned. "Knock on the door, and I'll take a look around the greenhouse."

He pushed open the white-painted iron door of the greenhouse and was greeted by a dry, musty smell. The old beds were completely overgrown with large plants growing in wild disarray, and in several places they had penetrated the cracked windows. There were small, old trowels lying around, and in the middle of the room was a worn wooden table with a single chair. On the table was a large advertising ashtray filled with butts.

Liam left the greenhouse and walked up to the red house, where Thorbjørn was standing with a petite, gray-haired woman.

"This is Edna," said Thorbjørn.

"Jørgen is a good boy." Edna continued her conversation with Thorbjørn in a rough voice that matched the smell of tobacco wafting out the open front door. She nodded briefly to Liam.

"Coffee?" she asked, turning resolutely and leading the way to a sofa in a small living room. She acted as though she had been looking forward to the visit.

"Yes, please," Liam said.

"Careful not to sit on Pearl!" she exclaimed, looking at the soft chairs around the coffee table. "She sometimes hides under the cushions."

"Pearl?" Thorbjørn asked as he lifted an embroidered cushion with a flower motif.

"My cat," she said, staring at them. "Didn't you want coffee?"

Thorbjørn looked in bewilderment at Liam, who nodded. "Yes, thank you."

"That's good. Then I'd like to ask for a cup too!" Edna said, and sat down carefully in one of the soft chairs.

Liam looked pleadingly at Thorbjørn and nodded toward the kitchen.

"Do you have milk?" Thorbjørn surrendered and smiled.

"The milk is sour," she said, pouting. "It's been a long time since Jørgen has been here, and he's the one who does the shopping. He wasn't here this week . . . and he wasn't here last week either . . . He usually comes."

"Do you have anyone else who can shop for you?" Liam asked, surprised that the two were still in touch. The older woman hadn't told him that when he'd called to arrange the visit.

"No, there's only Jørgen."

"Maybe you should consider a delivery service?"

"Are you crazy, Officer? They want fifty kroner for that!"

"I guess it's better than . . ." Liam hesitated and watched the older woman. She was neatly dressed and well groomed. The living room was also neat and well maintained. "Do you have food in the house?"

"Yes, yes, we have porridge and bread and lots of frozen food . . . and cheese." She looked at him with a sly smile. "And coffee . . . we can't do without coffee."

"Do you live alone with your cat?"

"Yes, it's been a long time since Torben died."

"And Torben was your husband?"

"Well, he was actually my sister's husband, but then she died and Torben and the boy moved in here with me, because my husband had also died a few years earlier, so it was convenient." She shook her head slightly.

"Coffee is ready." Thorbjørn placed an orange enamel tray with a red pattern on the coffee table and handed out mugs.

"What about the kid?" Liam said. "Does he still come here?"

"It's Jørgen," Edna replied, confused. "Didn't you come to talk about him?" She narrowed her eyes. "And what do you want with him?"

"So Jørgen has been living here?" Liam said, equally confused.

"Yes, that's what I'm saying. His mother died, and then he and Torben moved in here. Jørgen was twelve years old at the time."

"We were under the impression that Jørgen Andersen had worked here."

"Well, he helped out with the tomatoes, but it wasn't exactly a great success, and then we tried crayfish for a while, but it didn't go so well."

"Crayfish?" Liam stole a glance at Thorbjørn, who was watching them from his seat and seemed to be having a great time.

"Yes, we had them in big tubs out in the barn, and that was fine, but there was no money in it. No money at all."

"We understood that Jørgen was employed at the nursery?" Liam tried again.

"Ahhh!" Edna exclaimed. "But that was over the other side of the road . . . at the big one . . . Ebbe and Astrid's Tomatoes, they call themselves today. He was there for a few years, but that was a long time ago. They had a row."

"Do you know what their disagreement was about?" Thorbjørn asked.

Edna looked absent-mindedly out the window before announcing that it was something to do with the animals.

"But don't they grow tomatoes?"

"Yes, but they had so much extra heat from their facility that they decided they wanted to keep ducks too, so they were ready for Christmas." The words came slowly and a bit incoherently.

"And then they treated the ducks badly?" Liam asked tentatively.

Edna looked at him in wonder. "Did you know about that?"

Liam shook his head. "It was just a guess."

"Jørgen was so angry when he found out."

"What happened?"

"Some of the ducks died, and Jørgen believed they died because they were too hot and didn't get enough water. There were also too many; they were trampling each other to death."

"What did Jørgen say to that?" Thorbjørn asked.

"He was fired when he let all the ducks out. But he didn't care—he didn't want to witness that mess, he said." Edna lit up. "No, wait! He got some money from them, and then he stopped. They didn't want him to go any further with it."

"So they paid him to stop working over there?"

WOUNDS

"Yes, I think so."

Liam took a sip of his coffee. "We'll talk to them."

"I don't think they have ducks anymore," Edna said. "So you've come a tad too late."

"We just want to talk to them about Jørgen."

"Where is Jørgen?" she asked, looking around as if she had just realized he wasn't there.

Liam hesitated. "Don't you have anyone to come and keep you company?"

"No, it's only Jørgen who comes here . . . and then the mailman. Well, sometimes Laila comes down from up the road and says hello."

"A neighbor?" Edna nodded.

"We'll talk to her too," Liam said, "and then we'll come back to you."

"Before you go," Edna said, looking around searchingly. "Can you look at my phone? It's writing strange things and I press the wrong buttons so easily. Jørgen usually fixes it."

Outside the house, Liam surveyed the neighboring houses while waiting for Thorbjørn, who was tapping notifications off the screen of Edna's half-broken iPhone. It wasn't far to Laila's next door. He'd often noticed the house over the years. It was a visual feature on the road between Bellinge and Brylle, with its big pick-your-own strawberry signs in the summer and rather wild pumpkin displays at Halloween. Right now, their Halloween display was in full swing, with an inflated orange car hanging from the top of a pole by the highway and long stretches of orange pumpkins and spooky fun.

On the other side of the main road was the large nursery where Ebbe and Astrid's tomatoes were grown and packed.

"Someone has to tell her that she won't get any more visits from Jørgen," Thorbjørn said when he came out. "But I feel bad that she has to sit there alone when we tell her that Jørgen is dead."

Liam nodded. "Stay here with Edna, and I'll see if I can get hold of the neighbor before I go across the road and look around at Ebbe and Astrid's Tomatoes. Someone needs to be with her when we break the bad news about Jørgen."

CHAPTER

14

DYBBØL FOUND IT difficult to gather her thoughts. She looked up at the board where Lene Eriksen was placing a mark on a map.

"Our colleagues in Sweden have just launched a major police operation. An extended search has begun in the areas Amalie may have gone to," said the head of the investigation. "And here I mean a search that also covers lakes, bogs, forests, and empty buildings within a radius of thirty kilometers from where her jacket was found."

Dybbøl looked at her wristwatch. Her husband had texted that he was on his way to the police station. Something had happened. She had called several times, but he hadn't answered. It had now been almost twenty minutes.

"Just over an hour ago, I received a report that Amalie Vedel may have been traveling between Malmö and Skurup." She looked again at the board, where a map of Skåne county had been hung, and drew a red ink ring around the Swedish city.

There was a commotion in the room, and Lene held up a hand to signal that she wasn't finished.

"Several interesting witnesses have come forward in connection with the missing-child alert that was circulated in Sweden earlier today. Among them, we were tipped off that Amalie may have been seen in the vicinity of Skurup, but this has not been definitively confirmed. We are currently working intensively to obtain and review surveillance from Skurup station, the Øresund Bridge, and the ferry to Bornholm, as Skurup is right on the route from Malmö to Ystad, but I should remind you that the rest area where her jacket was found is not on this route." Lene looked down at her papers.

Dybbøl stood up as soon as she received a message from Søren. Her husband had texted that he was sitting in her office. "Sorry," she said, and looked at the others. "I'm afraid I have to go. Let me know if the surveillance yields anything."

* * *

"You have three calls," her secretary said as she entered the front office.

"I'll call them back later," Dybbøl said frantically, nodding toward the closed door to his office. "Is my husband waiting in there?"

"Yes, I got him a cup of coffee."

"Thank you!"

Dybbøl pushed open the door to the office. "What's happened? Has she come home, have you heard from her?"

She immediately sensed the uneasiness that lay heavy around him, and he seemed tense in the same way as when his work pressure threatened to push him over the edge.

"What happened?" she repeated, hearing for herself that her voice was sharp, bordering on shrill.

"When I came home earlier today to pick up some transcripts for the closed session tonight, our front door was open, and Lady was gone." He was pale and serious. "I looked all over the neighborhood, talked to all our neighbors, and I even went to the preschool down the road to ask if they'd seen her." He shook his head. "They hadn't."

"It's Zenia," exclaimed Dybbøl. "She's come home. She always goes with Lady when she comes home from school."

She felt her legs give way beneath her in a sigh of relief as she pulled out a chair and collapsed. "They're just out for a walk."

Her husband shook his head again.

"There are no signs that Zenia has come home," he said. "And the dog leash was hanging in its place." He hesitated for a moment. "Could you have forgotten to close the door when you left?"

"Of course I didn't forget to close the door," she said, but still picked up her bag with trembling hands to see if her keys were there. "Look, I have my keys. But maybe I forgot to set the alarm."

Right now, she couldn't even bring herself to be angry that Zenia had just disappeared. The relief was so overwhelming that she wanted to laugh with abandon. She couldn't wait to see her daughter and give her a proper hug.

"She hasn't come home," Søren repeated, and she could hear the irritation in his voice, as if he was trying to shake her. "If she had come home, I would have seen it. There's no trace of her in the house. She would have been in her room and would probably have been in the fridge; she usually does that. She's not there, Margrethe, and Lady is gone."

Dybbøl straightened up and looked at him. It wasn't often that he said her name like that.

"Do you think a stranger has been in our home and taken Lady?"

"I know it's fall break," he continued anxiously, "and I also know that she's run off with her friends before and disappeared without notice. But she's been gone for almost two days, and with the Amalie Vedel case and Lady's disappearance in mind, that's simply too long. We have to put out an APB. We can't just keep walking around waiting for her to show up. So yes, to answer your question: I think something has happened."

Slowly, the feeling of relief left her body as she realized Søren was right. They would have to put out an APB on their daughter and set the wheels in motion. It would be hell when the APB went out. The press would be all over her, and everyone would draw parallels to the Vedel case. Their lives would be turned upside down and become public property. There would be speculation about whether they were good or bad parents. Zenia's friends would be hunted down and interviewed, and no one knew what they might say. About wild parties or the activism she was so involved in. And when Zenia turned up and it turned out she'd been out sabotaging a chicken farm, that story would end up on the front page too.

She hid her face in her hands. She couldn't face it. "Amalie Vedel has been missing for almost three weeks," she heard her husband say. "And you said yourself last night that the chances of her being found alive are desperately small after so long. I insist that we report Zenia missing."

She straightened up and watched him as he pulled their daughter's laptop out of his bag.

"I brought this," he said, and asked if she could get their IT people to look at it. "Maybe they can see if she's been messaging anyone. Maybe they can get into her Messenger, Snapchat, TikTok, or whatever she uses with her friends."

Dybbøl cleared her throat. "I can't just go down and tell them to shove my daughter's computer in front of everything else they have," she said. "Can't you see how it's going to look when we haven't even put out an APB on her yet?"

"Then we'll put out an APB on her now," her husband decided. "And if you don't want to do it yourself, then . . ."

"Of course I want to do it myself," she interrupted him. "We can do it together. We just have to think about the consequences."

They sat in silence for a while before she pointed to the laptop. "Have you looked at it?"

"It requires a password, and I've tried the most obvious ones. When you reach out to IT, they might be able to track her cell phone too. We should have done that right away."

There was a hint of reproach in his voice.

"Just because I'm in this position doesn't mean that I can freely draw on all police resources. We have some big cases that are taking up all the staff's time at the moment. Everyone has plenty to do."

114   SARA BLÆDEL AND MADS PEDER NORDBO

Her husband stood up, and she looked away for a moment. Arguing wasn't helping, she knew that. She pulled herself together. "I'll talk to Piil. First, I'll ask her to look at the computer and start a trace. Then we'll have to consider whether we should file a police report."

Her husband came over and leaned over her. She returned the embrace and nodded as he whispered that they would find their daughter.

CHAPTER

15

WHEN LIAM HAD picked up Laila and left her and Thorbjørn with Edna in the small, smoky living room, he continued across Assensvej to the property that housed Ebbe and Astrid's Tomatoes. The nursery was on a completely different scale from Edna's, and everyone within a radius of twenty kilometers knew about it because of the light: An orange glow from the greenhouses stretched hundreds of meters into the air and could be seen far away at night.

There were several cars parked, and he could see that there were people in several of the greenhouses. Only one of the cars had Danish license plates; the rest were Romanian or Lithuanian. He stood for a moment and tried to get his bearings. The site was so large that it was impossible to survey it all at once, and as far as he knew, there were five or six different nurseries along Bindekildevej. Following Edna's instructions, he had walked a few hundred meters up the road and turned left, where there was a private residence with a small parking lot in front. Scattered around the house were greenhouses, several office buildings, and a large heating plant. There were disused silos. Newer silos. Containers. Chimneys. It wasn't exactly the picture you envisioned when you picked up a cute green cardboard box containing six tomatoes in a supermarket.

Liam had just started walking toward the residence when an old Audi with Romanian plates pulled into the parking lot. A muscular man and two slightly haggard women in their early twenties got out and looked at him quizzically.

"Do you know where the manager is?" Liam tried.

"Sorry . . . no English," the man said, and hurried after the women toward a two-story building. The building's many windows were blacked out from the inside with blankets or cardboard. He watched the three disappear into the building for a moment before pulling out his cell phone and taking a few pictures of the building and the parked cars. It was worth checking the license plates and work permits, he thought before turning around to move on.

"Hey!"

Liam looked up at the old, redbrick house, where a man was heading down the driveway. He looked agitated, waving his arms, and Liam noticed he was hobbling on one leg.

"What are you doing here?" the man shouted angrily.

"I'm from Odense Police," Liam said calmly, and took out his ID. "Investigation."

"Well, well, well," the man said, studying Liam's badge. "Do you have a warrant? If not, I'm going to ask you not to snoop around on private property!"

"Private?" Liam said in surprise. "I'm looking for a manager or supervisor who can help me answer some questions about a former employee here on-site."

WOUNDS

117

The man stared uneasily at Liam. "That would be me."

"Then maybe your employees own these cars and live in this house?" Liam continued.

"No one lives in the house," the man replied carefully as he slowly put on a plaid flannel shirt over his T-shirt with forced calm.

Liam looked at the covered windows.

The man continued to stare at Liam expressionlessly. "I want to see your warrant."

"I'm just looking for the owner of Ebbe and Astrid's Tomatoes," Liam said calmly. "You don't need a warrant to walk up a garden path."

"I'm having a bad day, so you've been warned," said the man, but he seemed to give in. "I'm Ebbe and Astrid's eldest son, Ole. What do you want?"

Liam looked at the man. He was probably in his mid-sixties and rather overweight. The dingy pale-yellow T-shirt under his shirt was snug, revealing an expanse of pale belly hanging over his trousers waistband. His poor legs were visibly swollen under his pants.

Liam abandoned the idea of suggesting they sit inside. "Can we talk here for a minute?"

Ole nodded reluctantly.

"I'm here in connection with a murder investigation," Liam said.

"Homicide?"

Liam nodded and looked down at his leg. "Are you hurt?"

"It's blood clots," Ole said. "Fucking shitty leg. I go to physio twice a week . . . in a fucking minibus, because I can't drive with that leg." He looked at Liam with his beady eyes. "What does our nursery have to do with a police investigation? Did one of my guys see something?"

"It's about a former employee of this place. Maybe it was during your parents' time. He's about your age."

"Fire away," Ole said, and looked toward the house, where a blanket was moving on one of the windows. But he seemed curious, and some of his reluctance had diminished.

"Jørgen Andersen," Liam said, and waited to see if the name rang a bell. "Like I said, it was quite a few years ago. He lived across the road back then."

"Jønne," Ole grunted. "You can't forget a crazy fool like him that easily."

"Did he work here?"

"For a few years, yeah, but he got crazier as time went."

"Can you elaborate on what you mean by that?"

Ole shook his head in resignation, as if it was something he struggled to take seriously. "At one point we tried a few ducks for Christmas slaughter, but we ran into some problems keeping them alive. Jørgen was convinced that we were mistreating the animals, but that was bullshit because we actually wanted to sell them at a good price, so of course we did everything we could to fatten them up and make sure they were healthy and well."

"How did he think you mistreated them?"

Ole held his palms up in the air dismissively. "Ask him."

Liam put his cell phone in his pocket to signal that they were talking off the record. "What I'm interested in isn't really about what happened to the ducks. I just want to talk to you about what Jørgen was like and why he was fired."

Ole sighed heavily. "One day Jørgen came into the building where the ducks were, and he found some of them

WOUNDS   119

dead or emaciated." Ole flailed his arms. "It was our irrigation system that had broken down. But he went nuts about animal cruelty. He was convinced that there were too many animals in too little a space and that they were squashing each other to death."

"So did you fire him?"

"It wasn't easy, because he got hold of his union, and it ended up with the police and vets paying an unannounced visit."

"Did you get a fine?"

Ole shook his head. "They didn't find anything illegal—we knew they wouldn't—and afterwards we agreed with Jørgen that he should stop working here."

"And he agreed to that?" Liam asked.

Ole stirred a little uneasily. "It was in my father's time, but yeah."

"We're under the impression that he left here with some kind of golden handshake?"

Ole looked dismissively at Liam without answering.

"Did you pay him to stop and keep quiet about what had happened?" Liam repeated.

"I don't remember that."

They both turned at the sound of a car turning into the parking lot. It was Thorbjørn. Liam raised his hand in greeting. The timing couldn't have been better. "That's probably the warrant you're looking for," he continued, looking at Ole again. "All these cars and the people who live in the house, is there paperwork on it all?"

"Of course," Ole sneered.

"Have you seen Jørgen out here after you paid him to stop?"

"No, we haven't seen him since then."

"So he hasn't come back for more money or to see if you still keep ducks?"

"I haven't seen him." He folded his arms across his chest and tilted his head back slightly.

"Apart from the ducks and animal welfare, did you find that Jørgen could be aggressive?"

"It's not something I've really thought about," Ole said, and his arms went down again. "But he was a strange guy. I didn't like him very much."

Liam gave up trying to get more out of the tomato gardener and thanked him for the chat.

* * *

Liam got into the car with his colleague. He nodded to Ole, who stood back in the parking lot and looked around a little, scowling.

"Did he have anything to contribute?" Thorbjørn asked as he slowly backed out of the small parking lot.

"Not really. He didn't seem very enthusiastic about Jørgen Andersen, but apart from the ducks, they didn't seem to have been at odds with each other," Liam said, sensing there was something Thorbjørn was dying to tell him. He seemed eager, the energy trembling in his well-trained body. "What?" Liam asked, looking at him.

"I got to talk to Laila before we comforted Edna," Thorbjørn began. "She told me that Edna is visited by a young girl at least once or twice a month. When I asked about it, Edna confirmed that she has a visiting friend."

Thorbjørn kept his eyes on the road, as if he enjoyed keeping Liam in suspense.

WOUNDS

121

"And?" Liam said, a bit annoyed. "So maybe it's someone who can help with the shopping, now that she no longer has Jørgen to do that."

"There's more yet," Thorbjørn said, winking at him as he slowed down. "It's a seventeen-year-old girl named Zenia, and as far as Edna understood, her mother is something with the police."

Liam frowned. "Are you saying it's Dybbøl's Zenia?"

"Yes, it must be," Thorbjørn agreed.

"Have you talked to Dybbøl?"

"Yes, I called her straightaway. But she doesn't know anything about Zenia being a visiting friend for Edna or anyone else."

CHAPTER

16

DEA WAS BACK at the station after her visit to Brandts Klædefabrik and had just opened the bag with the sandwich Rolf had bought her. She placed it on her desk along with a small chocolate heart in shiny red foil. She had called him several times, but he hadn't answered, so she texted him and sent him a picture of her blowing a kiss. Feeling girlish, she quickly looked around to make sure the other people in the open office hadn't noticed that she was taking selfies with her pouty lips and loving eyes.

She thought about her adult daughter for a moment. It had been months since they had seen each other. They hadn't even spoken on the phone, not since Dea had been told she was too old to fall in love with a man so much younger than her. Her daughter had gone to great lengths to tell her that it was to be expected that a man so young still dreamed of having children.

It had stung, and it still did when Dea thought about it. She had defended herself by saying that Rolf did have a daughter but unfortunately had a complicated relationship with the girl's mother. They had split up before the daughter turned two. He had moved to Zealand shortly after and, as far as she knew, had not had contact with either the girl or his ex since.

Dea had sensed from the moment she and Rolf started seeing each other properly that it wasn't something he liked to talk about, so they didn't. But nevertheless, it had hurt when her own daughter read between the lines that Dea was somehow wasting Rolf's time. Katrine had also managed to foresee that Rolf would no doubt leave Dea when he found a younger model. A younger, fertile woman, she said. Dea had been so furious and hurt. Katrine was twenty-seven and had no children of her own, so the argument had ended with Dea childishly shouting that maybe her daughter should just have children of her own, since she suddenly seemed so concerned about people reproducing.

Dea missed Katrine and knew they needed to move on and put this mess behind them. She had just decided to call and invite herself to Copenhagen when Liam walked quickly toward her and interrupted her thoughts.

"I just got a call from the North Zealand Police," he said, and shrugged off his jacket. Behind him came Thorbjørn, as if he'd just caught up. "A colleague has recognized the scars on Jørgen Andersen."

Dea pushed her sandwich aside and pulled out a notepad. "Recognized? Have they seen this kind of thing before?"

Liam nodded.

"They had a death in August this year, and the man had two similar scars on his torso. He has sent the report from the site investigation."

"Only two? Was he found in the same way as Jørgen?" Dea was fully paying attention now.

"He was found in a forest. The cause of death was a blood clot in his heart, so there was no suspicion of homicide. We will follow up immediately."

She nodded and got to her feet as he held out his cell phone to her. He zoomed in with his fingers and showed her a picture with a triumphant expression.

"It looks very similar," she admitted, and nodded. Thorbjørn had stepped forward to take a look. "Where was he found?" Dea handed the cell phone to Thorbjørn.

"He lived in Tisvilde, and his name is Jan Hansen. I've just asked Piil to get everything she can find on him. No actual police case was opened in August because the man died of a blood clot, so the call from North Zealand only came because the police officer who was at the location in the forest reacted to the picture we sent around."

Thorbjørn handed the phone back to Liam and glanced at Dea's untouched sandwich.

"Just take it," she said. The adrenaline had started pumping through her body, and she was no longer hungry.

"Jan Hansen was found in the woods on August eleventh. According to the report, he was wet and dirty at the time of his discovery. He had not taken his heart or diabetes medication since he disappeared from home on August seventh. According to the pathologist's report from the site investigation, it was likely that he could have self-inflicted the wounds we are interested in with a sharp object. Our colleagues spoke to the widow, who told us that he had left their home just after noon. It is unknown why he disappeared and why he was in the woods."

"Could he have wanted to die?" Dea suggested. "Is there anything in the report?"

"It doesn't say that directly," Liam replied. "But the case probably didn't get much attention because of the likelihood that it was a suicide. According to the widow, he lost his job a month before he died. He was fired just before the summer vacation, and he had been depressed in the time leading up to his disappearance."

"So it was considered a suicide because he had left home without his vital medication?" Thorbjørn crumpled the sandwich wrapper and sent it in a perfect arc to the trash can as he ate the last bite of Dea's sandwich.

"Yeah, something like that," Liam admitted.

"And the wounds?" Dea asked.

"They were superficial, and as I said, there was no suspicion of a crime, since he died of a blood clot that he got because he didn't take the medication that prevented that. The case was subsequently closed."

"I guess we would have come to the same conclusion," Thorbjørn said.

Dea and Liam nodded.

"But then Jørgen showed up."

"Yes, then Jørgen showed up," Dea repeated, looking at her boss. "Shall we get to Tisvilde?"

CHAPTER

17

"VISITING FRIEND? ZENIA isn't anyone's visiting friend. She would have said so; we always talk about what we're up to," Dybbøl exclaimed, and looked at Thorbjørn in bewilderment. "It must be a misunderstanding. She never mentioned a tomato nursery. Where did you say it was?"

"Between Bellinge and Brylle," Thorbjørn replied. She could feel that he was watching her intently and got the feeling he was withholding information because he hoped she might tell him herself. But she had nothing to say. The situation took her completely by surprise, and she was absolutely sure he was wrong. Still, a sense of unease closed in on her.

"I've just looked into it," the broad-shouldered officer continued. "Your daughter is a visiting friend through the Red Cross in Odense. And over the past year and a half, she's been coming to Edna Clausen's farm once a month."

Dybbøl shook her head and realized her breathing was too shallow. She took a controlled deep breath to calm herself. "I've never heard her talk about a woman by that name. Who is Edna Clausen?"

"Edna . . ." Thorbjørn began, as if he could spare her with his slow unfurling of the case. ". . . is Jørgen Andersen's aunt. He grew up on the nursery where Edna Clausen lives. So that's where Zenia goes regularly."

"Jørgen Andersen?" she repeated, feeling completely disconnected.

"Yes, the man who was found behind the abandoned inn in Verninge, with . . ." Thorbjørn fell silent.

Dybbøl threw her hands up in front of her face in shock. She had an overwhelming sense that she had made a huge mistake, that she had been sleepwalking through life since her daughter's disappearance. She had made all the wrong decisions. When Zenia didn't come home, she should have gone downstairs and reported it to the police immediately, so that Zenia would already have been reported missing and all resources to find her would already have been set in motion. Instead, she sat here wasting time. To top it all off, she'd just realized that she knew nowhere near as much about her daughter's life as she thought she did.

"But that doesn't make sense," she said, letting her hands fall heavily on her desk. "Why would my daughter be connected to your abused murder victim?"

Dybbøl looked away as she felt undiluted fear rolling in. "The animals," she whispered to herself. The office fell silent. She didn't know how long they sat across from each other in silence, but finally she looked up and looked directly at Thorbjørn. "My daughter is missing."

She saw his eyes widen on the other side of the desk.

"Zenia has been missing since Monday night. We need to put out an APB on her. I've already delivered her computer to Piil. Please wait to put out an official APB until we've received mast information to see if we can track her whereabouts."

She felt his serious gaze and suddenly felt strong and empowered. "I want you to find my daughter. Now."

* * *

"Should I turn off here?" Liam asked, nodding toward a side road. At least they had made it all the way to Tisvilde without taking a wrong turn.

"The next left, and then I think we have to turn almost immediately again." Dea peered out the windshield. "Skovridervænget. Mogens actually had a friend who lived here."

"Your husband?"

"Yes."

"But this wasn't where you were staying when he . . ." Liam stopped.

"When he died? No, it was in Jutland. It's okay to talk about it. It was a long time ago."

Liam nodded to himself. Dea had been in a similar position to his in Copenhagen when her husband died in her arms, and it had devastated her so much that she had ended up in Greenland for a few years. She couldn't handle life in Denmark. "Did you actually get hold of the North Zealand Police?"

"Yes, and I agree that there was no need for a more thorough investigation then, but there probably will be now. I spoke to his wife, who said that we can just drop by. She'll be there until five o'clock." She leaned forward in her seat to look up at the road sign. "It's going to be hard on her, us showing up and ripping into her grief so soon after. I could hear it in her voice when we spoke." She pointed out the windshield. "It's here!"

Liam turned onto the narrow road and parked the car next to the house Dea had pointed out. For a moment he sat and looked at the small white-plastered villa, hoping that they would be presented with a logical explanation for the two scars on Jan Hansen's chest.

Dea opened the car door. "Shall we?" She started walking up the garden path and waited for him to catch up, then knocked on the door and took a small step back.

"Yes?" said the woman who answered the door. She was dark haired and pale. Her eyes were blue gray and heavy with fatigue.

"We're the police," Dea said. "I'm the one who rang you a couple hours ago."

The woman stepped aside and let them enter. "Berit." She held out a cold hand uncertainly. The house seemed dark and tired, with brown ceilings, small windows, and carpeting on all floors.

"Have you lived here long?" Dea asked chattily, trying to get Jan Hansen's widow to relax.

"Seventeen years," said Berit, pointing to a couple of armchairs. "Would you like some coffee?"

"That would be great," Liam broke in.

Shortly after, Berit Hansen was back with three mugs with teaspoons in them. "It's Nescafé; we've never really drunk anything else. Milk?"

Liam shook his head.

Berit smoothed down her beige corduroy pants with restless hands before sitting down on the sofa opposite them. She didn't take up much space between the cushions and blankets, Liam noticed.

"We understand that your husband was missing for four days before he was found in the woods," Liam began.

"Yes." Berit sat motionless before continuing in a subdued voice, "It took four days before we knew for sure. But we had already reported him missing on the first day. It wasn't like him to disappear like that. He would never skip dinner without telling us, and when he wasn't home for evening coffee either, Maria and I called the police."

"Do you know if he had any personal reasons for being away for four days?" Dea asked.

Liam could hear that it was difficult for the woman to talk about this. She didn't flinch, but her voice became thick.

"I don't understand why you're asking about all this now," she exclaimed with her hands clasped in her lap. "My husband died of a blood clot. That's what we were told after they found him."

"There is no doubt that your husband died of a heart attack," Dea said. "We are here because of the wounds your husband had on his chest."

"I don't know anything about that." She looked at Dea in bewilderment. "They explained to us that he probably died because he hadn't taken his medication while he was away."

"You don't know anything about the two wounds on his chest?"

She shook her head uncertainly. "I didn't see any wounds. It was the undertaker who dressed him; Maria and I just gave them the clothes we found. It was our daughter who chose the suit he had worn for her confirmation."

WOUNDS   131

"I'm sorry for coming here with all our questions," Liam said. "But it turns out that your husband had two rather distinctive wounds on his chest." He briefly considered showing her the images from the autopsy report but instead pointed to his own chest.

Berit stared at him silently.

"Is it correct that he didn't have those wounds when he disappeared?" he asked gently to make sure the woman understood what they were asking.

"I certainly hadn't noticed them," Berit answered hesitantly, as if she was afraid of saying something wrong.

"Had you noticed any kind of wounds on his body before?"

She seemed perplexed, and Dea explained that the wounds were cut to look like a small flap of skin. Berit shook her head vigorously. "No, I'd definitely not seen anything like that."

"Do you think he could have cut himself?"

"Why on earth would he do that?" she exclaimed with a small, uncertain laugh.

"How was he mentally in the weeks before he disappeared?"

Jan Hansen's widow looked down at the coffee table. "He was more quiet and sullen than he used to be. I didn't know it at the time, but after he died, I learned that he had been fired from his job. He hadn't told me—I think he was embarrassed or ashamed—and he was probably afraid of the future too. I . . ." Her voice broke. "I really wish he had told me. So I could have supported him and we could have been in it together instead of him brooding over it alone. Without him, I can hardly afford to keep this house. I also blame myself for not noticing that something was wrong; we could have solved it together. I could have gone back to work, he could have found something else."

"I don't know if you know this, but you can get free financial advice from your local council," said Dea. "You just have to google it. There may also be some options through Jan's pension scheme."

"I haven't really had the energy to look at it properly yet," Berit confessed.

Dea took out her cell phone and tapped the screen a few times, found a number, and sent it to Berit. "Call them tomorrow."

Berit looked at the number. "Thank you."

"Where did your husband work?" Liam asked.

"He was the financial manager at Stålværket in Frederiksværk."

"How long was he there?"

"At least ten years."

"So he was happy there?"

"I'm sure he was, yes."

"Do you know why he was fired?"

"No, I didn't even know he'd been fired, so he didn't talk to me about it."

"Do you know if he was well liked at his workplace? Did he speak well of his colleagues?"

"I didn't notice otherwise, and when we went to Christmas parties and those company races, we always had fun with the others."

Liam leaned forward a little. "What was your husband's attitude toward animal welfare and cruelty to animals?"

The woman looked at him in amazement. "He wasn't an animal abuser, if that's what you're asking!"

"No, I actually mean the opposite. Did he actively fight for animal rights? Was your husband an animal activist?"

Berit blinked in confusion.

"Not that I know of! Why on earth would you ask that?"

Liam failed to answer and instead asked, "Did he ever talk about an art exhibition that consisted of taxidermy?"

She shook her head and looked like she had given up trying to understand where this was going.

"No, that doesn't ring a bell, and it was very rare that Jan had an opinion on anything political . . . He was mostly interested in football."

"Does the name Jørgen Andersen mean anything to you? Has Jan ever mentioned that name?"

"Is it someone from work? I don't know them all by name, although I was there every time there were events."

"No," Liam replied, explaining that the man lived on Funen.

"I don't think we know anyone around Funen," she said, shaking her head. "So what is this all about? Has my husband done something illegal?"

"We don't think so," Dea said quickly. "But the wounds he had on his chest could possibly be connected to a murder case. And that's why it's important we find out if your husband had any connection to the murder we're investigating."

"Jan killed someone?" She sounded desperate but still moved her face minimally when she spoke.

"No," Liam said quickly. "This happened after your husband's death. But we are trying to find out if there may have been a connection between Jørgen Andersen and your husband. If you don't mind, we would like to take Jan's computer, cell phone, and any other communication devices in for examination."

"Go ahead," she said softly. "It's all in his office. But I don't know his passwords. That's where all our vacation photos are and so many other things I never thought of transferring to my own computer. Now I can't access it at all."

"We hear that a lot," said Dea. "It's not something you think about in everyday life until it's too late. You'll get it all back, of course."

Berit stood up stiffly and disappeared through a door next to the kitchen. A moment later she returned with a dark-blue tote bag with a steel mill logo on it.

"I've gathered everything in here," she said, and held the bag out to Liam.

"Berit, you've been a great help," said Dea. "Thank you for letting us come."

"There wasn't much I could contribute," she said, and followed them out. She had opened the front door and had stepped aside when a thought seemed to strike her. She turned to Liam and asked with the same expressionless face, "Was my husband killed?"

CHAPTER

18

MARGRETHE DYBBØL WAS sitting in the front seat of the dog handler's car, facing Rolf. A car from the National Forensic Service had already been sent ahead. She had contacted them herself and had them send a man to her home address. Not the whole team, just a single forensic scientist who might be able to confirm or deny whether there were fresh clues that Zenia had been home. She had told them about Lady being gone but explained that it wasn't because of the dog and the open front door that she wanted her house searched.

She was also the one who had stopped Rolf in the hallway when she was on her way down to the department to find someone to go home with her to search the villa. When she spotted him, it occurred to her that it was even better to get a police dog out there. And she had been very clear that this was not a task the dog handler could say no to.

"I just want to know if it's my daughter who's been home," she said. "Right now it's not so much about whether we've been burglarized or not."

136   SARA BLÆDEL AND MADS PEDER NORDBO

She saw that he nodded. It had spread like wildfire when it became known that her daughter had disappeared. Dybbøl had asked Søren to stay behind at the police station to make sure the investigators got all the relevant information and pictures of their daughter they might need. She had decided to wait to initiate a trace on Zenia's cell phone until they issued an official APB. She couldn't shake the idea that her daughter had chained herself to a chicken coop in protest. And she certainly wasn't going anywhere if it turned out that that was why she was missing. At the same time, she felt the unease rumbling in her stomach.

"It's the next road," she said, pointing. They had barely stepped out of the car when a younger man from the National Forensic Service came walking toward them from the garden path.

"A basement window has been broken," he announced, and for a moment she didn't know whether to feel relief or the opposite. If it was a break-in, it had nothing to do with Zenia, she thought, feeling a strange disappointment. "I'm done back there, and I'm going inside now."

As far as she was concerned, people could ransack the whole house if they wanted to. She just wanted Zenia home. But then it occurred to her that it could be her daughter who had gone in that way. If she had lost her keys, it was not unlikely that she would try to get in through the basement. Dybbøl quickly ran toward the garden and sensed that Rolf was following. "How did it break open?" she asked as he squatted by the low window.

"It looks like the latches have been knocked open."

"Knocked open?" She sank down next to him.

WOUNDS 137

"You see this a lot. If the wooden frame of old windows is hit at the right angle, the latches will pop off."

The window was intact; none of the panes were broken.

"It's the window to the laundry room. Maybe my husband forgot to close it," she said. Her breath formed a white cloud in the air. The evening dusk was settling around the house and garden, and the grayish light distorted the appearance of the bushes, making them look like people standing still all around the garden. She looked at the forensic markings on the ground. It looked like someone had been kneeling in front of the window. She stood up and turned to the technician, who was walking back toward her and Rolf.

"There are traces of soil on the floor just inside the window, but there are no immediate signs that anyone has searched the house," he said. "But you'd better go in and confirm that yourself."

Rolf had also stood up and asked her to get some of Lady's dog toys. "Or the dog basket. I'll walk around the neighborhood with Ask and see if we can find your dog."

For a moment, Dybbøl had completely forgotten about Lady. Now she rushed in after the turtle that was the Labrador's favorite chew toy.

"It could have been hit by a car," Rolf said when she came out again.

"She," Dybbøl corrected. "Lady is a bitch. She could have been hit by a car." She felt the tears rising and quickly turned away. She cleared her throat and took a few steps toward the road. She knew it was an unfair comment—Rolf obviously didn't care if Lady was female or male, as it wasn't relevant to his work—but she felt powerless, alone and groggy, and needed to hold on to something she knew. "Lady doesn't usually run away," she said. "We can have her off the leash, and she won't go anywhere."

Rolf had let Ask out of the car. For a moment, Dybbøl watched the dog and the interaction between the two. She was always impressed by the trust and understanding between the police dogs and their handlers. She handed Rolf the turtle and turned to go back to the house to tell the technician what she had remembered.

"We actually have a small boathouse with old windows similar to the ones in the basement," she told the detective when they met in the kitchen. "My husband uses the boat when he goes fishing. And sometimes, before we put a key box out there, he forgot the key and broke the window in the same way. Or he had something he stuck in the gap between the window and the frame so he could lift the latches. Once, when he had taken our daughter fishing and they got in that way, she came home and said they had broken into the boathouse. And I remember her teacher telling us that Zenia had proudly exclaimed that she had learned how to break in somewhere when the teacher asked what she had done during the winter break. They didn't expect that from the police chief's daughter."

Dybbøl noticed that she was babbling and kept quiet. She was about to ask if he wanted a cup of coffee but decided against it. It was way past his quitting time; normally you wouldn't get a forensic technician out to a simple burglary where there was no sign that the thieves had taken anything. So she had already gone to great lengths over

WOUNDS

potentially nothing. "Thank you so much for your help," she said instead. "I'm very grateful that you're here."

He smiled politely and muttered that she was welcome, and then he was gone. She knew it and he knew it: She had pulled the boss card, and it was all a bit much. Once Zenia was officially reported missing, the case would be handed over to an investigation team and all available resources would be deployed to find her. All by the book, and all completely out of her hands.

CHAPTER

19

LIAM WRAPPED THE towel around his waist and grabbed his cell phone, which was on the edge of the sink. Thursday's morning briefing was still an hour away, so he had plenty of time. He opened the small skylight to let some of the steam from his shower escape. There was a text message from Helene, but he didn't have the energy to look at it this early in the day. His thoughts revolved around the connection between Jan Hansen and Jørgen Andersen. Two men of roughly the same age from two completely different parts of the country. North Zealand and Funen. Something had to connect them, and until he figured out what it was, they couldn't move on.

He studied himself in the mirror and tried to smooth down his red beard, which was no longer possible. Other methods had to be found, and he went to work with the trimmer. He also had to do something about his hair. Downstairs, he had heard his mother pottering around. He knew there would be more nagging about him working too much. He wondered if he should just rush out the door, but

WOUNDS

then the smell of freshly brewed coffee began to permeate the bathroom.

He went into his old boyhood bedroom and quickly got dressed. He had a little farther to travel to get to work than from the house in Dalum, so he had to leave soon. His cell phone vibrated again. Dea was letting him know that she was at Autogården in Tommerup Stationsby waiting for them to open. When they had returned from Tisvilde late the night before, they had agreed that she would go out and go through Monika le Fevre's written-off car, but it had completely slipped his mind.

He gave her a thumbs-up and texted that they would catch up in the department. Rolf had gotten nothing from his search of the farm. No clear indication that Jørgen Andersen had been out there. Liam did his belt up, straightened his shirt, put his cell phone in his pants pocket, and walked down the stairs to the waiting coffee.

"Good morning!" he said, smiling at his mother, who was already sitting at the table.

She looked up from her iPad. "Good morning, son. There's bread. Your dad baked it yesterday." She pushed a cutting board with bread toward his usual place at the table. "Helene came by last night with some boxes of stuff. We put them in the back, so you can see for yourself."

Liam looked at his mother in surprise.

"She seemed angry," she continued, "and I understand that they don't see you at all. Couldn't you at least call the kids once in a while so they know you're alive?"

It was her reproachful tone that made him see red. It was one thing that the exact same reproaches about his inadequacy as a father had been hurled at him in a steady stream from Helene since they had had children, but now his mother was apparently taking the relay. He regretted that he hadn't just left, and today he was going to make a real effort to look for a place to live.

"We are in the middle of a murder case," he said angrily.

"It sounds harsh, Liam, but it's been like that for years. There's always something violent going on . . . something more important than your children and the rest of us." She sounded like an echo of Helene.

"That's not true." He stopped, suddenly feeling that he was taking up too much space in the cozy little kitchen. "But it must be nice for Helene to feel that you are on her side."

He set the mug down hard next to the sink and left the room without saying goodbye. He could hear her saying something behind him, but he didn't want to hear what it was. He pulled on his jacket and walked out into the dark, chilly October morning.

* * *

"Hey!" Liam knocked lightly on the doorframe of Piil's domain. The door was half open, so he stepped inside and asked if he could interrupt.

"Yes, please!" she exclaimed sarcastically. "If you're here about Jan Hansen's computer, I haven't gotten to it yet."

"I didn't expect you to," he said quickly, realizing that apparently he wasn't the only one who was grumpy in the morning. He made an effort to soften his voice. "I just wanted to know if you'd had a chance to look at the one we brought in from Jørgen Andersen's apartment."

Piil nodded. "I'm also in the process of searching his computer for any connections to Jan Hansen."

WOUNDS

143

"Great!" Liam exclaimed.

"It's not like we're just sitting in here, drinking coffee and eating croissants," she said a little less grumpily. "Oh no, I almost forgot! We don't have croissants—only the real investigators get them with their morning coffee from the boss!"

Liam took the rebuke to heart. Because he had left so early after his run-in with his mother, he had stopped at a bakery on the way to the police station. But the bag hadn't made it any farther than the large, open-space office, where he had held a short morning briefing. Piil gave him a small smile when she realized that she had been a bit harsh. He actually quite liked her straightforward manner. There wasn't a lot of bullshit, and you always knew where you stood with her. And she was diligent. And talented. And, uh . . .

"They definitely had a shared passion," she said.

"Passion?" he repeated with interest, and stepped over to her screen.

"Yes, they both seem to have found great pleasure in spewing hateful messages online. If we look at Jan Hansen's online presence, he, like Jørgen, has also been after Monika le Fevre. But they both cast a wide net," she said. "It wasn't just Monika le Fevre they were after. They have been against all forms of human use of animals. I'll name them all: caged hens, mink farms, fox farms, snail farming, milk calves, zoos . . . everything! And they have both gone way overboard with their attacks. That's why Jørgen got his restraining order. It seems that both of them didn't care who was reading—they even handed out really crude death threats on more than one occasion. They must have belonged to the same hateful community."

144   SARA BLÆDEL AND MADS PEDER NORDBO

"So you have managed to look at his computer!" Liam exclaimed, and smiled at her.

Piil nodded with mischief in her eyes. "I came in early as usual."

He smiled at her. "Thank you!"

* * *

Dea looked at her watch as an old, blue Volvo turned into the square in front of Autogården in Tommerup. The car's headlights shone through the high gates so you could see the workshop on the other side. Adjacent to the workshop was a square, low-rise building that looked like a store.

She got out of the car and started walking toward the man who had gotten out of the Volvo. He was in the process of unlocking the store door.

"Are you the owner of this workshop?"

The man looked at her. "Yep. Is there something wrong with your car?"

"No, I'm from Odense Police, and I've come to look at the wreck from the traffic accident near Verninge."

"I did wonder . . . We don't get many cars as new as yours in here," he said, glancing at the Passat as he pushed the door open. "Do you want to come in? It's a bit chilly this morning."

Dea nodded and followed the man through a long, narrow hallway with shelves on one wall filled with engine oil, coolant, and hundreds of odds and ends.

"We got an older Mazda 5 in on Monday. Is that what you mean?"

"I think so," Dea said, reading the license plate number of le Fevre's car to the man.

WOUNDS 145

"That's right," he said. "It's not going back on the road, but there hasn't been an appraiser on it yet."

"So it's a write-off?"

"You're damn straight it is. The undercarriage is warped, and the roof has been crushed down."

"Do I need a key to get into it?"

"No, the windshield and both side windows are broken, so it didn't make sense to lock it. You can look at it inside and out."

"If we end up taking it in for further examination, we'll need your fingerprints and a photo of the soles of your shoes."

"We haven't even sat in it." He smiled at her. "It's early in the day to be out looking at car wrecks. Can I make you a cup of coffee?"

"I can't say no to that," Dea said in surprise. "Thank you."

"Milk?"

"No thanks, just black."

"It'll be waiting for you when you come back in."

Dea nodded and went outside. The wrecked Mazda was parked by itself behind the workshop. The mechanic was right that it didn't look like a car that could be driven again—it was a miracle Monika had escaped the accident with her life.

Dea pulled on a pair of blue rubber gloves and, with a bit of force, got one of the front doors open. There was broken glass on the front seats. In the passenger footwell was a lipstick, a pen, several receipts, and a few tokens of the kind used in shopping carts. Dea opened the glove compartment: driving log, wet wipes, and a protein bar. Searching, she reached under the car's front seats, but there was nothing but the obligatory pieces of lost candy and missing screw caps.

"I forgot this!" The mechanic came storming toward her, waving a brown envelope eagerly. Dea struggled to get out of the car and took the envelope. "We took it into the workshop, didn't want it to get wet in the car."

He looked at her expectantly, like a little boy expecting praise.

"Thank you so much," Dea said as she opened the envelope and pulled out a note and a small plastic bag. She could feel a chill run down her spine. She looked at the friendly mechanic. "I have to leave right away, but thanks for your help. I'll have to save the coffee for another day!"

* * *

Liam looked up from the paper with a look of consternation and asked if she was sure there was nothing else in the car.

"Absolutely sure," Dea replied. "I searched all of it."

"We need to get this skin flap to the forensic geneticists right away, and then the two of us will drive out and talk to Monika le Fevre's parents."

Dea nodded, taking the small plastic bag and confirming she would send it off immediately.

The patch of skin in the bag was the size of the square cuts made in Jørgen Andersen's and Jan Hansen's bodies. In this case, the skin had been cut deeper, so it was a fleshy patch of skin, dried out and clearly not recent.

"They just need to be able to tell us if it's human or animal at first," Liam said before she left. "If it's human, we need to run a DNA test as soon as possible."

WOUNDS   147

Dea nodded and mumbled in agreement as Liam looked down at the note that had been in the envelope. He said he would ask Piil to check if there was a document with that wording on either Jørgen's or Jan's computer.

The list is long and you are on it. Nothing stops until someone takes responsibility.

The sentence had been printed out from a computer. It had been sent anonymously, and those words were all they had to go on.

CHAPTER

20

DEA LOOKED OUT over the narrow strip of moorland that meandered between the road and the beach at the South Funen Archipelago. There was a row of small houses on the other side of the road, and they were here to visit the penultimate one.

Liam slowed down and stopped the engine. It had surprised her how comfortable she was outside the city limits. When she and Rolf started seeing each other, she had felt that the farm was incredibly far out in the sticks. She had felt almost claustrophobic when the evening darkness fell and stars were the only thing that stood out. Now, though, she loved it. The landscape, the open spaces, the edge of the forest and the trees reaching for the sky. She liked living in the countryside, and it had taken her by surprise that she had become homesick on the days she spent in her own apartment in Odense. Living in the countryside. Living with Rolf. She felt herself smiling and sensed Liam's gaze on her. She hurried to get out of the car before he could ask her what she was thinking about.

WOUNDS 149

The wooden house Monika le Fevre's parents lived in was large, painted black, and weathered. Toward the garden, there were several large windows that were taller than the others. It looked like an extension that had been added later.

They walked up the small staircase together, and Dea knocked. They waited for a moment before she knocked again. "They're probably at the hospital. I called the consultant before we left. She's still in a coma."

Liam went to look in through one of the large windows near the garden. "They're home," he said. "At least there are candles lit." He walked to the next window. "He doesn't seem to have stopped stuffing animals. That's what I was led to believe."

"That's what I thought," Dea said, and followed him to the window. She put her hands up to the glass to block out the light. In the middle of the room was a large, round dining table filled with fur and skin. It looked like someone had turned an animal inside out.

They went back to the front door and knocked again. When nothing happened, she went and grabbed the door handle. It was unlocked. She gently pushed it open. "Hello? Is anyone home?"

"What are you doing here? Who are you?" The voice was gruff and came from the corner of the house, where an older man appeared with a load of firewood in a basket.

"We're from the police," Liam said, showing the man his badge. "We're looking for Holger le Fevre."

"That's me," the older man said. His face appeared to shatter. "Is it my daughter? Has her condition worsened?"

"No," Dea said quickly. "We've come to talk about the accident."

The man gathered himself, and his face fell back into its usual creases. He put the firewood basket down. "That was a nasty one! My wife is with Monika; she left early this morning. She's there most of the day. I was there myself yesterday. But it's hard for me to see her lying there. She's not even breathing on her own."

He showed them into the room with the large table. The fireplace was lit, and the room was warm and cozy. Muted classical music was playing from the speakers, and bowls of fruit and lit candles were placed around the low shelves.

"They say she'll get better and she'll regain consciousness. But right now she's just lying there. My wife is singing to her. They say hearing is the last thing to go, so maybe she can sense that we're there."

There was something touching about the vulnerability in his voice when he talked about his daughter. It was as if his heart was wide open, revealing his great love for his child. A tender and gentle love that stood in stark contrast to the brutality of the flayed animal skin on the table. Dea stood by the window.

"What is that animal on your table?" Liam asked, looking curiously at the large piece of skin.

Holger stretched his arms out. "It's a wild boar."

"So you're still doing taxidermy?" Dea said. He looked at her as if he didn't quite understand whether it was an accusation. "I spoke to your wife at the hospital, and I got the impression that you had quit after the outcry that arose against your daughter."

He nodded and seemed to consider what he wanted to tell them.

"We tell everyone that I've quit," he replied. "I couldn't handle all the fuss. But this is what I do, what I know, so now I just keep a low profile and sell my animals under a different name." He looked at Dea. "I don't think I'll ever be able to let it go completely."

On a small side table, a green cloth was spread out, and on the cloth lay an arsenal of sharp tools. Scalpels, scissors, knives, and various pliers. "Does it always look this macabre?" she asked.

Holger looked at the boar skin. "I don't think of it that way, but yes, from the outside, this phase is a bit macabre." He seemed to perk up a little. "It was the Victorians who started stuffing animals to keep in their homes. The Victorians loved death; they were almost obsessed with it, and through taxidermy they created the illusion of immortality, perhaps to convince themselves that they could circumvent impermanence." He ran a hand over the skin. "What really fascinated them was the grotesque. The deformed being."

"Deformed beings?" Liam repeated. "Like your daughter's scarred-animal exhibit?"

"When I was young . . ." Holger le Fevre said without answering. He walked toward a large cabinet. "I was also fascinated by the more macabre. Now it's more the beautiful and pure that speaks to me." He opened the closet, where stuffed animals were neatly lined up in several layers. He took out an animal and handed it to Dea. It was a rat that looked like it had been run over. "I had a roadkill series, but I kept it mostly to myself."

Dea looked at the rat.

"What about human taxidermy?" Liam asked, causing Monika's father to wince. He stepped away from the table.

"Not many years ago, there was a stuffed Inuit in the Westfries Museum in the Netherlands," he said. "So it has happened. And then there's Dr. Gunther von Hagens' world-famous Body Worlds exhibitions, where human bodies are donated to his art. But that's something else, because everything is peeled off so that only the skeleton, muscles, and tendons remain. My wife told me about Jørgen Andersen and the scars that were found on his body. She said, 'I think they look like the ones our daughter showed in her exhibition.'" He stopped talking abruptly and looked at them with a wary gaze. "I guess I never got to ask what you wanted? Why have you come here?"

"We're here for two reasons," Dea said, and jumped right in. "Firstly, to ask you if you think it could be your daughter who abused Jørgen Andersen up until his death. And then we'd like to know what you were doing on Monday between four and six PM."

She felt Liam's gaze on her, but he remained silent.

Holger le Fevre stood for a moment staring ahead of him, then he turned and walked to the window. "No," he said. "It is not Monika who cut the man, even though she had every reason in the world to loathe and hate him. But she doesn't have that brutality in her. And that's what people can't understand!"

He turned to face them again. "For her, the stuffed animals are art. They are beautiful and pure in themselves. But Monika is also politically driven. A political artist who wants to put issues on the agenda and shake up how we humans think about ourselves and our own actions. But she is not brutal and cruel, and she would never hurt another human being."

He was silent for a moment before explaining that he had been home all day Monday. "My wife was in the hospital with Monika, and I was just here. On Monday, we didn't even know if our daughter would survive." He shook his head. "I can't believe that my daughter's exhibition is connected to Jørgen Andersen's death. I think you need to look elsewhere."

"There's also another thing," Liam said, taking over. "Your daughter drove at very high speed into a tree. We suspect that she received a threat before she got in the car. Did she mention anything about a letter?"

Holger le Fevre straightened up and shook his head in disbelief. "That means nothing to me."

Dea looked over at Liam, curious if he would tell him about the skin tag, but he didn't mention it.

"I wasn't with her the last few days before the accident," Holger le Fevre continued, "so I can't say if anything had happened just before. I know that she had started cleaning up her workshop. Her plan is to shut it down completely. She won't start up again, even though I keep encouraging her to do so. I think it's a waste of an excellent talent if she stops now. But she doesn't think it's worth the risk."

"Do you know if there is surveillance at her farm?" Dea asked on a sudden impulse.

The father shook his head. "During the years we've been buried in threats, hatred, and vandalism, she talked about it several times. But it never materialized."

"Do you know where she was going when she left home on Sunday?" They were heading toward the hallway. He

154 SARA BLÆDEL AND MADS PEDER NORDBO

had already opened the front door and was waiting while they got their shoes on.

"Well, she was going to see you!" he said, as if surprised they didn't know that. "She said she was on her way to the police and would come out here afterwards."

CHAPTER

21

A GUST OF WIND caused a pile of dry autumn leaves to swirl up under the lamppost below Dybbøl's window. She stood in her office and looked down toward the intersection at Overgade. A group of children ran past the police station, shouting. Several of them had their faces painted. Their parents followed, chatting at a more leisurely pace with cups in their hands. They had probably been to an autumn event at the museum, she thought, thinking back to when Zenia was little and had often attended children's events at Møntergården with Søren. Zenia had made decorations out of felt and had her face painted like a tiger. Dybbøl rarely had time to go to these kinds of events, but she clearly remembered how excited Zenia had been to go with her father.

Dybbøl clicked back into Zenia's Instagram profile to see if anything new had been posted. The latest post was still from Monday. A picture from school.

"Chief?"

She looked up. Thorbjørn poked his head into her office. She often left the door to the front office open to signal that she, like everyone else, was part of the team at the police station.

Thorbjørn had Zenia's laptop in his hand along with a stack of printouts. "I think it would be appropriate for you to see this first." He seemed serious.

She put the phone down, felt her heart race, and waved him closer.

"Now I'm getting nervous, Thorbjørn. Come in . . . and close the door."

Thorbjørn pushed the door shut with one foot, walked over, and put the computer on the table. "We'll both be able to watch."

"Grab a chair." She pointed to the round table with the seven chairs, trying to read his face with a tightness in her chest.

Thorbjørn put the sheets down and pulled the chair over. He opened the screen and opened Zenia's email. "You told us to look, so that's what we did. You'll have to take the heat from your daughter if she gets angry that we've been snooping through her stuff."

"Of course," said Dybbøl impatiently. "What have you found?" She could feel the anxiety building inside her.

Thorbjørn hesitated. She could see that he didn't like what they were about to do. She wanted to shake him, but at the same time he infected her with his discomfort. "What is it?" To her annoyance, she could hear her voice trembling.

"It seems your daughter is an activist," he began.

Dybbøl felt a great wave of relief wash over her entire body, and she suddenly felt almost exhilarated. "We know," she said as calmly as she could. "And yes, she's a bit square about it. We try to explain to her that it's not all so black and white and that it will settle down when she gets a little older. Young people have their phases. Woke. That's how they are. Do you have children of your own?"

Thorbjørn shook his head quickly. He still looked very serious.

"So you already know?" he asked.

"Yes," confirmed Dybbøl. "She is an animal rights activist and regularly participates in protests and demonstrations, and sometimes she and her activist friends take their protests to animal farms where animals are mass produced under unfair conditions, but it is my opinion that their protests are fairly innocent. I think Zenia and her friends are mainly in the activist community for the community." She felt like herself again, and her voice no longer wavered.

"There's also a lot online," Thorbjørn continued, looking at her intently, "and it's not quite so innocent. Do you know anything about that too?"

Dybbøl frowned. "Of course there will be a lot of comments when she posts her messages, but debates on social media are often like that. The debates can easily get heated when you're not sitting opposite each other and presenting your opinions."

Thorbjørn fiddled with the printouts he had with him.

"Your daughter is very crude in her language and attacks," he said. "I can't describe it as anything other than online hatred."

"That sounds violent!" Dybbøl could hear that it sounded a little sharp. She suddenly felt cold and exhausted. "Let me see it!"

Thorbjørn nodded without looking at her. "Zenia also appears on le Fevre's Facebook profile." He glanced at her and pulled himself together before continuing. "She appears in several of the very violent threads that are part of the online assaults the artist ended up dealing with."

"Are you saying that my daughter participated in the online hate campaign against Monika le Fevre? I don't believe that. It simply can't be true. The exhibition was shown four years ago, right? Zenia was only thirteen at the time."

"This was in the last year. The campaign didn't stop just because Brandts Klædefabrik decided to take her exhibition down."

Dybbøl took a deep breath and tried to gather her thoughts and get an overview of the situation. "Has there been any contact between Zenia and Jørgen Andersen?" She thought of Edna and the tomato nursery and wondered if that was where her daughter had been inspired to use such crude rhetoric. Was it Jørgen who had managed to make Zenia turn her back on common sense and the values Dybbøl and Søren had tried to raise her with? She had been brought up to speak to other people with respect. To be inclusive and understanding despite disagreements. To always try to understand the reason for other people's actions. In other words, solid humanistic values that until recently, as far as Dybbøl could tell, had been a natural part of Zenia's behavior. It was hard for Dybbøl to imagine that her gentle, gifted, and lovely daughter had developed into a keyboard warrior. An almost radicalized person. She wasn't like that.

"So far we haven't found anything to show that Jørgen Andersen and Zenia were in contact with each other, but I think you should look into this thoroughly," Thorbjørn replied, and again seemed as if he had to pull himself together to continue. It was clear that he didn't like being in this situation with his boss. "And I would also suggest that you check your daughter's Messenger, Snapchat, and Instagram messages as well."

He avoided her gaze as he leaned over the desk and pushed the papers over to her. Then he stood up abruptly and left the office before she could say anything else.

* * *

Dybbøl sat for a long time with her eyes closed. It wasn't hard to understand what it was that Thorbjørn hadn't wanted to tell her. After reading the printouts he had brought with him, she had started trawling through her daughter's messages. Thorbjørn had flagged some of the ones addressed to Monika le Fevre, but there were many more. It wasn't just the artist and her exhibition that Zenia had directed her anger at. Like an immature and spoiled child, she had spewed her immense rage in all directions. A completely uncontrolled aggression against anyone who had either come to Monika le Fevre's defense or had dared to interpret le Fevre's art in a different way than her.

It wasn't a pleasant read, and it wasn't easy in the slightest for Dybbøl to sit there and gain insight into the behavior of the person she felt most connected to and thought she knew so well.

It shocked her that this side of Zenia's personality existed. But it shocked her almost more that she hadn't been aware of it. That she hadn't made sure she was more involved so she could have realized that her daughter had developed into the head of her own little aggressive one-woman army. She had such a hard time recognizing her loving and sweet girl in all this but had to face the irrefutable and relentless facts: She didn't know her own daughter, who was behaving like an unhinged and cold monster online.

Why hadn't Zenia talked to her about the terrible thing that had happened? She must have known, and it cut Dybbøl to the quick that her daughter had walked around with that knowledge all alone.

Dybbøl tried to calm herself down so she could think clearly. She remembered Julie from Zenia's class. Zenia had been outraged that Julie had written an assignment about Monika le Fevre's exhibition of mistreated animals. She thought Julie was in favor of animal cruelty, and during many evening meals, she had harped on how little Julie understood. Dybbøl had to admit that she and Søren had filed Zenia's rage at Julie with the other things her daughter expressed resentment about.

Dybbøl looked at the papers scattered across the table. This changed everything. Zenia hadn't just expressed her indignation and anger at the dinner table at home. It was there in black and white that she had been at the forefront of an outrageous bullying campaign against Julie Villadsen.

It was all dawning on her now. Dybbøl remembered that Julie had been bullied throughout the winter and had finally dropped out of school. Dybbøl skimmed the nasty messages Zenia had written again. *Bullying* was almost too mild a word to use for the endless series of hateful messages Zenia had sent to Julie. Sometimes up to ten messages a day. It seemed almost violent, and the poor girl must have

WOUNDS 161

been going through hell. She had become the object of mutual hatred, because Zenia wasn't the only one who had harassed Julie. But Zenia was the worst; she had definitely whipped up an uncontrollable feeding frenzy with Julie as the prey.

CHAPTER

22

LIAM LOOKED AROUND at the others in the large meeting room. He felt that he was having a sugar crash and could see that several of the others were too. The morning croissant hadn't hit the sides when the workday was so intense. There was no time for lunch, and as they approached six PM, he had considered ordering a ton of pizzas, but time had run out anyway, and now here they were. Half the department, tired and probably as starving as he was.

"Good evening," he began. "As you already know, there has been a development in the Jørgen Andersen case. It has taken a turn, which means that we can now remove Jan Hansen of Tisvilde from the list of those who have been after Monika le Fevre."

A hand went up. "Are we now investigating the murder solely on the theory that it happened as revenge for his incitement against the artist?"

"We're not ruling out any motives," Liam quickly replied. "Everything remains open; however, right now our main focus is on the scars and wounds found on the bodies of Jørgen Andersen and Jan Hansen."

He paused for a moment and looked at Piil, who had sat down on a table at the back of the room.

"This evening, Piil has presented me with our first breakthrough in the Verninge case. It turns out that Jørgen Andersen created a fake Facebook profile in Jan Hansen's name—just as he has created a number of other profiles on social media in the names of different people. He stole their identities, used their profile pictures, and pretended to be them when he bombarded the world with his hateful messages."

Several of the investigators nodded, while others seemed to be stumped. Liam asked Piil to explain.

"One of the profiles that was used to spread hate and harassment had Jan Hansen's name but was created and controlled by Jørgen Andersen. He was the one writing, the one behind the hate," Piil explained. "And it's been going on for a number of years," she added.

"And probably without Jan Hansen ever realizing it," Dea added.

"Are there more fake profiles? What about Zenia's?" Dybbøl asked.

"Zenia herself is behind her profiles. I can see that she would log on from her IP address, and its location is identical to your address."

Liam sensed that Piil was finding it difficult to meet Dybbøl's gaze. Everyone had been informed that the police chief's daughter had actively participated in the internet harassment of Monika le Fevre for some time. He felt for his IT investigator, because even though she was one of the most experienced on the team, it was clear that she found it disturbing to have been given this unpleasant insight into Dybbøl's private life. He himself would have preferred not to know this about Dybbøl's daughter. It was as if he suddenly knew something about Dybbøl that revealed more about her than he wished to know.

"We now know that Jørgen Andersen, posting under his name and that of Jan Hansen, along with Zenia, were behind some of the online campaigns against Monika le Fevre," Liam continued to move on. "Two of them are dead, and Dybbøl's daughter has now been missing for three days."

"But Jan Hansen was a fake," someone exclaimed. Liam nodded.

"But the perpetrator may not have known that . . ." he said, and fell silent when he noticed how Dybbøl turned her face away. It wasn't hard to imagine how she must feel.

"I have been in contact with the twelve people who unwittingly added their names to the fake profiles that Jørgen has used," Piil said. "None of them were aware that their names and pictures were being misused in this context. I have given them my direct number and told them that they can contact me twenty-four hours a day if they experience any kind of threat."

"Does this mean that we now have reason to fear that Dybbøl's daughter may be subjected to the same mistreatment as the wounds and scars found on the two victims?" someone asked.

"It's too early to conclude anything, but it's a possibility we need to work on," Liam replied.

"And what about Amalie Vedel?" Dea asked. "I guess we have to consider whether she can also be connected to this."

Liam nodded and noted to himself that Dea didn't seem to be tired at all yet, even though it had been many hours since she had stopped by the garage to examine Monika's car. It suited her to be newly in love. In a flash, he was struck by a longing for his own family. He missed the feeling of belonging, of being loved. Being a lone wolf was not at all suited to his temperament.

"At first glance, there is no obvious connection between the two cases, so we continue to run them as two separate investigations. Vedel is Lene's case. But it is clear that we are currently investigating whether Amalie, like Zenia, may have taken part in the harassment of Monika le Fevre."

"If this is about revenge on Monika's behalf, why wait four years?" asked one of the female investigators who hadn't been in the department that long. Liam couldn't remember her name, but he liked her.

Liam thought for a moment before shaking his head. "I can't answer that, but I'm no longer entirely convinced that this has a direct connection to Monika," he replied. "The scars do point in Monika's direction, and she most likely plays an indirect role, but I'm more inclined to believe that we need to investigate whether we're dealing with a vendetta against people who misbehave online." He smiled wryly at his own understatement and was silent for a moment, wondering if it was foolish to go directly against the investigative direction he had set himself, but he decided it was time to open up all possibilities, so he continued. "It has become so easy to smear other people online and ruin their lives. Maybe we're dealing with a perpetrator who has had enough of it."

Dea raised her hand and talked about some interesting things she had seen on TV.

"I can't remember if it was *Aftenshowet* or *Go' aften Danmark*, but it was about famous people who came forward and talked about the hate messages they regularly received. It was pretty wild and eye-opening, because several of the people who had sent the hateful messages were interviewed and asked why they had done it and whether they had considered the fact that it was real flesh-and-blood people they were smearing. Several of them were genuinely shocked that their messages had scared or hurt the celebrity in question. In several cases, they ended up apologizing. I think some people lose sight of how cruel the messages they send are and how hard it hits you when you're attacked by people you don't know or have never met. But apparently it can be hard to understand when you're just sitting in your living room getting angry."

Liam nodded; he had seen the same footage himself. "However, I still believe that Monika le Fevre is the focal point of this case. We've had a canine unit out on her farm with no results. But now I want to start really digging deeper. Tomorrow we'll get a warrant so we can conduct a search of her property. We need access to her cell phone and computer, but we also need to look at the bigger picture—maybe we'll see something new. She couldn't have killed Jørgen Andersen herself; we know that for sure because she was in a coma when he died. But I would like to know who delivered the threat Monika le Fevre was carrying in the car when she crashed."

He looked around at the team before thanking them for today.

* * *

Liam was already in the hallway with his jacket half on when he realized that Dybbøl was still slumped in her chair in the meeting room. He turned around and walked back toward her. She sat motionless with an exhausted expression on her face, and it seemed as though she hadn't realized that the meeting was over and the others had left the room. He gently pulled up a chair next to her. "Are you okay?" he asked gently.

"No." She shook her head and hid her face in her hands. "I keep thinking about where she could be. If she's being abused and killed in the same way as Jørgen Andersen. Is she under a tarp somewhere? Have they cut her?" The last question sounded almost like a shout, and Dybbøl broke down sobbing in front of Liam. He looked away. It felt too intimate to witness his boss completely losing control, but there was nothing to do but wait for her crying to subside. Finally, Dybbøl raised her head and wiped her eyes. Then she cleared her throat and said in a near whisper, "I don't understand!"

Liam gave her what he hoped was a supportive look as they sat in silence for a while.

"You have to believe me when I say that I am genuinely shocked that my daughter has been involved in such disgusting harassment. I didn't have the slightest clue . . . It's a complete surprise to me that she behaved so horribly toward other people." She cleared her throat again. "I probably should have been more involved in her activism. Demanded to know what she was up to. And who she was corresponding with. But I don't check her messages. She'd never allow that, and if I were to insist on it, it would ruin our relationship."

He nodded. "Of course you can't check her messages." He understood that it wasn't possible to know everything about what your grown-up children were doing, but it was also clear that Dybbøl hadn't had the trusting relationship with her daughter that she had thought she had. Maybe she had had a clue after all, Liam thought, but he could recognize the desire to only see your children's good side.

"I haven't spent enough time with her," Dybbøl admitted, giving him a look of despair. "I have let my daughter down! I neglected her because I chose to believe that she was self-reliant and sensible. I should have been there back then with Julie. I should have asked more questions about what was happening, but I didn't even realize that my daughter was so involved in the bullying. It's just awful. And so tragic." She sobbed.

"And it started after Julie presented her paper on Monika le Fevre's artwork?" Liam asked. He had managed to get a brief summary from Piil and Thorbjørn, who didn't think the suicide could necessarily be directly linked to the girl's schoolwork. It happened almost six months after she had left school, and in those six months she had been on sick leave and had been diagnosed with anxiety.

"Yes, it started just after the fall break last year," Dybbøl said. "In Zenia and Julie's class, the students had been given the task of writing an assignment that had to be presented and defended in front of the class. I remember Zenia came home and was furious that Julie was allowed to present. She wanted their teacher to boycott Julie's

WOUNDS 169

presentation because it was about le Fevre's stuffed animals. Zenia felt that their class teacher was pissing on her values. She showed me a video she had recorded on her phone of Julie relaying and analyzing le Fevre's message with regard to the exhibition. I remember being quite impressed with her performance—she was factual and thorough, and it was clear that she really cared about the subject matter. At the time, I didn't even realize that it was going to turn into a huge drama. Which Zenia obviously helped create. Julie took her own life on March eighteenth this year," she concluded tonelessly.

They sat in silence for a while. Then Dybbøl spoke again.

"Are you sure there is a connection between Jørgen Andersen and my daughter?" She turned her face toward him. "It could be a coincidence that they both care about animal protection. After all, a lot of people do."

Liam shrugged it off and said that so far there was nothing other than the fervent hatred of animal cruelty that tied Dybbøl's daughter to the Verninge case. But then he added the fact that they had both come out to Edna Clausen's at the abandoned tomato nursery. "They may well have met there," he said.

"We should probably also investigate Amalie Vedel's social media channels, emails, and text messages even more thoroughly," she said, straightening up a little. "Just to see if she might have had contact with Jørgen Andersen or Zenia."

Liam agreed with her and said he had put Lene Eriksen on the case. He was actually more interested in talking to Julie Villadsen's mother, but he didn't tell his boss that. Thorbjørn had already been in contact with her and had reported how Annette Villadsen had not minced her words when she said she hadn't felt that the police took her concerns seriously when the harassment against her daughter was going on. She had contacted them several times to get them to put an end to the violent online attacks against Julie but had received no help whatsoever.

"Right now we are waiting for the technical results after the break-in at your home, and we are of course constantly keeping an eye on any new information that has come in in connection with the alert we have sent out. We will find your daughter and bring her home safe and sound, I promise," he said in his most reassuring police voice. He knew there was no way he could make such a promise. She knew that too. But right now it felt like the right thing to say.

CHAPTER

23

ON FRIDAY MORNING, Dea quickly scribbled down the woman's information on her notepad. The message from the Forensic Genetics Department had just arrived in her mailbox. It wasn't unusual for forensic geneticists to be able to create a DNA profile in less than twenty-four hours if the submitted material was of good quality, as had apparently been the case with the skin tag from Monika le Fevre's car, but it would have required them to put everything else on the back burner. They had even run it through the system and found a match. Dea quickly stood up and made her way to Liam's office.

"Lise Bruun," she said. "Born in 1961. She lives down by Haarby."

He looked up at her in confusion and put his glasses down on his desk.

"The piece of skin from le Fevre's car! The one that came with the message that she herself was on the list." Dea waited impatiently for him to understand what she was talking about, but when he still didn't get it, she continued:

"Lise Bruun is also one of the people who was after Julie back then. Piil has checked her profile, and it's real—she took part in the harassment."

Liam straightened up when he finally realized that she was referring to the envelope from the car wreck.

"And why do we have her in the system?" he asked.

"A few years ago, she took part in a protest against one of the farms here on Funen that supplies scrambled eggs to Danæg. Lise Bruun was arrested but not charged. She was arrested, however, after sending several serious threats to the bison farm. She complained that they advertised a bison safari and at the same time invited people into the restaurant where they could eat the bison meat. They also have a farm shop where they sell bison meat, and she wanted that stopped. The owner of the place ended up withdrawing the complaint, and the charges were dropped."

"So a piece of that woman's skin was the reason why le Fevre canceled her dinner date with her parents and drove off toward the police station at such high speed that she smashed herself into a tree?"

"I can't say if that was the reason," Dea replied, annoyed at suddenly being called to account for such conclusions when she'd just provided a new piece of information that might help them answer the question he himself had asked the night before during their briefing: namely, who had delivered the threat that had prompted Monika le Fevre to get in her car to drive to the police station with the envelope?

Dea regretted that she and Rolf had stayed up until three o'clock. He'd had dinner ready when she got home after the late briefing, and they'd shared two bottles of wine while she told him about the le Fevre case. Ask hadn't caught Jørgen

Andersen's scent at Monika's farm, but now that they had obtained a search warrant, Rolf was going back out there with Thorbjørn and a team assigned to search the property.

Dea thoroughly enjoyed the late evenings when they sat together in his living room and talked about the day. She had long tried to convince herself that she enjoyed the solitude and silence after a long, busy day, but with Rolf, it was different. She relaxed in his company, and when she had the opportunity to evaluate the day with him as a gifted and qualified conversation partner, she could think more clearly about her work. But now she was feeling the fatigue, and she regretted that they'd talked so late into the night.

Liam got up and stood energetically in front of her.

"Have you got the address?" he said, reaching for the note she held in her hand.

Dea nodded and handed him the paper.

"Should I come?" she asked, thinking about the deal she had just made with Julie Villadsen's mother.

"I'll take Thorbjørn with me," he decided. "I want you to talk to the girl's mother. Is she bringing her daughter's computer and cell phone?"

Dea nodded. Julie's mother had seemed reluctant and dismissive when Dea had spoken to her and had explained that it was about Zenia Dybbøl and the fact that she was missing. Dea couldn't quite understand the woman's attitude, but at the same time, she had a feeling that she had spoken to her before. She had wondered about it for a while but had dismissed it. In her line of work, you met a lot of people, so you could offend someone without even realizing it. She had to give the matter her full focus. Monday night into Friday morning was a long time for a seventeen-year-old girl to be missing without a trace.

She had heard Liam suggest to Dybbøl that she take a few days off so she wouldn't have to come in to the police station and be at the epicenter of the investigation. But Dybbøl hadn't wanted to hear of it. The press had made a big deal about the police chief's daughter's disappearance, and they were having a field day. Pictures from Zenia's Instagram profile were already circulating online, and there was a lot of speculation about where the young girl had last been seen. None of the guesses had the slightest basis in fact, but that didn't stop the newspapers from trumpeting one theory after another. Piil had made Zenia's Instagram profile private, but Dybbøl didn't want either it or her Facebook account to be closed down completely in case her daughter suddenly became active on one of them.

"Annette Villadsen will be here in half an hour," Dea told Liam. She then went in to ask Piil if she had gotten anything out of her search. She was checking if there had been a connection between Jørgen Andersen and Julie, and she was also looking into who the fake profiles Jørgen had created had communicated with. Now Dea would also ask her to find out everything she could about Lise Bruun.

* * *

A pair of dainty sparrows took flight from a nearby feeder as Liam and Thorbjørn walked down the path to Lise Bruun's house. Behind the garden, the trees in the forest that surrounded the house creaked in the wind. The half-timbering on the low house was crooked and the thatched roof was old, covered in vivid green moss in several places.

The windows were low, and even from a distance, Liam could see that Thorbjørn would have to bend his long body indoors.

"I bet she's got her hands full with all those birdhouses," Liam said, pointing to the edge of the forest where the house's small but very wild lawn met the forest. "And hedgehog houses."

"Those are for hedgehogs?" Thorbjørn asked, and laughed. "Cute!" Liam stepped onto the stepping stone in front of the front door and knocked.

They stood and looked around for a while, but nothing happened. "Let's go for a walk."

They walked past the house. The brickwork was weathered and the woodwork was in need of a lick of paint. Lise Bruun might think it was important to fight for animal rights, but her old farmhouse could also use some attention. Liam walked behind the house, where he came across some long grass and some old garden furniture. The chair cushions looked like they had been left out for a long time, and on the table was a glass filled with murky water and several dead insects. Just then, Thorbjørn called out to him.

Liam's colleague stood at the terrace door and waved him over. "There's a fucking dead dog in there."

They both walked over and leaned their foreheads against the window. The dog was almost directly in the doorway. It was emaciated and shriveled up, its fur looking matted and moth-eaten. Skin and bone, Liam thought. "We're going in."

A moment later, Thorbjørn had cleverly picked up a stone and smashed the window. Carefully, he reached for the latch with one hand through the shattered glass and opened the door. A violent and foul stench immediately wafted toward them, and there was no doubt that the dog had been dead long enough for decomposition to be at its peak. Around the dog's head, the floor was mottled, and all over the rotting body Liam could see maggots feeding.

Thorbjørn pulled his sweater up over his nose and hurried through the living room to open the front door to create a draft. Liam quickly surveyed the room and then went to open one of two doors at the end of the room. There was a possibility that the occupant of the house was in there, so he mentally prepared himself to be met with anything and everything. Both rooms were empty. The same was true of the kitchen and the small bathroom. They realized they had been through the entire house. Liam sent Thorbjørn outside to do another round, this time to see if Lise Bruun had collapsed somewhere near the property. He himself went back to the room where he had noticed her computer.

* * *

The screen lit up and the fans immediately started making noise as soon as Liam turned on the PC. It was an older model—a big box on the floor. He sat down on the office chair and was pleased to see that Lise Bruun hadn't bothered using a password. He opened her mailbox, where there were unopened emails dating back to August 5.

"What have you found?" Thorbjørn asked, standing behind him. He had carried the dog outside and told Liam that he had covered it with a blanket.

"It's been over two months since she last opened emails," Liam said. "We'll take the computer to Piil, and then we

WOUNDS 177

need to search the house. Will you call the National Forensic Service?"

Thorbjørn nodded and pulled out his cell phone. The stench still hung heavily in the air, even though a cool wind swept through the living room. "Then the dog must have died of thirst and hunger. It looks like it tried to eat its fill of pillows and blankets."

He went to the kitchen and opened the fridge. The milk was way past its expiration date, and all the other fresh food had long since gone bad. A rotten cucumber was all smashed up and about to spill over the glass shelf. The date labels were consistent with the fridge having been untouched since early August.

Liam went back to the living room. On the coffee table were books on birds and dogs. On the walls were framed pictures of animals of all kinds, even a gigantic spider looking back at him from a gold frame. There were piles of old Animal Protection Society magazines lying around, looking like they had been read over and over again. There was no doubt that the house was inhabited by an animal lover. Lise Bruun would never just leave her dog behind.

He went outside, got hold of the duty manager, and asked him to send a canine patrol unit to Lise Bruun's address in Haarby.

"We need them to search the forest in a five-kilometer radius," he said. "There may have been an accident, and I fear she may be out there somewhere."

"Five kilometers?" the watch commander repeated.

"Yeah, that's plenty," Liam said. "There are several canes in her hallway; I don't think she was the kind of person who walked far."

178   SARA BLÆDEL AND MADS PEDER NORDBO

"Roger that," the watch commander confirmed.

"And then I want an APB on her." He thought for a moment. "We'll go out with dogs, the Home Guard, drones. The whole shebang, because now we're looking for Amalie, Zenia, and Lise Bruun."

"Roger that," the watch commander repeated.

Liam had just finished the conversation when Piil called him back. "I haven't been able to find any relatives, but I have found her former workplace. They must know something about her."

"Thank you! Thorbjørn and I will head out there right away, and her computer will be with you within the hour."

CHAPTER

24

"I HAVE NOTHING GOOD to say about Zenia Dybbøl," was the first thing Annette Villadsen said when she sat down opposite Dea. "She's a disgusting and unfeeling person. I would actually call her callous."

She looked angrily and implacably at Dea.

"And the police did nothing to help me either. Absolutely nothing. You were completely indifferent and just said that there was nothing you could do when there were no direct threats. And then I got a long rant about how young people were exposed to far worse things online than what Julie experienced. You told me about untraceable foreign traffickers who blackmail young people. And you talked about videos with compromising content that are shared and in many cases can ruin young people's lives. But you wouldn't listen when I explained that this is exactly what had happened to Julie. Her presentation had been filmed. Without her permission; she wasn't even aware of it. They cut it and made her look like a terrible and evil person, and they wrote things over it that made her look ridiculous. But apparently it wasn't serious enough. Because it didn't involve anything sexual." Julie's mother looked at Dea coldly. Then she added, "Actually, I think it was you I spoke to several times when I called."

Dea listened, completely unprepared for the torrent of rage that poured out of Julie's mother. Before the meeting, she had read the material Thorbjørn had printed out. The messages to Julie were indeed disgusting. They were crude, hateful, and degrading, and it was unbearable to think what it must have been like for a teenager to be stalked like that. But the videos were news to her.

"I'm really sorry about that," Dea began. "Did you also tell us about those videos when you called?"

"Too right I did!" Annette nodded vigorously. "Several times. But no one seemed to take it seriously. I also went to the police station and talked to a young man, but he told me, like all of you, to contact the school. He even gave me a leaflet and recommended that I go to Save the Children's website and read about fighting cyberbullying!"

She shook her head and looked at Dea.

"You made it sound like an everyday occurrence that everyone had to go through." She slumped a little. "But it wasn't like that for us. It was serious; my girl couldn't take it. She was breaking right in front of my eyes, and I couldn't get any help to stop it."

"Didn't you get any help at all?" Dea asked sympathetically.

Annette Villadsen nodded. "We got in touch with a Save the Children employee who was a fantastic support and who took the time to talk to Julie. But it wasn't enough, because the attacks continued. The video and images

WOUNDS

continued to circulate online, and new abominations were added. I took her out of school and she went on sick leave. I hoped that it would stop with time and when she was no longer part of the bullies' daily lives. But it didn't."

She stared insistently at Dea.

"Do you have any idea what it feels like to see your child disappear right before your very eyes?"

She remained silent, actually waiting for an answer to the impossible question. Dea shook her head. If someone had hurt Katrine, she probably would have jumped down their throats.

Annette looked down.

"It's a nightmare," she said quietly. "It was so hopeless, and there was nothing I could do. Nothing! Julie was my only child; it's always been me and her. And now she's no longer here."

"What about her father?" Dea asked, but Julie's mother just shook her head and said that he had never been involved. They had split up when Julie was eighteen months old, and they hadn't had any contact since.

They sat in silence for a moment until Dea asked Julie's mother to tell her about what happened.

Annette Villadsen leaned forward across the table. She had folded her hands in front of her, and Dea struggled to read the expression in her eyes.

"Why?" she began, pausing for a moment. "Why do you suddenly want to talk to me now? Why has Julie's case suddenly caught your interest?" She held her palm up to Dea before she could answer. "Because," she continued. "Because it's now the chief constable's daughter you're worried about. Am I right?"

182   SARA BLÆDEL AND MADS PEDER NORDBO

Dea thought for a moment but then nodded.

"Not because it's her," she added. "But two girls your daughter's age are currently missing. We don't know if the two cases are connected, but we do know that Zenia Dybbøl for various reasons can be linked to a man who was found murdered on Monday. Both his murder and Zenia's disappearance are currently linked to the hate campaign that hit Monika le Fevre after her exhibition at Brandts Klædefabrik. And we have just realized that both the murdered man and Zenia participated in the harassment against your daughter."

Now that she had told it like it was, Julie's mother's expression changed, and she looked at Dea with horror and compassion written all over her features.

"Did someone kill Zenia because of what she did to Julie?" she asked slowly, as if it suddenly hurt her to speak.

"We don't yet know what happened to Zenia or where she is, but we fear that this may be what happened."

Dea prepared herself for a rant about Dybbøl's daughter getting what she deserved, but instead Annette's eyes glazed over.

They sat in silence for a while, but then Julie's mother straightened up and moved her shoulders a little, as if she was getting ready to go.

"It all started, as you know, when Julie gave a presentation at high school based on Monika le Fevre's exhibition of stuffed animals. It was in no way her intention to defend the mistreatment of animals. It was all about the way artists express themselves and the tools she used to get her message across. Julie had done so much work on that assignment. She had interviewed le Fevre and visited her workshop. She was so proud of her assignment, and she was looking forward to presenting it.

WOUNDS

It really was an amazing and incredibly talented assignment—her teacher thought so too. My daughter dreamed of becoming a journalist." Annette smiled a little to herself. "Then it all went wrong . . . it was as if her classmates intentionally misunderstood her. Julie tried to explain that for her it wasn't about the animals and that she was only interested in le Fevre's effects, i.e., the art theory behind the exhibition, but it was no use. At first, the others in the class distanced themselves from her just a little bit. They started to exclude her and make little remarks about her having a sick attitude. It was already bullying, but we thought it would pass. That it was something Julie could handle. She thought so herself."

Annette looked a little ahead of her.

"I think it was a week, maybe two, before the case really started circulating on social media, and it spread so quickly that it took some time before I realized that she was now being subjected to increasingly severe bullying both at school and on social media. And now it wasn't just those at school who had her in their sights. Videos of her talking about the le Fevre exhibition were circulating, and what she said had been completely distorted and edited together with the most disgusting images of both animals from the exhibition and animals that had been violently abused in other contexts. It made it look like Julie supported cutting up live animals and putting them on display afterwards. It was horrible. And completely, completely wrong."

"Do you know who was behind it?"

"I know it was Zenia who recorded the presentation, but I don't know who manipulated the images and videos. Many of the people who smeared her online were adults. I can't understand how they could behave so horribly toward a young girl."

"Did you try to stop them by contacting them?"

Annette nodded and shrugged her shoulders in resignation. It had obviously done no good.

"I contacted several of them. I wrote to them and asked them to stop, but they didn't care. And they were also really rude to me. Somehow they had all agreed that Julie just needed to stop being an animal abuser."

Annette looked at Dea for a long time before continuing. "My daughter was in no way an animal abuser. It was quite clear that they had targeted her to vent all their hatred. I think they just needed a scapegoat; it really had nothing to do with my daughter. It could have happened to anyone."

Now she leaned back a little in the chair and folded her arms in front of her chest.

"That's when I contacted you."

Dea looked down. She could understand Annette's anger.

"My daughter always loved going to school, but in the end I couldn't get her to go at all. She ended up locking herself in her room and sitting there until the bell rang. That's how her days went. At first she cried a lot, but that stopped. Eventually she would just lie in her room with the curtains closed, apathetic."

Annette could no longer hold back her tears and cried silently until she looked up again.

"I went to Monika le Fevre to ask her to come forward and support Julie. She had helped her with the assignment, so I thought that she, if anyone, understood what it was that Julie wanted to convey. But she didn't; she just turned her back on us and said she didn't have the energy to do more. No energy! Ha!"

Julie's mother snorted contemptuously.

"She wanted to bask in Julie's interest, and she probably imagined that she herself would gain something from a gifted young woman trying to shed light on why she had experimented with live animals. But she didn't want to support us when I explained to her that Julie was being bullied because of the presentation. I thought that was so horrible. She's a grown woman, and it was her choice to do the exhibition. I was furious!"

"So you went to see Monika le Fevre at her farm?" Dea asked.

"Yes, you're damn right I did!" Now Annette's voice had renewed vigor. "I got so angry, I could have killed her."

Dea glanced at the recorder on the table to make sure it was still running.

"Eventually Julie stopped eating altogether. There was almost nothing left of her; she weighed just over forty-four kilos. The plan was to hospitalize her, but we didn't get that far. Because one day while I was at work, she went to the embankment a few hundred meters from our house and threw herself in front of a train."

Annette stood up abruptly and picked up a bag from the floor, handing it to Dea.

"Here is my daughter's computer and cell phone. The password for both is 102030."

She took her coat from the back of the chair, adding, "I don't care what happened to Margrethe Dybbøl's daughter, because I will never get my own daughter back." The

186 SARA BLÆDEL AND MADS PEDER NORDBO

compassion from before was gone, and her voice was hard. "But I hope Dybbøl feels the fear people feel when they realize they are about to lose the person they love the most. And that no one will do anything to stop it from happening."

She pulled on her coat and had started walking toward the door when Dea stopped her.

"What did you do Monday afternoon and evening?"

Annette looked at her, expressionless. "I was at home, and I have no witnesses to that."

CHAPTER

25

LIAM GREETED A group of elderly people playing cards in the common room at Sydmarksgården, where Lise Bruun had once worked.

One of the women looked at him for a long time until one of the others at the table sneered at her.

"It's your turn, Birthe."

"Oh . . ." The woman looked down at her cards again. "Is this blackjack we're playing?"

"Fish!"

Liam and Thorbjørn looked at each other with a smirk and continued toward the office up ahead. They reached it at the same time as a woman came to the door.

"My name is Lizette, and I'm the director here on-site. Welcome. I understand that this is about Lise Bruun."

"That's correct," Liam said, nodding. "It seems Lise hasn't been home in over two months."

"My goodness!" the principal exclaimed, and asked them to follow her into the office. "Two months? What about her dog?"

"Unfortunately, it's dead, and it's because of that that we fear something may have happened to Ms. Bruun."

Lizette sat down heavily in her chair and motioned for them to sit opposite her. "That's horrible. She loves that dog." Lizette looked up. "When Lise worked here, she regularly brought Rollo with her. The residents loved him. He was a lovely dog."

"We're trying to find people who might be able to help us find out where Lise might be," Liam said. He then asked when Lizette had last been in contact with Lise.

"Uh, it's been a while now. It must have been before the summer vacation, because I was traveling all July in my caravan."

"As far as we know, Lise Bruun had no family, but she was employed here for many years, so you must know her well."

"Yes." The manager nodded quickly. "She had been here the longest when she left, so everyone knows her."

"Why did she stop?"

"Her arthritis had gotten so bad that it was difficult for her to do her job. In fact, in the end it was impossible. I offered her a part-time job, but she wouldn't take the place of a real position instead of someone new with a good skill set." Lizette looked at Liam. "She was like that."

"Can you tell us anything more about her? What did she do when she wasn't working?"

"She was a somewhat quiet woman, happy but quiet. For several years, she was behind an embroidery festival at the Linen Museum on the Krengerup Estate. That work took up a lot of her spare time, but she gave that up when the arthritis got too bad." Lizette sighed as she thought about it. "She was well liked by everyone here. I really don't like to think that something might have happened to her."

WOUNDS 189

"We don't know anything for sure," Liam said quickly. "But of course we'd love to know why she hasn't been home for so long. And why she left her dog behind."

Lizette shook her head. "Yes, that's hard to understand."

"When did she stop working here?"

"That was about two years ago, but she kept coming to visit for a while."

"But not lately?"

"No, like I said, it's been a while since I last saw her."

"And no one noticed that she no longer stopped by?" Thorbjørn asked.

"No, not really, I'm sorry to admit. We've had some cutbacks and more elderly people, so we're busy doing our jobs. Many of the residents who knew her have also passed away since she stopped working."

"Do you know if Lise had a special interest in animals and animal welfare?" Liam asked. On the way to the care center, they had received a call from Piil. Lise Bruun had been part of the chorus of keyboard warriors, as Piil called them. She had participated in the public outcry against Monika le Fevre following the exhibition, and she had also been involved in the harassment of Julie Villadsen over the winter. Piil had already investigated whether it could be Jørgen Andersen who had been at it again and had created a profile in Lise Bruun's name, but that wasn't the case. All the evidence was on the computer they had found in her home, which they had to assume belonged to Lise.

"Yes, she was very concerned about the proper treatment of animals, and she could get angry when she read about neglect and other kinds of animal cruelty in the newspaper. But there's nothing wrong with that, is there?"

"No, absolutely not," Liam said, and smiled at her. "Did any of you socialize with Lise in private?"

"No, not as far as I know. I don't think she went out that much. She was good at looking after herself."

An employee poked her head into the office. "Oh, I'm sorry, I didn't realize you had company."

"It's okay, maybe you can help," Lizette said. "The police here are looking for Lise. Have you seen her around lately?"

"No, I haven't seen her since she was last here." The woman shook her head and seemed a bit confused by the question.

"Have you ever witnessed Lise being rude to others?"

Liam looked at the two women, who both promptly shook their heads.

"Rude? Lise? No, she certainly wasn't," the manager replied quickly. "Lise was polite and very well liked."

"Last question," Liam said. "Do you know if she had a falling-out with anyone?"

Again, they shook their heads.

"I can't imagine that," said Lise's former colleague.

"Me neither," Lizette said in agreement.

Liam nodded briefly to Thorbjørn. They stood up and said goodbye. "We didn't learn much from that," Thorbjørn said on the way out to the car.

"No," said Liam. "Except that we can now establish that Lise Bruun has almost two personalities. And it's obviously only one that her former workplace knows about. It would be interesting to find out who knows about the other, less charming side of her."

CHAPTER

26

Dybbøl waved Dea in when she spotted her in the front office. She put down her cell phone and asked her to sit down.

"Are you okay?" Dea asked, pulling the chair to the other side of the desk.

She could feel the pitying looks of her colleagues all over the police station, and sometimes she was convinced she could feel their disgust, but maybe she was imagining it. When Liam had suggested she stay at home for the next few days, it was exactly those looks that made her reject his suggestion and go to work. She didn't want them talking about her behind her back. She wanted to stand tall, stand by her daughter, and force the entire team to do their very best to find her. Shying away from confrontation had never been her thing, and she wasn't going to do it now, even though she was ashamed of Zenia's behavior. But she missed her more than she was ashamed, and it was the missing that helped her keep her head above water and her nose to the grindstone.

"I'll be fine," she said calmly. "What did you get out of the conversation with Annette Villadsen?"

Dea shrugged a little nervously, and again it became clear to Dybbøl how uncomfortable it was for her employees to report to her when it was her daughter they had to report on. Just as it had been for Thorbjørn after Piil accessed Zenia's computer. Dybbøl tried to nod and signal that she was ready to listen to whatever Dea had to say.

"She mostly talked about the time leading up to Julie's death. About the period when she tried to ask us for help. I'm actually surprised that she didn't file a formal complaint against the Odense Police. Did she do that?"

"No, she didn't file a complaint," Dybbøl replied, slightly annoyed. "There was nothing we could do. As I understand it, we referred her to various bodies where she could seek knowledge and help."

She was well aware that it might look like she had covered up for her daughter. She felt a sudden anger. Was she going to sit here and be held responsible for something that hadn't even made it to her desk? She looked at Dea sharply. She'd be damned if she was going to be intimidated. She was the chief constable, and if any of her people at the time had felt the matter required directorial intervention, they should have come to her. The direct request she had received from Annette Villadsen had bypassed her and been immediately passed down the hierarchy, so no one could now blame her for not reacting.

She took a deep breath and returned Dea's gaze.

"I haven't tried to cover for Zenia," she said as calmly as she could. "I didn't know anything about Zenia's involvement in all this until yesterday. It's a terrible tragedy, and I can see now that we should have reacted. We should have taken Annette Villadsen's cry for help more seriously. My daughter's behavior was way over the line and very unpleasant, but not criminal. If writing nasty things about and to other people online was criminal, the entire police force would have no choice but to catch such criminals. And I would like to remind you that Zenia is not hiding behind fake profiles; she has written in her own name and has not tried to hide her identity and thus make it consequence-free for herself. She stands by her opinions."

Dybbøl stopped herself and regretted what she'd just said. Here she was, defending her daughter.

"We might always want to protect our children . . . and then we might turn a blind eye," Dea said tentatively.

"Yes, but I'm a police chief. I can't have a blind eye." She looked at Dea. "I'm just trying to say that I'm not going to try to cover for Zenia. I realize that she's behaved really badly, and I'm not afraid to talk about it, but she's my daughter, and she's gone, so we have to do everything we can to find her, no matter what she's done or who she's hurt."

Dea nodded slowly. "Of course, of course."

"What was she doing when Jørgen was killed? I understood from Piil that he had also been active in the comment sections of the posts that portrayed Julie Villadsen as a crazy animal abuser."

The expression in Dea's eyes changed when she dryly suggested that Annette Villadsen was a slender woman who might have found it difficult to tow Jørgen Andersen behind the disused inn single-handedly. "As far as I know, there was no trace of her in Verninge, but of course I'll look into it further."

194 SARA BLÆDEL AND MADS PEDER NORDBO

There was a knock on the door, and Dybbøl's secretary poked her head in. "An envelope has arrived for you."

"Who from?"

"I don't know; they brought it up from reception." Dybbøl stood up and took the envelope. She felt Dea's gaze while she examined the envelope. There was nothing on the front or back. Then she tore it open, pulled out a photo, and stopped dead.

She didn't know how long she had been staring down at the smiling young girl standing on the sidewalk outside Cathedral School when Dea cleared her throat.

She handed the picture to Dea; *#thinkbeforeyoutype* was written on the back in ballpoint pen.

"Is that your daughter?" Dea asked.

Dybbøl nodded absently and walked with stiff movements toward her chair before sitting down. The last faint hope that there was a good and natural explanation for why Zenia had disappeared for so long was now gone. The threat was unmistakable, and it was no coincidence that it came now. Someone was to blame for her daughter not coming home.

CHAPTER

27

LIAM WAS CHILLED to the bone as he exhaustedly walked up the stairs to the station after spending the last few hours searching for Lise Bruun in the woods behind her home. Now darkness had fallen and the search was suspended until the next morning.

He and Thorbjørn had bought a couple of pizzas on the way back, and his plan was to go to his office to get his laptop before heading to his parents' house in South Funen, but he stopped and listened to the voices from inside the large open office.

"What's going on?" he asked when he spotted Lene Eriksen.

"It's Amalie!" she replied eagerly, pointing to the meeting table, where a young girl was sitting. "She's come home."

Liam walked over and stood next to Dybbøl.

"She was picked up by a patrol down by the train station fifteen minutes ago."

"Did something happen to her?" Liam asked, looking at the girl. She was sitting on a chair with a blanket around her but didn't seem too badly hurt.

"I didn't realize I'd caused so much trouble," the girl snorted.

"Trouble?" Lene repeated sharply. "Half the country has been running around looking for you! You can't just disappear like that."

Amalie Vedel began studying her nails and avoided looking at the lead investigator.

"My dad watches everything I do," she said quietly. "I just want to be left alone."

"You're about to turn eighteen," Lene continued. "Move away from home! Change your cell phone number! Anything that doesn't lead to us having to launch major searches in several countries to look for you!"

Dybbøl shook her head.

"She tells us that she's been to Sweden, where she stayed with some friends. She can't tell us exactly where the place is, but it sounds like it's a remote farm somewhere in Skåne. She had gone there to participate in a silent retreat. There seems to be a holistic community behind it. But there's also something about a guy, and she stayed longer than she had planned."

Liam looked at his boss.

"I think there's been a lot of smoking weed or taking something that she's not too happy to get into."

"Have you talked to her parents?"

"They're on their way."

Lene Eriksen approached them. "I want to have time to question her before her parents arrive. I think something

WOUNDS 197

doesn't quite add up, and I'd like to get her alone before she changes her story because they're listening in."

"You think she was forced to go?" Liam asked, suddenly realizing just how tired he was. At the same time, he was struck by the uplifting feeling he always got when a case of this nature had a positive outcome, which was rare.

"I think there's something she's not telling us, and I'd like to know if she was forced to do something she didn't want to do. Do you want to join me?"

He really wanted to go, but he could also figure out who would have to deal with the press when they announced that Amalie Vedel had returned home safely, so he nodded and followed Lene, who had put her arm around the girl and had started walking toward interrogation room one.

CHAPTER

28

DEA QUICKLY READ through the press release on Saturday morning.

It succinctly announced that Amalie Vedel had returned home safely and was now reunited with her parents. She knew it was Liam who had insisted that no more details be released. He had called her late at night and told her that the girl had come home. Or at least almost home; she had taken the train from Copenhagen Central Station to Odense, and outside the station a patrol had spotted her and brought her in.

"She's been stoned for two weeks," he had said. "Sex, drugs, and rock 'n' roll." He had explained that during yesterday's interrogation, they had learned from the girl that she was in love with a much older hippy who had invited her to participate in a kind of therapy program where they didn't talk for days and had no contact with the rest of the world. Amalie had also talked about various drugs that the retreat participants had taken to achieve a higher level of consciousness, and it had slowly emerged that Amalie had also been on that path. She knew her parents wouldn't approve, and she mumbled something about leaving a note on the kitchen table so her parents wouldn't get nervous, but later in the interview it became clear that the note was something she wished she had done. The short of it was that the girl hadn't been forced to do anything and had actually had a wonderful trip, so there was nothing more to talk about in that respect. After all, it wasn't the first time in history that a young person had gone on a trip that hadn't been fully thought through beforehand.

Dea was shivering. She was sitting on Rolf's sofa with a big blanket around her, it was freezing cold, and she hadn't managed to get the pellet stove going. She had texted him several times to get some long-distance support, but he had yet to reply. Now she was warming herself with a cup of tea and procrastinating about going to the cold bathroom, even though she had to get going soon.

She had barely heard Rolf when he got up. It was still dark when he left. He had prepared her for the fact that he and Ask would be out the door early because they were going to participate in the large-scale search for Zenia Dybbøl and Lise Bruun that would begin in the morning. Sniffer dogs, water search dogs, drones. It was Liam who had set the expensive package in motion.

Dea thought of Dybbøl. It seemed as though the envelope containing Zenia's picture had fallen from the sky. Dea had hurried to get hold of the people who had been sitting at the information desk, even though they had both just finished their shift when the envelope was delivered. Neither of them had noticed who handed it in.

Dybbøl had insisted on sitting in when Dea and Piil were given access to the surveillance tape from the entrance to the police station. But they had not found out who had placed the envelope in the chief of police's pigeonhole and settled for the fact that mail delivery was no longer considered important because everything was done by email. No one cared about printed matter, advertisements, or thin anonymous envelopes anymore.

Dybbøl had struggled to hold it together, even though it was obvious to everyone that she was falling apart. Dea thought about what was written on the back of Zenia's picture: *#thinkbeforeyoutype*. Before going home, she had messaged Piil and asked her to search the hashtag. It popped up on some Instagram posts, but there hadn't really been anything she could use. Dea hoped that Piil could dig up something more substantial.

She stopped dead as she stepped into the bathroom. The narrow, tiled room was next to the toilet. Two closed doors right next to each other, and the only area of the house Rolf hadn't had time to do up yet. He had written *Love you* across the mirror with the red lipstick she hardly ever used. It was the first time those words had been used between them. A happy smile spread across her face as she leaned over the sink, took the lipstick and drew a curved heart next to his declaration.

CHAPTER

29

LIAM STARED TIREDLY at the phone when it rang again. No one seemed satisfied with the brief message that Amalie Vedel had returned home. He wanted to direct all inquiries to Lene Eriksen. She was the one who had handled the case and had been responsible for reuniting the girl with her parents. "No," he said calmly. "We have no further comment on her whereabouts. As I said earlier, she is home safe and sound. We are all pleased about that, and the matter is now closed."

Liam had just stood up when the phone rang again. This time it was his private cell phone.

"A dog unit has just reported that a possible body has been found," Thorbjørn said breathlessly, as though he was running or walking at a fast pace as he spoke. "We're near Gadsbølle . . . close to Vissenbjerg."

Liam grabbed his coat and made a beeline for the office where Dea was sitting, beckoning her to follow him. He caught a brief glimpse of Dybbøl before they hurried down the back stairs into the courtyard and jumped into his car.

"We're searching a larger forest area and are currently standing by a boathouse," Thorbjørn continued, explaining that the elongated forest lake stretched about a kilometer farther west. "Call me when you get closer, and I'll guide you. It's a bit difficult to get down here," he added.

* * *

Thorbjørn stood waiting by the side of the road, where the canine patrol unit cars were lined up. On the other side of the road were plowed fields as far as the eye could see, and a wild blackberry thicket stretched along the road. But where they stood, the forest rose abruptly and densely in front of them, and had he not known better, he would never have guessed that a large lake lay beyond. Liam stood for a moment and listened. The traffic noise from the highway cut right through.

Four dog teams had combed the area. Liam noticed how Dea was quickly inspecting the cars, but Rolf was working in an area near Fåborg. It hadn't been more than half an hour since he had reported in and announced that they were moving on. Liam couldn't criticize Dea's work, yet it bothered him that she had changed. It was completely unfair, because you couldn't be annoyed that someone suddenly seemed happier; he was well aware of that. There was an energy about her that he had never seen before. Not even when they had a one-night stand after they met on a training course before Dea moved to Odense Police. At that time, they were both in relationships, and it should never have happened. They hadn't seen each other again until Liam heard about what had happened to her husband. They'd had coffee together a few times after his death, and it hadn't been easy seeing her go to pieces. He chuckled to himself. He should be happy for her! Rolf was her first boyfriend since Mogens passed away.

"What have we got?" Liam asked, shivering in the cool wind. He held a branch for Dea and walked past the police cordon before they continued down the overgrown path that ran through the orange-and-red autumn leaves of a willow tree. Soon they stood in a clearing. The area consisted of long, withered grass and a large lake with a heavy mist resting just above the surface of the water.

"We have a body," Thorbjørn replied. "We've only looked in through the windows; I wanted to wait for you. Forensics have been called and are on their way out here."

Liam nodded. He had also gotten the message that a forensics team was on its way to the scene.

"The forest area is publicly accessible and used for hunting. But it seems that the boathouse is private; there's a padlock on the door. There are nets and traps inside, but there's no telling how often the cabin is used. The body is in the dinghy."

"And we still don't know who owns it?" Liam asked.

"No," Thorbjørn replied. "We're working on finding that out."

The boathouse was a low, oblong log cabin with two small windows on each side. It almost looked like a small allotment house, Liam thought. Half of the house went out into the water, where it was supported by several beams that went down into the lake. He imagined how you could sail the dinghy straight in and leave it dry-docked through the cottage.

"Are there any signs of a break-in?"

Thorbjørn shook his head.

204 SARA BLÆDEL AND MADS PEDER NORDBO

"So whoever placed the body must have had the key to the padlock," Liam said, moving aside as a colleague came to cut the lock open.

"We're ready to go in." Dea handed him a protection suit, hairnet, and gloves, and Liam accepted the flashlight that was held out to him. One of the officers turned on the light inside the boathouse. Liam had only been able to see the fishing tackle through the window, but when he entered the low-ceilinged room, he saw that there was a table, chairs, and a dartboard on the wall. The place was clearly used for more than boat storage, although right now there was a visible layer of dust, indicating that it had been a while since anyone had been there.

Thorbjørn and Dea waited outside while he walked past the table to the dinghy, which lay between two wide beams. Liam stepped onto one of the beams and looked down at the body.

"We need to call the pathologist," he shouted out to the others. The body had been lying there for some time. So long, in fact, that all facial features had long since disappeared. It was hard to tell if it was Lise Bruun they had found, but this couldn't be Zenia. The person in the boat had been dead for at least a month, probably more, he estimated. The eyes were gone, almost all the tissue under the skin was gone, and the skin had large, brown patches in it.

The air flowing into the boathouse through the doors facing the lake, which had now been opened, carried the autumnal fog into the house. The milky mist settled over the naked female body, emphasizing the cruelty and horror of the situation. Liam leaned over the body and scrutinized the battered torso. Although the skin was brownish and

WOUNDS 205

leathery, he could clearly see wounds of the same type as the ones they had seen on Jørgen Andersen. On this woman, the many wounds were almost healed in some places, and black nylon thread had fused with the dried skin flaps.

"It's a white, middle-aged woman," he announced as he rejoined the others. "With the same wounds and scars we've seen on the other two. And she's been lying here for a long time."

"Is that Lise Bruun?" Dea asked.

"That's probably very likely." Liam nodded.

"Don't people fish anymore? Why hasn't she been found?" It was a dog handler who asked the question. Liam shrugged his shoulders and thought that it wasn't that unusual for places like this to be used periodically.

"And why here?" Thorbjørn asked. He had walked down to the lakeshore and was looking out over the water. "Jørgen wasn't exactly hidden away. But she would only be found here when the owner of the boathouse showed up."

"Maybe the perpetrator didn't expect her to lie there for so long," Dea suggested. "It's possible they knew that the boathouse is used regularly?"

"I had started working on my own little theory that our perpetrator might want to exhibit something, want to be seen . . . maybe to scare someone." Thorbjørn joined them again. Liam nodded; he had been thinking along the same lines himself. The perpetrator hadn't gone to the slightest effort to hide the bodies.

"If we go with it, who needs to be scared? What is it that needs to be on display? And for whom?" Dea asked. They moved a little to make room for the forensics team, who had just arrived. "There was a message behind Monika le Fevre's exhibition. A message that we need to think about how we treat animals in the Western world. What could the message be here?"

"Well, I guess the message right now is that the deceased was found in the chief constable's boathouse. I guess that's a direct way of communicating with us," said Liam.

Thorbjørn seemed to agree. He nodded toward the dinghy. "She's naked," he pointed out. "Jørgen was dressed."

"Jan was also dressed," said Dea.

"I don't think the perpetrator finished what he started with Jan Hansen," Liam said. The thought had crossed his mind before, and as he stood inside the cabin looking at the body in the dinghy, he thought it again. The abuse of Jan Hansen must have been interrupted earlier than the perpetrator had anticipated. Perhaps that was why he hadn't had time to stitch his wounds.

"Or maybe he realized that Jan Hansen had not been involved in the internet harassment. Maybe he realized it was a fake profile," Thorbjørn said.

"Or she," Dea said. Liam and Thorbjørn looked at her questioningly. "The perpetrator could also be a she," she elaborated.

Liam nodded and felt a twinge of frustration that you had to spend energy on something he felt was self-evident. But she was right; you were supposed to use the correct terms. "The perpetrator," he corrected himself.

* * *

The line of police cars, civilian cars, and the ambulance signaled from afar that this was where something serious had happened. Blinded by tears and breathless with fear, she swerved behind the rear car, jumped out, and started running toward the path blocked by the red and white police tape. She didn't think of locking the car or taking her bag; she just ran and felt the soft forest floor under her feet.

Twigs and dry leaves stuck to her jacket sleeves and branches whipped her face as she ran as fast as she could without realizing it. Several times she almost lost her balance. She skated across the greasy forest floor in her biting shoes, gasping for breath. In the distance, she spotted the blue jumpsuits of the forensics team. Then she recognized the back of the pathologist standing talking to Liam. Although the forest whirled past her at lightning speed, she took in these glimpses like small events happening in slow motion.

She had been sitting in her office with Amalie Vedel's parents. They had insisted on knowing whether the police could establish with certainty that their daughter had not been the victim of a crime. They had repeatedly requested that the man who had invited Amalie to Sweden be questioned on suspicion of kidnapping. Throughout the conversation, Dybbøl's thoughts had been with Zenia. She had imagined how she had been forced to leave by an unknown perpetrator. She envisioned her slight, delicate body being mutilated and cut up. She heard her screams and imagined several times that she could actually feel her daughter's fear as vibrations running under her skin, that she could feel Zenia's fear in her own body because they were connected as mother and daughter.

"We are considering filing a complaint that it took so long before you managed to locate our daughter," was the

208 SARA BLÆDEL AND MADS PEDER NORDBO

last thing Dybbøl remembered from the conversation with Amalie's parents. The moment she read the message about the discovery of a woman and recognized the address, she had stood up without further explanation and run out of the office.

* * *

Dea turned around in a startled jerk when she heard a muffled scream and saw Dybbøl running toward them through the trees. "Is it my daughter?" sobbed the chief constable, gasping for breath so violently that it was hard to understand what she was saying. She bent over and rested her hands on her knees, trying to control her breathing. She was pale, had small scratches on her cheeks, and her face was wet with tears and snot. Neither of them had time to respond before she straightened up and strode purposefully into the boathouse. Liam jumped forward and gently stopped her as she was making her way through the forensics boxes and equipment.

"That's not your daughter in there," Dea heard him say. He gently led their boss away from the cabin, where the technicians were doing their forensic work. Just then, a stretcher was lifted into the boathouse and two paramedics prepared to move the body. The boat had already been pulled out, and the site investigation was nearing completion.

Together with a forensic photographer, the forensic pathologist described the surroundings in which the body had been lying. The dinghy and boathouse were photographed, the temperature of the water and air was determined, and only then was the body lifted out of the boat and placed on its stomach on the ground sheet that had

WOUNDS 209

been unfolded, allowing Frank to complete his on-site examination.

From where Dea stood, she could see that the body had the same kind of wounds on the back of the body as on the front, but not nearly as many. She heard Dybbøl's cries and the pathologist's monotone voice as he meticulously examined the back of the body while delivering short, sharp observations.

"If it's not Zenia, then why is it happening here?" Dea went back to join Liam and Dybbøl. He still had his arm around her, as if he was still afraid she would run into the boathouse. Dea noticed the splashes of mud on Dybbøl's pants and dirty shoes. She exchanged a quick glance with Liam.

"What can you tell us about this place?" she asked, looking at Dybbøl.

There was something apathetic about the chief's movements as she slowly nodded. She didn't look at the boathouse but stared out over the lake. Darkness was beginning to fall, and above the trees the setting sun had set fire to a wide band of thin clouds.

"This is our boathouse," Dybbøl whispered. "My husband has fishing rights to the lake and also has a dinghy out here."

Liam removed his arm from her shoulder and turned to face her.

"When was the last time he was out here?" he asked.

At first she didn't answer, then she shrugged and shook her head.

"I don't know," came the reply. "He used to come out here with Zenia; they used to fish together. But that was a long time ago. She no longer wanted them to catch fish for fun, even if they threw them back in again. For my husband, it was more about them having fun and spending quality time together. But that stopped when she no longer wanted to come out here."

She hid her face in her hands for a moment. "When I saw the address, I knew right away that it was a signal for me. I spent my childhood in this boathouse. I inherited it from my father. My parents had a farm down the road." She pointed behind her. "This is our private getaway. We come out here in the summer and enjoy the silence. It's our sanctuary when we need a break."

Dea had never thought of Dybbøl as someone who had grown up in the countryside. She had a hard time picturing her as a little girl walking through the woods. On the other hand, she had just as much trouble picturing her stern, penny-loafer-and-houndstooth-blazer-clad boss playing darts and drinking beer out here in the boathouse, but the last few days had turned her image of Dybbøl upside down anyway. As the chief constable stood there disintegrating before their very eyes, Dea really became aware of the person behind all the correct and logical thinking for the first time.

"It's been a long time since I've been out here myself," Dybbøl continued, "but my husband and his friends use it regularly. He's also kind enough to lend it out when people want to go fishing."

"Then we would like a list of everyone who has had access to the boathouse," Liam said. Gone was the gentle and comforting tone. He looked at his boss expressionlessly and said he would appreciate it if the list was as accurate and complete as possible.

WOUNDS

It was as if he was pulling himself together, Dea thought, following him with her eyes as he joined the pathologist at the lakeside.

Dybbøl stood for a moment, looking lost, and then spotted Thorbjørn, who immediately came toward them with a technician. "You've used the boat too, haven't you?" she asked.

The muscular investigator shook his head.

"Sometimes my husband invites people on fishing trips out here. He posts an announcement on Facebook, and people just show up. Several people from the police station have been along, and I was sure you were one of them. Those who have been here know the key is out here."

CHAPTER

30

LIAM TOOK A deep breath. "What do you think? What's your first impression?"

The pathologist had packed his bag and signaled that the woman was ready to be carried to the ambulance.

"Yes, what do I think?" Frank looked over at the body. "Female, somewhere between sixty and seventy, but it's hard to tell because of the condition of the body." He pulled off his hairnet and mask, and his blond curls fell onto his forehead. "I assume you're fishing for a description to confirm that this is the woman you're looking for."

Liam showed Frank a photo of Lise Bruun. "Could this be her?" The pathologist looked at the photo for a moment before handing it back. "It's not unlikely, and as you noticed, the body has the same injuries as the ones we saw on Jørgen Andersen and Jan Hansen. However, I can't stand here and say that the injuries are identical, even though they look similar."

Liam liked Frank and was comfortable working with him. The pathologist was always careful not to jump to conclusions.

WOUNDS   213

"We first need to analyze the cut surfaces of the wounds to be able to say for sure if the same procedure and perhaps the same tool was used."

"I understand that," Liam said, "but I don't think we can doubt that the message is the same, right?"

"No," Frank admitted, "there's no doubt about that. And this woman's hands and ankles are bound in the same way as the body behind the Verninge Inn had been."

"Cause of death?" Liam tried.

"Too early to tell." The pathologist shook his head quickly, as expected, and took a step in Liam's direction. "I've heard about the situation with Dybbøl's daughter," he said quietly. "Any news?"

Liam looked toward the boathouse and said that they would have to take Søren Dybbøl in for questioning. "And we also need to find out if there has been any contact between him and the three victims."

Frank thought for a moment before saying what Liam was already thinking. "But how does Zenia's disappearance fit into this development?"

Liam shook his head and felt the autumn chill creeping in under his coat's collar. "I just don't know," he admitted, and was about to say something about Dybbøl and her daughter, but then caught the glint in Frank's eye and kept it to himself. It wasn't appropriate to speculate about Zenia— there was still hope, and they needed to hold on to that.

*   *   *

Liam greeted Søren Dybbøl at the door to the Reactive Department and showed him to his office, where he pointed to a chair.

"Would you like a cup of coffee?" he asked, looking expectantly at the police chief's husband.

Søren shook his head. He seemed shaken but composed, and had already reported to the police station before Liam made it back from the boathouse.

"I understand you've been informed about the find out there?" Liam began, and Søren Dybbøl nodded. At the same time, the door opened. Dybbøl stuck her head in and waved Liam out into the hallway with impatient gestures.

"I want to sit in," she said, looking insistently into Liam's eyes.

"I don't know if . . ."

"I'm in," Dybbøl interrupted, and was about to push past him.

"No," Liam decided firmly. "I'm in the middle of an investigation, and now you have to let me do my job."

He was about to add the obvious about her being too personally involved in the case, but simply put a hand on her arm and pushed her away. Dybbøl was well aware that all rules dictated that she shouldn't participate in the interrogation of her own husband under any circumstances, but Liam could understand that it was difficult to remain within the boundaries of protocol, given the situation Dybbøl found herself in.

"I . . ." she began again, and he saw the desperation in her eyes.

He let go of her. "If I was the one so deeply involved in a case, you would have sent me home immediately."

He held her gaze until he sensed that she had had time to compose herself. Then she nodded slowly, exchanged a glance with her husband, and walked down the hall toward her own office.

* * *

Liam went back and sat down opposite Søren without commenting on the scene.

"I'm fully aware of the difficult situation you're in," he said instead, with all the compassion he could muster, "but right now I need to know everything you can tell me about the boathouse you own. Who knows about it? Who has access out there?"

Søren Dybbøl leaned forward slightly, folded his hands over his knees, and said with a touch of arrogance, "Shouldn't you be out looking for my daughter instead of sitting here with me? Surely one of your subordinates can take this information, which is not difficult to understand. You're the head of the department, my wife's closest—"

Liam grimly raised one hand in the air to stop him. "When was the last time you were in the boathouse?" He could hear that he sounded harsh, but he'd had enough of people trying to tell him how to do his job.

He could see that Søren Dybbøl was getting ready for another rant, but he beat him to it.

"The woman we found out there today has been there for months. Long before your daughter disappeared. We are currently investigating a case with three fatal victims who have been seriously mistreated, so if you are at all interested in us making progress in this investigation, which may also involve your missing daughter, please answer what I'm asking you right now, in as much detail as possible, so that we in the police can do our job to the best of our ability."

It was as if some of the air went out of Dybbøl's husband, but Liam wasn't quite finished.

"I've decided to bring you in for an informal interview here in my office, but we can also arrange a formal interview with two officers from my department. It's up to you."

Søren Dybbøl shook his head, a little embarrassed, and leaned back.

"I'm sorry," he said, rubbing his eyes. "I haven't slept the last few nights. In the beginning I was out looking for her, but the last two I've just sat up waiting. I can't stand it."

He rubbed his eyes again, which were now completely red. "Have you seen the photo my wife received of Zenia in front of the high school and *#thinkbeforeyoutype* on the back? I think someone knows where she is. Someone is doing this to her. And against us."

Liam let him finish, but as soon as Søren was done, he returned to his line of questioning.

"Who knows about the boathouse?"

"People in our circle of friends do," Søren replied, now more cooperative. "Most of the time it's just our friends, but it does happen that some people bring a guest."

"I got the impression that you sometimes organize fishing trips out there. Can you tell me a bit about that?"

He nodded quickly. "Yes, we've had fun in the past, but not so much this year."

"Why not?"

"Too much work," Søren said, a little stunned.

WOUNDS 217

"Do you remember the last time you were out there?" Liam asked. "We're having a bit of a hard time understanding how the deceased has been lying there for so long without being discovered."

"I was there during the summer vacation, at the end of July, I think."

"Was the dinghy there?"

"Yes, it was there. It hasn't been out much this year."

"Who has a key to the boathouse?"

"I have, and I've put a duplicate above the door out there, because Zenia and I experienced coming out there and realizing that I had forgotten my key a little too often. We got a bit tired of climbing in through the window."

A brief twitch that looked like a smile slid across his face.

"So basically anyone can come in," Liam stated.

Dybbøl's husband nodded. "But there's nothing to steal out there," he said. "I think the more alarms and locks you install, the more people think there's something to steal. And there isn't. I've never had anyone abuse the fact that they could get into the house out there. Inside is the key to the padlock that locks the gate to the lake, so if you want to take the boat out, you can do that too. There has never been any vandalism, and people moor the dinghy and lock it behind them if they've borrowed it."

Liam had the padlock from the gate in a bag, and he emptied it out on the table so Søren could see it properly. "Do you recognize it?"

Søren stared at the broken lock without touching it while Liam explained that the police had cut it.

"Yeah, that's mine, that's the one hanging out there. It's got a little spot of paint on the bottom and then that dent there." He pointed to the dent. "I can get my key from the car if you want it."

"You don't have to," Liam said. "I just wanted to make sure it was your lock and not a lock the perpetrator put on after killing that woman out there."

He leaned slightly forward over the desk.

"Søren," he began. "What do you know about your daughter's relationship with the girl from class who ended up committing suicide?"

"What's that got to do with it?" Søren exclaimed, the arrogant edge back in his voice. "Why in the world do we have to get into this now? Isn't this about the dead woman you found today? My wife and I fear that it could be the same perpetrator who is currently holding Zenia captive. Or worse." He swallowed hard. "And then you sit here and accuse our daughter of all sorts of things that belong to the past. She's a victim; don't you realize how serious this is?"

"Yes, we certainly do," Liam replied. "In fact, we hope that by understanding the case of Julie Villadsen and the hatred that arose against Monika le Fevre in connection with her exhibition, we will have a better chance of finding your daughter. Maybe the cases are connected; that's why we're investigating both of them."

"Just find her." Søren Dybbøl's voice cracked, and he started rubbing his eyes hard again.

There was an awkward silence. "Has your dog come home?"

Dybbøl's husband shook his head in resignation.

WOUNDS

"No, Lady is still gone . . ." He stopped, and Liam sensed that they were thinking the same thing: that it was completely unlikely it was a coincidence that it was just now that Lady had run away. But he hoped it was just him taking the thought a step further: that it was possible Lady was being turned into a stuffed animal that would have fit in well with le Fevre's exhibition.

CHAPTER

31

DEA SLUMPED IN her office chair and stared at the email that had just landed in her inbox, an email that had been sent out to everyone in Odense Police: "Chief Constable Margrethe Dybbøl has resigned indefinitely for personal reasons." She wondered if she should send her boss a message. Maybe just a heart emoji. It hadn't been more than a few hours since they had walked back to the police station from the boathouse. The decision must have just been made.

Dea reached for the phone on her desk and tried again to reach Julie's mother. Annette Villadsen wasn't answering her calls or returning her messages. Before Liam had started his conversation with Dybbøl's husband, he had made it clear that if she couldn't reach the girl's mother, she would have to drive to Holmstrup and bring her in for questioning.

Piil had presented them with a series of attacks that Lise Bruun had aimed at Julie. It was possible that the dead woman in the boathouse, who had to be Lise Bruun, had been well liked at her previous job, but she had behaved disgustingly and aggressively toward Julie online, and the attacks had gotten worse and worse as the chorus of haters egged each other on.

Dea had just reread her report from the conversation with Annette, and at no point had the mother tried to conceal her anger toward the people who had helped drive her daughter to her death, as she put it.

"Interrogation with the rights of a defendant," Liam had said. He wanted the mother to account for her whereabouts during the time of the victims' disappearance. "If she can't, we'll arrest her and search her home."

But Dea didn't believe it for a second. There had been nothing in Annette Villadsen's behavior during the conversation that would indicate she was trying to hide anything. Quite the opposite, in fact. Three deaths, two of them certain homicides, brutal abuse. Dea trusted her investigative experience and knowledge of human nature enough to be sure that she would have known if Annette Villadsen had carried out these crimes or had the slightest connection to them. She was on board with the two obvious revenge motives Liam saw. The mutilations could act as revenge for either Monika le Fevre's exhibition or the harassment Julie had been subjected to. Assuming that the motive was the latter, Annette Villadsen was an obvious suspect. But maybe it was a little too obvious, Dea thought as she patiently let the phone ring. She had barely let go of the receiver when her cell phone started ringing in her bag. An unknown number.

"Dea Torp," she said.

"Carstensen, Neurology Department," said a dark and authoritative voice, which she immediately recognized as the chief physician's. "Monika le Fevre woke up from her coma this afternoon. The diagnostics are very positive. I have just come from her room myself, and as our preliminary examinations also support, I believe that her brain has not been traumatized as a result of—"

"Can I talk to her?" Dea interrupted.

"—the accident," the chief physician continued unchallenged. "The patient is doing well, considering the circumstances. And you are welcome to have a short conversation with her. However, I need to prepare you for the fact that she won't remember anything from the accident itself. It's possible that in time she will remember more. But right now, pushing her won't help."

"Does she remember anything from the time leading up to the accident?"

"Fragments," he replied. "But among other things, she doesn't remember that she was driving the car when the accident happened."

"I'll be right there," Dea said quickly, and grabbed her jacket. The door to Liam's office was still closed, and she wasn't sure if he was still in there with Dybbøl's husband, so she didn't want to disturb him. She ran toward the stairs down to the courtyard and almost ran into Rolf's arms.

"Hi, honey!" she said, thinking about the lipstick message on the mirror at home with butterflies in her stomach. "Are you on your way home?"

He pulled her into a kiss and rested his chin on her head for a moment.

"I actually came to ask if you've eaten or if we should go to that Italian together."

She had texted him about the body they had found in the boathouse and prepared him for the fact that she could

WOUNDS 223

be home late, but he had been out with the search team all day and had not responded.

"I'm sorry," she said, and explained that she was on her way to the hospital. "Monika le Fevre has woken up from her coma. I don't think it will take that long. Do you want to wait here, or are you going home? I can bring some food home when I'm done."

He kissed her again. "I'm driving home, done in—and hungry. It's been a long day. I'll get some food and see you at home."

Dea felt joy and security surge through her as she crossed the courtyard and made her way to the service car. She thought for the first time how unusual it was for her to feel connected to another human being. At the same time, she had to admit that she hadn't thought about him much during the day. But now that she was getting off work soon, it was a nice thought that it was him she was going home to.

* * *

The hospital corridor was quiet when Dea entered the ward where Monika le Fevre was admitted. The large door had only just closed behind her with a mechanical suction sound when consultant Carstensen met her from the other end of the corridor.

In his authoritative manner, he announced that Monika's parents had been there since she had woken up from her coma, but they had just driven home. "Maybe it would have been better to wait until tomorrow, because she's sleeping right now," he said.

"I want to check on her," Dea said quickly, and asked if there was a chance she would wake up in the next hour.

He nodded and offered to go in to see if they could wake her. "If she's a deep sleeper, we'll let her sleep, but it's also possible that she just needs to rest and she'll surface when we call her name."

Dea had been very insistent when she explained to Carstensen during her first visit how important it was that she got to question Monika le Fevre. But at the time, the question was whether Monika could be an accomplice in the murder of Jørgen Andersen. That possibility was of course ruled out, as Monika had been in a coma both when Jørgen was killed and when Zenia disappeared. However, it seemed important to find out who could have delivered the envelope with the letter and the small piece of Lise Bruun's skin that Dea had found in Monika's car after the accident.

Carstensen knocked gently before opening the door to Monika le Fevre's room. The room was darkened, but the bedside lamp shone directly onto the floor in a sharp beam.

"Monika," the consultant called, and walked over to the bed. He called again and put a hand on her shoulder. "You have a visitor."

Dea stayed by the door while Carstensen talked to Monika, who replied, mumbling, in a cracked voice, after which the chief physician came over to Dea and nodded affirmatively.

"I've explained to her that you're here to talk to her about the accident. You can bring up the murder in Verninge yourself if you feel it's important. But feel your way and be considerate of her condition. And no more than ten minutes," he said.

* * *

WOUNDS   225

"Hi," Dea said, pulling a chair over to the bed and introducing herself. "I'm here to talk about what happened Sunday night. About your accident."

Le Fevre's head rested heavily on the pillow. Her face was bruised and severely swollen on one side. She had an oblong bandage over one eye, and the skin around her swollen lips had a bluish tint. She seemed drowsy and didn't move at all, but her eyes were sharp and focused intently on Dea.

"The doctor has told me what happened," came the rushed reply. She cleared her throat awkwardly. "I was due to go to my parents' house. We were going to have beef stroganoff. We take turns deciding the Sunday menu, but my mom does the cooking." She moved her face slightly; maybe it was supposed to be a smile.

"Had you been home during the day?"

Monika le Fevre nodded once before resting her head on the pillow, exhausted.

"I think so . . ." she said hesitantly, but then interrupted herself. "I'm a little unsure about the days. I'm packing up my workshop—I've been doing that all week. But I was also in the woods, maybe it was Sunday." Suddenly she half stood up and reached out for Dea, who took her hand in surprise.

"Do my parents know I'm lying here?" She sounded scared and looked at Dea with wide eyes.

Dea hastened to reassure her that everything was fine. "They've only just left," she said.

"There was light out there." Monika's arm went limp, and she pulled it back and let her hand land on the sheet. A shadow slid across her face. She grimaced, and her gaze flickered fearfully for a moment into the room, which was still in darkness.

226 SARA BLÆDEL AND MADS PEDER NORDBO

"Should I turn on more lights?" Dea asked, but Monika didn't respond. She lay with her eyes closed, and Dea just had time to think she had fallen asleep when she started talking again in her cracked voice.

"The lamp on the workbench in my workshop was on. That's what puzzled me. I had turned off all the lights there myself. I'm always very careful that they're not on when I'm done working."

She was breathing heavily and almost breathless, and it seemed as though she was using all her strength to produce words. "I thought my father had been there. We sometimes borrow tools from each other. When I'm not home, he just lets himself in. So I called and asked if there was anything else he needed, because I would bring it with me when I drove over to them."

It was slow, the words were obviously coming to her painfully, but Dea had straightened up and was listening attentively and patiently.

"But it wasn't him who had been there." She opened her eyes and looked at Dea with an anxious look. "The lamp was pulled all the way across the table. I knew that's not how I had left it. I never leave it like that!" She fell silent and paused for a long moment.

Dea nodded encouragingly at her.

"The envelope was in the middle of my work surface," Monika continued with difficulty. "I wanted to throw it out. I've stopped reading what people write about me. I don't read reviews or comment feeds. The vicious tone against me had flared up again after a young high school girl wrote about my exhibition in an assignment for school. When she approached me for help with her assignment, I

WOUNDS

warned her that she might be uncomfortable dealing with my art because people only see and hear what they want to. But she said she thought nuance was important. She knew what I had been through in the wake of my exhibition, and I was touched that it meant something to her to pass on and explain what I had originally intended in exhibiting my mutilated animals. I myself have long since given up trying to explain that my message was exactly the opposite of what people thought. The people who were and are violently angry with me are not interested in being reasoned with. They are interested in war."

She gently turned her face toward Dea.

"There's a whole army of keyboard warriors out there, you know that?"

Dea nodded. She wanted to go back to talking about the envelope, but she had a feeling it was best to let le Fevre talk at her own pace.

"They don't stop once they smell blood. They are ruthless and relentless, and I can't take it anymore. My doctor says I've developed a form of posttraumatic stress. She's the one who has advised me not to read what they write and not to engage in the attacks being directed at me. I want to retreat. And on Sunday I would have told my parents that I am putting my farm up for sale. I have found a small house in Fratticciola. It's in Tuscany. I can't take it anymore. I have no more strength."

"But you opened the envelope," Dea said to bring her back on track. Now they had to move on.

"Yes, I opened it," Monika said, her voice almost disappearing, but then she cleared her strained throat. "There was a piece of skin in it, and I just had enough. I remember calling my parents and saying that I wasn't coming anymore because I was going to go to the police. I'm not going to put up with any more of this. It's gone on long enough and I wanted the police to take it seriously. No one has ever taken it seriously. Not even when the young girl who wrote about my exhibition jumped in front of a train. It's as if cyberhate doesn't count because you don't face each other directly and have personal contact while the violent harassment takes place. As if it's an extenuating circumstance that it doesn't happen in 'real life.'" Monika le Fevre made quotation marks with one hand still resting on the bed.

Behind them, the door opened. It was a nurse who stuck her head in and said it was time for Monika to rest.

Dea nodded quickly.

"Do you have any idea who might have left the envelope in your workshop?"

Monika le Fevre shook her head.

"It could be anyone. There's enough to go around." She closed her eyes, almost squeezing them shut, as if she didn't want to think about the number of people who could have left the envelope on her desk.

"Okay, Monika," the nurse continued, and Dea stood up.

"I remember getting into the car," Monika continued. "I also remember thinking that I couldn't take it anymore." She opened her eyes, which were now filled with tears. "I was driving fast. Too fast; it was as if a strange and external force was chasing me through the evening darkness. I was so determined to put an end to it all. My only wish was to get to the police with that disgusting patch of skin and maybe finally be taken seriously."

WOUNDS

"Okay," the nurse said efficiently, guiding Dea toward the door while reassuring Monika with caring words.

Dea took one last look at Monika le Fevre, who was quietly crying into the sheet she had pulled up around her chin.

CHAPTER

32

THE WEEKEND HAD left the Institute of Forensic Medicine in Odense deserted.

Liam's footsteps echoed down the hallway past the many closed doors. His body felt stiff, and his neck was sore after a restless night with too few hours of sleep on the office couch. When he woke up, his shirt was wrinkled and the T-shirt he wore under it smelled of sweat. He had thrown the soiled clothes into a duffel bag before washing himself in the sink of the department's restroom and pulling a sweatshirt with the police logo over his head.

He hadn't meant to stay in the city; he had even looked forward to sitting alone in the darkness in his parents' kitchen with a cold beer and peace to clear his head. But suddenly that was no longer an option.

He had gotten into his car, but his hand wouldn't respond when he reached out to press the start button. His feet wouldn't reach the pedals. At first, he had sat motionless, waiting to regain control. Then he realized his body

WOUNDS

had begun to tremble with reluctance. Or fatigue. Or . . . He hadn't felt the tears, but realized his cheeks were getting wet.

His mom had sent a text message that there was a late-night snack in the fridge. They expected him to be home around eleven PM. Liam had sat in the darkness of the car, thinking about his children. About how wrong it was that he was heading home to his parents to sleep in his old room instead of heading home to them.

He hadn't seen Laura and Andreas for weeks. Helene wouldn't talk to him. When he tried to make an appointment to see the children, he got a short text back saying that she wasn't ready yet. That she wasn't ready! He had raged and ranted at her about that.

But then, out of the blue, she had messaged that he could come and get them—as if they were still small, as if time had stopped when everything was good between them. But nothing was good. There was no longer anything between them. He was out, and she was in charge.

I can't, he had written back. He had tried to call to explain that he was standing outside a boathouse with a dead body and a forensics team that had just arrived on the scene, but she hadn't answered, so he had left a message.

She hadn't answered that one, which didn't surprise him—this was exactly the kind of situation she could no longer tolerate. So he wrote that he would talk to Laura and Andreas himself and arrange to see them. *No,* came the short reply. *Don't contact our children until we're ready for it.*

It wasn't so much the intransigence of her tone. What was tearing him apart was the powerlessness he felt that she had managed to turn their children against him. How had it happened? How had things gotten so out of hand?

He had gone to the Irish Pub and ordered a double Scotch. And another. He had managed to take the first sip of the third before he finally gathered enough courage to admit he was well aware of how it had come to this. He was the one who had hurled himself out of the family that was his life, and that realization stung. For years, he hadn't listened to what Helene said when she wanted to be with him. He hadn't paid enough attention. Hadn't taken it seriously enough. There had always been something he had to deal with at work before he had time to deal with and take care of her and the kids. Before he . . . "Blah, blah, blah, blah," he said so loudly to himself that he felt the bartender's gaze and shook his head defensively.

And then he had gotten angry. You would have thought Helene had known he was on the verge of another murder when she sent her message. As if she had been sitting somewhere watching, waiting for the right moment when she was sure he would have to say that he was dealing with something more important than his children and her.

After the fourth double whisky, he'd had the presence of mind to go back to the police station, where he'd thrown himself on the sofa with anger coursing through his veins. Stupid as he was, he had texted a furious message to Helene, and he had been determined to put an end to her deciding when he could see his teenage children. No more dancing to her tune, no more being found guilty of willful neglect.

WOUNDS 233

She hadn't replied, and when he woke up with a heavy head and a bitter taste in his mouth, it was too late to recall the message.

Once in the hallway, Liam could smell the pungent odor of the autopsy rooms. He pushed open the door to the large, white tiled room and greeted Frank. The pathologist gave him a searching look before turning his attention back to the autopsy table. It was covered with a cloth.

"There's not much left of Lise Bruun, but the identification is positive: It's her. We can say that with certainty based on her dentition and a number of other characteristics. She had surgery for a herniated disk seven years ago, and there was a fracture of a carpal bone." Frank respectfully removed the cloth with both hands.

Liam held his breath for a moment as he looked down over the mutilated female body. "How long has she been dead?"

"Somewhere between nine and eleven weeks; that's as close as I can get yet. It's likely that the warm weather in August accelerated the degradation."

"Did she get those wounds before or after she died?" He pointed to the woman's torso.

"Without a doubt, before she died. Most of the wounds were in the process of healing. I can also tell you that she was probably starved over a long period of time. It's hard to be absolutely certain, as it's easier to tell if a person has starved when the body is fresh, but in my autopsy, I have found a high concentration of ketone bodies in the victim's muscles. These substances are excreted during prolonged starvation. Unfortunately, they are also excreted by diabetes or sudden alcohol withdrawal, so we need to rule out

234 SARA BLÆDEL AND MADS PEDER NORDBO

that Lise Bruun was a diabetic or alcoholic before we can know anything about how long she starved for."

Liam thought about it. Jørgen Andersen had also been starving—his stomach and intestines had been completely empty—but because the body was fresher, Frank could have been more certain. Therefore, it was naturally likely that Lise Bruun had also been starving.

"Is there anything else you want to tell me?" Liam looked at Frank, who, as usual, was standing to his side, waiting patiently for Liam to finish his thought process.

"Her wrists and ankles were also bound with zip ties. The wounds on her torso are similar to the ones we saw on Jørgen. However, it's interesting that the wounds and scars on Lise are not as nice, if I may say so, as the ones we saw on Jørgen." He smiled a little apologetically at his choice of words.

"So they're not the same?" Liam took a closer look at one of the wounds and could see that it wasn't covered by a flap of skin in the same way he remembered from Jørgen's body. The piece of skin that had been cut free was currently in an evidence bag after they had removed it from the envelope that had been delivered to Monika le Fevre. The pain must have been unbearable, he thought, dwelling on the battered torso and the ugly open wound. She had been cut in thirteen places, and twelve patches of skin had been reattached. Like a brutal patchwork, they lay scattered across the pale, grayish skin.

"Yes, they are almost identical, but it's as if the wounds we see here are an earlier version of the ones we examined on Jørgen Andersen. As if the perpetrator just had to get to grips with the technique. The cuts are less secure on this victim." Frank pointed to where the photos of the other two victims lay next to each other on the table. "Some of her scars are more similar in execution to the two we saw on Jan Hansen."

"It matches the dates of the disappearances." Liam nodded, looking at the photographs of the dead bodies. "The perpetrator continuously developed their technique and gradually became more confident while working on Lise Bruun."

"Yes, that makes sense." Frank gently covered Lise Bruun again.

"What about the cause of death?" Liam asked. He was having a hard time connecting the three victims. The distinctive wounds obviously tied them together, but there was no consistent modus operandi in the way the victims had died. He felt his overarching view of the case crumbling, and he realized that it was too early to rule out the possibility of multiple perpetrators. It was still possible that each of the three victims had their own perpetrator, even though his intuition told him otherwise. There could also be one perpetrator who'd lost interest once the abuse had been carried out. A person who was not interested in death itself but rather saw it as a necessary evil, something to be overcome or something that came naturally as a result of the abuse. Liam tried to keep his thoughts together. It was a matter of sorting and remembering the ones that might be useful and lead him forward.

The forensic pathologist went to the sink and began zealously washing his hands and forearms.

"Jan Hansen had a blood clot," he said. "Jørgen Andersen suffocated. When you have investigated whether Lise

Bruun was an alcoholic or a diabetic, I can state with greater certainty what my theory is so far. And if I'm right, I would say that the two gentlemen died a compassionate death compared to Lise Bruun. I believe she starved to death. A brutal and merciless death."

CHAPTER

33

DEA SAT ON the sofa and stared ahead of her, her dried tears tightening the skin on her cheeks. She was cold and shaken to the core. He had rushed out the door without closing it behind him, and now a cold wind blew in from the hallway and wrapped itself around her bare feet. She couldn't bring herself to get up to close it and instead sat trying to understand what had happened, replaying the last hour over and over in her mind, frantically searching her memory for something she had missed.

The pizza boxes and the empty red wine bottle from yesterday were still on the kitchen table. When she returned home after visiting Monika in the hospital, he had made sure the candles were lit and the table was set. The wine had been opened, and the living room was filled with gentle bossa nova music coming from the speakers. They had both been tired after an intense week. He had talked about how he and the other handlers had coordinated the search with water search dogs and how he had led Ask through a densely wooded area. She said Monika had woken from her coma and Liam wanted to bring Julie's mother in for a formal interview with a view to charging her. "She's the one with the strongest motive—avenging what happened to her daughter. I just don't believe it," she had said, explaining how the girl's mother had not for a moment hidden the fact that she wanted all those who had been after her daughter and had indirectly driven her to her death to rot in hell. She and Rolf had talked about how well they understood her— that they could vividly empathize with her anger.

After eating, they had sat on the sofa and talked about everything and nothing. A little about dreams for the future. About the old factory building that could be turned into a fabulous home. About his handyman skills and her lack of interior design flair. They had talked about her daughter. And about his. She had gathered her courage and asked if he dreamed of having more children. He didn't. Maybe that was it? she thought. The whole having-more-children thing. She shouldn't have brought it up.

Dea let her eyes rest on the unopened bag from the bakery on the coffee table in front of her. Today, she had woken him up with a cup of coffee by the bed before driving to the bakery for bread. They had agreed to get up early enough to have a quiet morning together before she had to leave. She was to pick Thorbjørn up in Odense at half past nine so they could drive to Holmstrup and Annette Villadsen's together. Dea still hadn't gotten hold of her, but the last time she talked to her, she had prepared her for the fact that they might need to talk to her again, and she had seemed very cooperative.

Dea felt the tears welling up again. Maybe there had already been small signs last night that something was

WOUNDS 239

wrong. It wasn't something she had noticed, but now that she thought back and dissected the situation, she could perhaps remember that she had felt a hint of irritation from him that she had to work all weekend when he was off. He had suggested she call in sick and leave the questioning of Julie's mother to Thorbjørn.

"We can go away for a few days. To an inn, or maybe find a nice seaside hotel. How about Bornholm?"

She had felt a wave of warmth wash through her body, and she had leaned into him with abandon, saying that the Sunday allowance could help cover a little getaway. She had taken out her phone and checked her calendar before suggesting a weekend in November, but by then it seemed like he had lost interest. Instead, she had tempted him by saying that she would bring sandwiches home when they had finished questioning Julie's mother. He had smiled at that—it was their little joke that she loved sandwiches—and then he had kissed her and asked for an open-faced roast beef sandwich. No matter how hard she thought, she couldn't think of what she could have done.

This morning she hadn't felt anything either. He had pulled her in when she brought him the coffee, but when she returned from the bakery, he was gone. The coffee she had carried onto his bedside table was untouched and the bed was messy, even though they normally took turns making it when they got up. She had been wondering what was up, but had started setting the breakfast table and boiling eggs, when he suddenly appeared in the doorway.

Dea closed her eyes.

Rolf had broken up with her and kicked her out almost in one breath. She had barely recognized his voice when he told her to pack her things and leave the farm. At first she had thought he was joking, but he hadn't flinched and had said in the same strange voice that he meant all her things, with a wave of his hand toward the bathroom and the bedroom to let her know he was talking about her toiletries and the clothes that had crept into his closet over the past three months. On a shelf he had cleared out for her.

She had put the pot of eggs down on a heat mat and stared at him, speechless.

"You need to pack and leave now," he said. "When I get back, you and your stuff will be gone, and you and I will be history."

"What the hell is going on?" she had shouted, but by then he was already out the door. She watched him cross the courtyard with a wagging Ask at his heels.

* * *

Dea pulled herself together, wiped her eyes, and stood up. On heavy legs, she walked into the bedroom and pulled out her weekend bag from under the bed. For a moment she stood looking at the comforter. It was one he had bought for them. Quickly she cleared her shelf and then went to the bathroom for her toiletry bag and the toothbrush that shared a cup with his.

She realized that her hands were shaking. Bit by bit, she was removing herself from the life they'd had together and that she had loved so much. She grabbed her cell phone from the bedside table to see if he had texted. He hadn't.

The anger came rolling in a wave that made her gasp for breath. What the hell did he think he was doing? That asshole! In three long strides she was on his side of the bed, grabbing the cup of cold coffee and throwing it against the wall so that the brown liquid cascaded over the white bedding.

Furious, she slung her weekend bag over her shoulder, grabbed her handbag from the armchair and her coat from the hallway. She threw open the front door and stomped out into the courtyard without looking back at the house she was beginning to think of as home. At the car, she dropped everything in a pile on the ground and stood looking at the closed doors to the factory building and the low barn.

Then she started calling out to him, her voice echoing between the buildings as she walked with long strides over the cobblestones. Even if she had to beat it out of him, she would make him explain what she had done wrong. She wasn't going to put up with this. Suddenly, the age differ-ence between them felt colossal. Did he think he would get away with behaving like a spoiled teenager and treating his girlfriend like this? He sure as hell wouldn't if she had any-thing to do with it.

She pulled open the door to the workshop and called again. It was dark and as empty and deserted as it had been when he showed her the room with the large, idle machines and the beautiful gable window. She continued in the dark-ness toward the office.

There was a dull hissing sound from inside the pellet stove, but otherwise all was quiet.

"Asshole!" she shouted, tearing at a heavy, black-painted wooden sliding door. It led into the low barn and didn't budge an inch. She looked out the windows toward the field, but didn't see him or Ask. She shook with rage and shouted again, calling his name and kicking the door.

Anger made her sweat profusely, and tears filled her eyes again, blurring her vision.

She felt desperate—he was also her colleague, they had to talk; otherwise it would be impossible to see each other at the police station when they had parted like this. She cringed. How she would hate to see the look of triumph on Liam's face when he was right—he had never had much faith in their relationship. She let go of the sliding door handle and was about to go out to look for him behind the house when she heard a noise.

It came from the other side of the heavy door, sounding like a moan, a complaint. She stood still in the darkness and listened. Then there was another faint sound—a kind of drawn-out sigh. For a moment she thought it sounded like Rolf and a woman, but then there was silence again. In a flash, she could picture him with another woman. Naked and completely absorbed in each other. Irrational jealousy surged through her in a moment of madness. Then she pulled herself together and listened again.

"Hello," she called. "Are you in there, Rolf?"

There was a scraping sound, as if something was being dragged across the concrete floor. Dea abandoned the sliding door and walked back through the workshop, calling Rolf's name. From the courtyard, an old-fashioned two-part stable door led into the barn. From the window where she stood, she could see that it was closed. He wasn't usually in there either. She thought maybe it was an animal she had heard. A rat he was catching. She shuddered. Dea stopped for a moment and tried to compose herself. She didn't want Rolf to see her in that state, so she forced herself to cool down before joining him. She took a deep breath as she pulled out her cell phone. Exhaled heavily a few times. She had to text Thorbjørn and warn him that she would be ten minutes late.

Dea had just unlocked her phone when the blow struck. The phone flew out of her hand in an arc. Instinctively, she reached for the shelf in front of her to keep herself upright. Another blow hit her head, and blackness fell around her as she lost consciousness.

CHAPTER

34

LIAM HAD JUST said goodbye to Frank and had gotten into his car to drive back to the police station when Thorbjørn called.

"What do you mean, Dea didn't come and get you?" He had filled himself with the mediocre forensic institute's coffee to chase away the fatigue, but his head was still pounding and he was fully aware of the need to call Helene as soon as possible and apologize for the previous night's messages.

"She just didn't show up and I couldn't get hold of her, so I drove down alone to bring Annette Villadsen in for questioning." Liam didn't have time for employee bickering. It was Sunday, he hadn't slept properly for a week, and now that Dybbøl had resigned—probably after a strong recommendation from higher management—he could see that his workload wouldn't exactly ease when what had been on her plate would be transferred to his desk.

"Fine," he said shortly. "Then she owes you another favor." He was about to end the call.

WOUNDS 245

"Annette isn't here," Thorbjørn continued. "And I can't reach her."

Liam sighed. The hangover was like a tight band around his forehead.

"She's probably gone away for the weekend. We'll bring her in tomorrow."

"You'd better come down here." Thorbjørn sounded serious, and only now did Liam realize that something was wrong.

"Something happened in the house. I don't think she left her home voluntarily."

* * *

Liam parked behind the patrol car parked in front of Annette Villadsen's red villa. He looked out over the fields and felt the drizzle that mercifully cooled his hungover face. He glanced into the open carport, where a bicycle and lawn mower were sheltered from the rain, and saw Thorbjørn coming to meet him.

"When she didn't answer, I opened the door," Thorbjørn began. "I called her several times, and when I opened the front door, I could hear her cell phone ringing inside."

He made room for Liam to enter. They both stood in the doorway and looked in.

Inside the hallway was a floor lamp. The glass shade was shattered and scattered in a thousand pieces across the brown tiles. A candlestick was knocked over on a low shelf under the hallway mirror, and a sweater lay on the floor.

"We're going in." Feeling distracted and incapacitated, Liam pushed open the front door and accepted the latex gloves Thorbjørn handed to him.

246   SARA BLÆDEL AND MADS PEDER NORDBO

"Hello," he called into the house. "It's the police, and we're coming in now!" There was complete silence. He called out again and nodded to Thorbjørn.

Carefully they walked over the shards of broken glass in the hallway. Liam took a quick glance into the living room. A chair had been pulled out from the dining table, where an iPad was charging in the fruit basket along with a crumpled paper napkin. He followed Thorbjørn into the kitchen, and they both stopped abruptly.

"What the hell happened here?" the tall investigator exclaimed, instinctively taking a step back and stepping on Liam's toes. On the floor, a bouquet of flowers lay soaked in water from a broken vase, and on the floor by the fridge lay a kitchen knife. There were no blood splatters and no other signs of a struggle. Next to the sink were a half-empty coffee cup and a tub of butter without a lid. The lid was next to the container, along with a knife and an open packet of crispbread.

Thorbjørn walked to a closed door next to the living room. Liam caught a glimpse of a desk in there, while he himself continued toward a dark room where the blinds were pulled down. Under the window was an unmade double bed. A T-shirt had been left on the comforter, and on the floor next to the bed were a pair of panties and a used towel.

He squatted down, pulled off one glove, and felt the towel. It was no longer wet in the way you would expect if Annette Villadsen had gotten out of the shower a few hours ago.

"Not from this morning?" Thorbjørn asked behind him. Liam shook his head and got to his feet. The room at the end of the hallway must have been Julie's.

The narrow bed was neatly made with a striped bedspread in pink and light green and covered with lots of pillows and teddy bears. Liam thought of his own daughter, who had also kept all her teddy bears from when she was little—they made her feel safe, she said—and he thought the same was probably true here. An attempt to prolong childhood. The shelves were crammed with young adult books with glittery spines, and on the windowsill a lot of small animal-shaped knickknacks took their place alongside colored glass bowls filled with beautiful stones and shells. If it weren't for the slightly stagnant air in the room and an indefinable feeling of being staged, Liam wouldn't have been surprised if Julie waltzed into the room with her school bag and sat down at the white-painted desk to do her homework. Everything was ready to welcome a teenage girl, even a narrow vase with a single fresh tulip on the bedside table.

* * *

He stood in the doorway for a moment, thinking about what Dea had said. For the last month of her life, Julie had refused to leave her bed. The girl had pretty much stopped eating, and anxiety had kept her locked in this room, living the last part of her life with the curtains drawn, until one day she had gotten out of bed, walked to the railroad tracks, and thrown herself in front of a regional train.

He carefully closed the door to the room when Thorbjørn called him from the living room. A purse and a magazine had been left on the coffee table along with the cell phone they had heard from the front door. There was no doubt whatsoever that the occupant of the house hadn't gone away for the weekend, Liam said, and he accepted the framed photograph from the bookcase that Thorbjørn held out to him.

248   SARA BLÆDEL AND MADS PEDER NORDBO

It depicted a little girl being held by a young man. It wasn't hard to imagine that the girl was Julie. But it was the man who made Liam step over and hold the picture in the light from the lamp above the dining table.

The girl was maybe two years old, he guessed. He did the math; back then, the man in the picture must have been in his early twenties, but he was not hard to recognize. The hair was longer, the face more boyish with rounder cheeks, the body less muscular. But the eyes and smile were the same. Rolf.

He felt Thorbjørn's gaze. "Family?" the tall investigator suggested.

Liam shrugged. "Or maybe a family friend. Either way, there's a connection. Get Dea on the phone. We need to know what his relationship to Annette Villadsen is."

Thorbjørn turned to the window with his cell phone to his ear, but he let his hand drop a moment later. "It's going straight to voicemail. I think it's off."

"Get hold of Piil, then. I want her to do a search on Rolf Lundgren. I also want her to find out who Julie's father is."

It was clear from Thorbjørn's body language that Piil was in the middle of something when he got her on the phone.

No, Liam signaled vehemently. "It can't wait! We need to clarify the connection between Rolf and Annette Villadsen. Tell them we're heading back to the police station right now. I'll meet you there."

CHAPTER

35

MARGRETHE DYBBØL LAY on the sofa, staring out the double patio door. Lady's empty dog basket sat on the floor next to her, and outside the rain poured down. The morning's argument with Søren still clung to her. They had argued violently and unfairly about guilt and responsibility.

Why hadn't they realized what their daughter was up to? Which one of them was responsible for Zenia's anger growing into an uncontrollable monster? Was it her or him who had failed to teach her how to behave toward other people—how inclusivity and acceptance were some of the most important qualities to take into adulthood?

Since she'd packed up her desk and logged off the police computer system, her self-recriminations had almost surpassed the fear she had felt for so many days, overriding any other feelings she had. She had a hard time separating all her emotions. Fear. And sadness, as if she had already lost her daughter. But these emotions were mixed with anger at Zenia's behavior. And then she was disappointed. But sometime last night, she had realized that the disappointment was actually more directed at herself. She had let her daughter down by not paying enough attention to her. She was disappointed in her own efforts as a mother. She had not lived up to her own expectations.

The landline rang, but she didn't get up. Until now, she had reacted to the slightest sound, the slightest sign that there might be news about Zenia. But now she was lying here as if her body had decided to die. As if it was unable to handle being in a state of readiness for so long, waiting so long for disaster to strike.

"Chief Constable Has Taken a Leave of Absence." The headline meant nothing to ordinary people scrolling through the online newspapers, but the journalists were chasing her for a comment. They wanted to know if there was any news about her daughter. They wanted Zenia's parents' opinion, but mostly hers, on what it was like to have just closed the Amalie Vedel case when their own daughter was still missing. She didn't answer the phone, wouldn't comment or talk to anyone.

Liam had texted to ask how she was, and she had no idea how to respond. She was happy for Amalie's parents, but at the same time she felt a tremendous amount of anger toward the young girl who had turned up and hadn't realized how many resources they had used to find her.

Resources that could have been used to find Zenia. They had wasted manpower and time searching for a girl who didn't even feel she had done anything wrong and who was almost oblivious to her parents' concerns.

While Zenia was gone and no one had been looking for her. Until now. She should have gotten a search underway straightaway. The very morning Zenia hadn't come home.

She should have gone out with a search party, all guns blazing. But she had been embarrassed at the idea that it was her daughter who might have gone on a trip with her friends without thinking. She hadn't wanted to show the world that she wasn't in control of her daughter, that she didn't know what she was doing. She had also been ashamed because it was likely that Zenia was taking part in a protest that would be embarrassing for Odense's chief constable to face. She had turned her back on her daughter instead of protecting her with her head held high. That realization was hard to come to terms with.

She thought about Søren. It was as if his life just went on. He had just gone in to the town hall to work, even though it was Sunday. He would be gone for a few hours at most, he had said, something to do with a Russian company that wanted to build offices at the old port facility.

*   *   *

The silence in the large villa was frightening. She got up from the sofa, feeling dizzy as she walked toward the kitchen and turned on the coffee machine with mechanical movements.

For a moment, she stood and watched a bird hopping happily in the pouring rain in the newly planted cherry trees outside the window. Then she went to the fridge and took out the milk. It slipped out of her hand almost in slow motion and spread in a puddle on the floor. Slowly she collapsed on the floor as she watched the milk run in a small stream under the kitchen cabinet.

She couldn't bear it, couldn't take it anymore. She sat motionless for a moment before she struggled to her feet and

252   SARA BLÆDEL AND MADS PEDER NORDBO

reached for a tea towel. Just then, she heard a familiar and missed bling from her cell phone in the living room. She gasped out loud. The text was from Zenia. Her daughter had added the special notification sound to messages that came from her so Dybbøl could always hear when her daughter wanted something from her. The same applied to her calls.

Dybbøl stubbed her toe on the doorstep as she ran into the living room with tears streaming down her cheeks and snatched her phone.

Hi mom! Ran out of juice, can't speak. Pick me up at the tomato nursery in Bellinge.

Her hands shook and she breathed frantically as she dialed Zenia, but the phone wasn't answered. Shortly after, a new text message arrived.

Mom, stop calling. Come right away.

CHAPTER

36

P IIL WAS ALREADY in her office when Liam and Thorbjørn returned.

Focused and wearing workout clothes, she looked intently at her two computer screens.

"I can see from the electronic traces that Rolf has been looking at Julie's case in our system—the reports from the mother and the reports about Julie's suicide. He has opened all the files several times."

"When did this happen?" Liam leaned over her shoulder to watch.

"The first time was three days after he joined us and was given access to the system," she said absently as her fingers ran over the keys and new windows opened. "Rolf Lundgren," she summarized as she read the screen, "is registered as the father of Julie Villadsen, who was born on May fifth, 2005. The mother is Annette Villadsen; she is the custodial parent. For a while they were registered at the same address, but he moved out one year and eight months after his daughter was born."

254   SARA BLÆDEL AND MADS PEDER NORDBO

Thorbjørn had pulled two chairs over to Piil's desk. "We still haven't located him?" Liam asked.

Thorbjørn shook his head.

"We need an overview of his schedule," Liam said. "Are you thinking that Julie's mom and Rolf have been working together to avenge what happened to their daughter?"

Liam shook his head hesitantly. "I don't know what the hell I'm thinking," he admitted. "Rolf has been here. We've spent every day working with him, but he hasn't said a word. Not even when it came out that it was Dybbøl's Zenia who was one of the driving forces behind the bullying of his daughter. Why the hell hasn't he said that he's the girl's father?"

Immediately, the printer started up. Piil stood up and returned with copies of the handler's duty schedule for the past six months. "Rolf was enrolled in a course with the Danish Police Dog Association from August seventh to eleventh this year. This was during the period when Jan Hansen disappeared from his home and was later found in the woods."

"Where was the course held?" Thorbjørn asked. He had stood up and was pacing back and forth restlessly.

"At the police dog school in Farum."

"Close to Tisvilde!" Liam stated. "Find out if he was there all day. We need to know the exact schedule for the course and get the names of the other participants. We also need to compare his schedule with the key times of the murders of Jørgen Andersen and Lise Bruun. And where was he when Zenia disappeared?"

"And where was he when Monika le Fevre crashed?" Thorbjørn added.

Piil turned in her chair. "Do you think it was Rolf who delivered the envelope with the skin patch to her?"

WOUNDS 255

"Him or the girl's mother," he replied.

"Shit," Liam exclaimed softly, and closed his eyes. His brain was working too slowly; he was lagging behind and couldn't get his thoughts in order. In a brief flash, he remembered how he had gratefully accepted when Rolf offered to take his police dog out to Monika le Fevre's farm to see if they could find any clue that Jørgen Andersen had been out there before they found him behind the inn. Not for a moment did he wonder why Rolf hadn't asked for an address before he left. Maybe he was reading too much into it, but le Fevre had a hidden number and a secret address, and she had had it since the hunt for her began. Maybe Rolf had just checked the system himself, but it would have been easier for him to just ask Liam, he thought.

For a moment, they sat in silence while Piil worked at the keys. Then Liam straightened up.

"Collect all available surveillance near le Fevre's home and find out if one of Julie's parents can be linked to the address a week ago. And if it turns out that Rolf Lundgren is involved in these crimes with the girl's mother, it will also explain how the envelope with the picture of Zenia could arrive in Dybbøl's pigeonhole without us being able to trace how it got into the station."

"Why don't we just drive out and bring him in for questioning?" Thorbjørn exclaimed, impatiently turning his big body toward Liam.

"Because . . ." Liam began slowly.

"Because," Piil took over, "when we bring him in, we need to make sure we have enough to hold him. If we jump to conclusions, we risk doing more harm than good."

"More speed, less haste," Thorbjørn teased. Piil nodded seriously.

"What happened at Annette Villadsen's address?" she asked, turning to Liam. They had been so focused on Rolf's connection to Julie that for a moment he didn't understand what she meant. But then he pulled himself together.

"There had been a commotion," he replied, telling her about the fallen lamp, the vase, and the kitchen knife on the floor. "But no visible signs of injury."

"No blood?" She leaned over the keys again.

He shook his head. "Her cell phone was out there, so there's no point in trying to track it." At the same time, his own cell phone started buzzing in his pocket. He rejected the call from Dybbøl. She had called a few times to ask for news, and right now he didn't have the time to tell her again that they still hadn't found Zenia. He noticed that there was a series of messages from Helene. He hurriedly pushed them off the display—he didn't have time for them now either. Instead, he called Dea.

She had called him the evening she left the hospital after her conversation with le Fevre. But since then, neither of them had been in contact with her, and Thorbjørn had even called several times without success. Her cell phone was still going straight to voicemail. An unsettling feeling crept up on him. She wasn't usually out of reach for so long, and with his new knowledge of Rolf, Liam felt an urgent need to hear her voice. "Set up a trace on Dea's phone, and then let's compare Rolf's schedules with the times of the deaths."

"No," Thorbjørn exclaimed, and slammed a hand on the table. "I'm not sitting here plowing through old records

WOUNDS   257

while there's a risk that Dea is alone with a possible perpetrator. We're going out there."

He grabbed his jacket from the chair and was out in the hallway before Liam could object. Liam quickly pulled on his fleece sweater and followed him. "Call me when you have information about her cell phone," he said to Piil. "I think it's turned off now, but I'd like to know where it was when it was still in contact with the towers."

She nodded without flinching, and he realized that his IT investigator was thinking exactly the same thing as Thorbjørn. If Rolf or Annette Villadsen was behind the brutal acts in this case, Dea should not be alone with either of them. He ran down the hall after Thorbjørn.

CHAPTER

37

DYBBØL GOOGLED *TOMATO* nursery. Five results. She quickly skimmed them until she came across the name of the elderly lady in Bellinge. It was still hard for her to believe that her daughter had been a visiting friend. Zenia had never told her or Søren about Edna, and now this small and essentially sympathetic thing felt like another contaminated drop in the ocean of events Zenia had kept secret.

She typed the address into her phone. Annoyed, she called Liam again, but quickly realized that he was rejecting her call. Dybbøl considered texting that she had heard from Zenia and that she was on her way to pick her up. But she wanted to tell him face-to-face, so that she could defend herself and her family from everything that followed in the wake of her daughter apparently being no better than Amalie Vedel.

Yet her relief and joy were so overwhelming that she had forgotten all about being angry. All the fear that she had been living with for so many days now had vanished the

WOUNDS 259

moment she heard the little beep from her phone that she had so longed for. Right now, she just wanted to enjoy the bliss of knowing that Zenia was coming home.

It was a seventeen-minute drive to the address. Dybbøl backed out of the driveway and called Søren, but he didn't answer either. She had reached the end of her residential road when she realized she was still wearing her slippers. She had forgotten all about the pool of milk on the kitchen floor and regretted for a moment that she hadn't spent an extra minute changing into pants and a sweater so she wasn't running through the neighborhood in her tatty home wear. Her short hair was unwashed, and she wasn't wearing any makeup. Under other circumstances, she would never set foot outside looking like that, but right now she couldn't care less. If she had to crawl around on her bare knees in the October rain, she was happy to do so, as long as she got her daughter home safe and sound. She tried Søren again, and when it went to voicemail, she left a message in a voice she found hard to recognize. "Darling, I'm on my way out to get Zenia; she's coming home. Everything is fine, she's just been an idiot." She immediately regretted the last part and quickly added that Zenia's cell phone had run out of power. "I'll see you at home," she finished.

* * *

Dybbøl slowly rolled into the makeshift parking lot and felt the tires sink into the soft mud as she parked in front of the farmhouse.

The gray haze of the afternoon hung heavy over the property, which looked like it was freezing in the pouring rain. She looked at her cell phone and checked the map once more; this was definitely the right place. She left the engine running, honked twice in quick succession, and waited impatiently, heart pounding, for Zenia to come out. She couldn't wait to hug her. As she sat waiting, she began to make plans. On the way home, they would stop by that great Vietnamese takeout place and buy the fresh spring rolls that Zenia adored. Then they would eat ice cream and watch a good movie while Dybbøl cuddled with her daughter on the sofa in their warm living room. The serious conversations they needed to have could wait until tomorrow.

A flickering television light streamed out of one of the farmhouse windows into the wet darkness. The rest of the house seemed deserted. She looked around. At the end of the dirt road was a low building with a tall chimney rising from it. There was no sign of life there either, and again she checked the address and map and realized that she was in the right place. She sent a message to Zenia: *Here now. In front of the house and waiting.*

When there was no response, she turned off the engine, ran up to the front door in four long jumps to avoid the puddles, and knocked. No answer.

She felt the rain seeping through her slippers and knocked again, irritated. It smelled of rain, fall, and mold, and the water from the gutter splashed against the stone steps and hit her soaked pants. She banged on the door again, then grabbed the handle and tentatively opened the door.

"Hello!" she called out loudly, and stepped into a small hallway where one wall was completely covered with coats hanging untidily on far too few hooks. It was cold and smelled overwhelmingly of smoke.

WOUNDS   261

Dybbøl pushed past the coats and opened the door to the room that led into the house. "Hello!" she called into an old-fashioned, blue-painted kitchen where used dishes were stacked in rickety towers around the kitchen sink. Some of the peeling kitchen doors hung precariously on their hinges, and the faucet dripped monotonously into a pot sitting in the sink filled with dirty water. Then she heard shuffling footsteps approaching.

"Hello," she said when an old woman finally came into view. "I've come to get my daughter."

The woman looked at her in disorientation and then nodded toward the kitchen table. "The home helpers usually just put the food there," she said.

"I'm Zenia's mother," Dybbøl explained, knowing that her smile was strained. She couldn't wait any longer now. "I've come to get her."

Edna Clausen slowly picked up a laminated note from the flowered oilcloth that lay slightly unevenly on the round dining table. "It's lobscouse today. You can get me more butter. The beets are always so bland, but don't buy a big slab; a small one will do."

"Have you seen my daughter?" Dybbøl asked tightly. She had had enough of talking about food and shopping.

The old lady's expression changed, and she suddenly looked both hurt and angry. She shook her head. "If the girl won't come out here now that they say Jørgen is dead, then she certainly shouldn't," she said, putting down the home care weekly menu. "Maybe they're all dead. In any case, no one comes to visit me anymore."

Her eyes glazed over, and she reached into her apron pocket and took out a cheroot, which she placed in her mouth with great concentration before slowly pulling out a lighter from the same pocket.

Dybbøl stood still for a moment, looking paralyzed at the small muddy lake her slippers had left on the floor, then she turned on her heel and ran out the way she had come. Something was very wrong. Out in the courtyard, she looked around desperately and, heart pounding, started running along the disused greenhouse, calling for Zenia.

She ripped open the doors to the smaller buildings and called out to the empty rooms. There was no sign of her daughter and no sign that there had been any humans at all for a good long while. Down by the building with the chimney, she turned on the flashlight on her cell phone with shaking hands before pushing aside the latch and pulling the door open. She was soaked now, her hair was wet on her forehead, and her fingers were cold as ice.

"Hello!" she called out loudly. "Zenia!" Old boxes and junk were piled up along the walls, smelling strongly of old dust, and in several places she almost tripped over large holes in the broken concrete floor. "Zenia!" Her desperate cry turned into a frightened scream when she sensed something large and alive behind her. The next moment, she was almost knocked over by Lady, who threw herself at her with a whimper.

Dybbøl gasped in shock and sank to her knees with her arms around the black Labrador, who twisted and turned in excitement to see her.

"Lady!" she whispered, overwhelmed. "Where have you been?" She hugged the dog to her for a moment before she was back on her feet and running toward the door. If their dog was here, it must mean that Zenia was around too.

WOUNDS 263

Again, relief washed through her. She waited in the doorway for Lady to join her, wondering why the dog hadn't already jumped ahead as she usually did.

"Come on!" Dybbøl shouted impatiently, and hurried on. Reluctantly and almost timidly, Lady slowly approached her. When she reached the door, Dybbøl wanted to grab her collar to pull her outside so they could close the door behind them, but as she bent down to get a good grip, Lady jumped aside with a violent movement, and Dybbøl screamed loudly.

The black Labrador was clean-shaven on one side of her body. The thin skin bulged out in uneven, burgundy-colored swellings in several places. The large wounds had not yet healed but were held together by coarse stitches in black nylon thread.

CHAPTER

38

T HE RAIN WAS still pouring down as Liam and Thorbjørn drove way too fast through Bellinge and Verninge as they approached Rolf Lundgren's farm. They had only exchanged a few words during the half-hour drive. Thorbjørn drove steadily and confidently, looking intently out the windshield, where the wipers were running at top speed. "I've never liked him," he said darkly. "He's always seemed so detached, like he thought he was superior in some way."

Liam had never thought about him like that. He had mostly been annoyed by all the times the dog handler had sat on the corner of Dea's desk and flirted so shamelessly with her. Now he wondered if she had been taken advantage of. His thoughts were interrupted when Piil called.

"Dea's cell phone was active until nine thirty-two this morning. It was at Rolf's address in Nårup when it was switched off."

Liam closed his eyes and couldn't make sense of it. The commotion in Annette's house in Holmstrup could not have anything to do with Dea. If she had chosen to pick up

WOUNDS 265

Julie's mother before she picked up Thorbjørn so they could do the interrogation together, she would have informed her colleague.

He asked Piil to locate Annette Villadsen's relatives. "And we need to get a team out to Holmstrup to talk to her neighbors. Does she have a car? Put out an APB."

"She doesn't have a car," Piil replied, saying that she had already told the officer on duty to send a patrol.

"We are interested in anyone who may have spoken to Annette Villadsen between when she was at the police station and now."

"Roger that," Piil said shortly.

It was barely two o'clock when Thorbjørn turned into the courtyard in front of Rolf's home. There was light in several of the windows of the low farmhouse, but the outbuildings were plunged in darkness. Liam stepped out into the rain and immediately felt a little calmer when he spotted Dea's car at the front of the house. There were no other cars in sight, but hers was there. If there really was something to fear, one had to assume that Rolf would have tried to give the police the impression that Dea was not on the farm by hiding her car. He realized he didn't know which car Rolf himself was driving. He almost messaged Piil to ask her to check, but didn't and instead headed for the front door. There was still the possibility that the loved-up couple were in there and had lost track of time. Enjoying Sunday, pulling the plug, and taking the day off like any other normal new lovers would. Like he and Helene had done in the early days. No, the first few years, he thought, remembering weekends when they had stayed in bed. Of course, even when he was newly in love, he would never have stayed in bed on a Sunday if he and his colleagues were in the middle of a murder investigation that so far had three victims and a missing girl. But Dea and Rolf might have different priorities.

He waved Thorbjørn over and wondered if he should have called for backup. He saw himself balancing between overreacting and not taking it seriously enough. His cell phone buzzed in his pocket; it was Dybbøl again. He declined when he saw that Piil had sent a message telling him that Rolf Lundgren drove a Volvo station wagon. She sent him the registration plate details and asked if she should put out an APB. *She's a star,* he thought, silently thanking her for her efficiency. It was a pleasure to work with people who thought for themselves.

Yes please, he replied, and resolutely grabbed the front door. It was locked. He walked toward the back door of the house but didn't even have time to put his hand on the handle before the big German shepherd burst out barking in the hallway. He could see the outline of Ask through the door's frosted glass. The police dog was standing on its hind legs and barked furiously until Liam backed away from the door. Just then, Thorbjørn called and waved him over to Dea's black Passat. He pointed to a pile on the rain-soaked, muddy ground. Weekend bag, handbag, her long light-brown coat. It had all been left in a heap next to the car, and it had been there for a long time. The coat was soaked through.

Liam quickly opened the weekend bag. It felt too private to rummage through, yet he let his hand search the bag. Underwear, sweaters, jeans, makeup bag, and a toiletry bag. It was stuffed full. There was also a hand blender and a small coffee grinder.

He looked up at Thorbjørn. The rain was pouring down his face. "Call for assistance," he said. "We need to get more people out here."

"I don't think he's here," Thorbjørn said, but he had already fished out his cell phone. Liam shook his head; he didn't think so either. In fact, he didn't believe that either Rolf or Dea was on the farm.

"But we have to turn everything upside down," he decided, and walked with quick steps back to the main house. With his elbow, he broke one of the barred windows on the front door and unlocked the door by sticking his arm in. He waited a moment to see if an alarm went off, but the only sound he could hear was Ask barking like crazy. He hoped the huge German shepherd was locked in the back hallway; otherwise it could be a problem. He had his hand on his service pistol as he continued into the living room. It was empty, and on the coffee table was an unopened bag from the bakery. He glanced into the empty bedroom and lingered for a moment on the brown splashes on the white comforter. The breakfast table was set for two, but the dishes were unused, and there were two eggs in a small saucepan left on the kitchen table.

He quickly searched the entire house, but he already knew he would find no one. The anxiety that had been simmering inside him at the police station was turning into full-blown fear. Dea would have let him know if something was wrong, if something had happened to make her forget her appointment with Thorbjørn.

Her daughter! Dea's daughter—it was so obvious that he stopped and stood still. If Dea had rushed out the door, it could be because something had happened to Katrine.

Piil answered immediately. "I'll find her."

He stood for a moment, staring out into the gray afternoon haze. He saw Thorbjørn enter the large building on the other side of the courtyard, and a moment later the lights flickered on over there. Liam took one last look around the kitchen and living room. He quickly scanned the bathroom and a small office but decided to leave it until help arrived so they could go through the house properly.

The rain was pouring steadily as he crossed the courtyard to join Thorbjørn. He remembered Dea telling him about the abandoned plastics factory, but he was surprised to see that it still looked as though the employees had gone home five minutes ago.

"The whole thing started when I turned on the main switch," Thorbjørn said, nodding toward the machines, which were slowly coming to life with ticking and hissing sounds. Liam looked around the large factory room for a moment. The CNC milling machine had rusty blades and a protective screen that had seen better days. There were stacks of molds and boxes of plastic balls and scraps that had been dumped in a smaller container. There was a faint smell of lubricating oil in the air, and at the end of the room under the large iron windows was the production oven flanked by desks. A faint warm light now emanated from the sooty oven door, and the oven hummed and buzzed. It sounded as though it were happy to finally be brought back to life.

Thorbjørn had gone into an adjoining room, and Liam followed him. In the room were a blue pellet burner and several pallets of pellets in bags. Liam started to investigate the area around the pellet stove and cringed when there was a huge bang from the other side of the room where Thorbjørn was. With long strides, he rushed over and spotted Thorbjørn standing with a fire extinguisher in his hands, which he was using as a battering ram.

"There's someone in the back," he said angrily. He lifted the fire extinguisher again and hammered it full force into the lock of a solid-looking wooden sliding door, but at the same moment the fire extinguisher was triggered and the room was instantly enveloped in a suffocating white cloud of fire-retardant powder.

"What the hell are you doing?" Liam took a few steps back. His eyes stung, and the white powder stuck to his wet clothes.

"We need to get that door open! Now!" Thorbjørn groaned and banged again and again, as hard as he could. There was a loud bang of iron on iron as the lock finally popped open and the door could be pushed aside.

* * *

The smell of urine was so intense that Liam immediately pulled the fleece sleeve over his hand and covered his nose and mouth. His gaze was fixed on the couch in the middle of the room as his eyes adjusted to the semidarkness. Slowly, the details of the room emerged. The couch was covered in brownish layers of dirt on its cracked black plastic surface. On the concrete floor beneath it were large stains in various stages of dryness and a glistening pool of something Liam couldn't make out. On the table next to the couch was a pile of used cloths, all soaked in a reddish-brown liquid.

It gave him a jolt when Thorbjørn let the fire extinguisher fall to the floor. The tall investigator stood for a moment with his arms at his sides and stared. Then he pulled himself together and turned on his cell phone torch. He shone the light around the walls, and Liam could see that he came across a switch, which he activated. A bright white light flickered on, illuminating every corner of the dusty and dirty room.

Still, it took him a moment to spot the person crouched on the floor in the far corner with her arms wrapped around her legs and her head resting on her knees.

Dea flashed through his mind, but the person didn't have Dea's hair color. He felt a hint of relief and signaled to Thorbjørn that they should approach the woman carefully.

"We're from the police," he said softly as they got a little closer to her. He gave his name and rank and introduced Thorbjørn. The woman didn't react, but he had no doubt that she was alive. Her body trembled, and she was breathing shallowly.

Thorbjørn pulled away slightly, and Liam could hear him using his low voice to call for an ambulance and summon the National Forensic Service.

"Who are you?" Liam asked, squatting down next to the woman. "What happened?"

She didn't lift her head but shook her head slowly. "Annette," he tried. "Are you Julie's mom?"

No reaction.

"We have reason to believe that Rolf . . ." he began, but didn't get any further because, with an abrupt movement, she turned her face up toward him and looked straight past him with wide eyes. Liam had to control himself not to let out a sound of shock at the sight of her battered face.

WOUNDS 271

"I didn't know he'd come back," she said in a shrill voice. "I haven't seen him since our daughter was little. I was hospitalized for two weeks and he was forbidden to visit us. I was only twenty at the time, and I was so scared. I didn't dare report him, but at the hospital they convinced me that it was necessary if I wanted to take care of myself and my daughter."

Liam took off his fleece sweater and handed it to the woman, who took it with stiff movements and placed it on her knees. Three of the fingers on one of her hands were at completely wrong angles and were obviously broken.

"I didn't know he'd become a cop. At first he came to see us a couple of times, but each time I called the police, and after a while, he stopped. I haven't seen him since Julie was three. The last time I saw him was when we met with a social worker to talk about how he could see his daughter during supervised visitation. But he told me that if he couldn't be a father to his little girl in a normal way, he didn't want to be in our lives at all."

She started crying so heartbreakingly that Liam didn't care about the filthy surroundings; he sank to the floor next to her and pulled her into his arms.

He heard a commotion in the hallway and could hear that backup had arrived, but he left it to Thorbjørn to deal with and concentrated on keeping Julie's mother together, as she was currently disintegrating in his arms.

"He didn't believe that I hadn't recognized him when I was up at the police station talking to the policewoman. He said I had looked directly at him in the hallway. But I'm sure I didn't see him. I'd recognize him anytime." Her breath was uneven. "Not a day has gone by that I haven't feared he would show up. Right up until Julie's death. When I lost her, I stopped being afraid."

She made a guttural sound that sent chills down Liam's spine.

"Nothing mattered to me after Julie died, so I thought I wouldn't care. But then suddenly there he was. Yesterday morning. I had just gotten out of the shower and hadn't heard that a car had arrived. I was so scared that I didn't have time to slam the door."

The crying started again. Liam waved away a paramedic and signaled that he should come back later. Julie's mom wiped her face on his fleece sweater before continuing. "He accused me of killing our daughter because I wasn't able to take care of her well enough. He said that I should have defended her. That I should have shielded her. And that he had now come to teach me a lesson because I had been the worst mother in the world." Her voice cracked. "He recounted in detail what Monika le Fevre and the others who were disgusting to Julie did. He even knew about the bullying video that was shared."

She wiped her face again.

"He's been watching us. With Julie. It's terrifying to think about. He was so aggressive and threatening as he stood there on my doorstep again. Just like he was when we were young. It took me completely by surprise when he hit me; I had completely forgotten how cold he was." She paused, and Liam studied her bruised face. She had several open cuts from heavy blows and was so pale and swollen that Liam guessed even those closest to her wouldn't recognize her.

"Especially when I tried to get him to stop hitting me by telling him that I had begged the police for help to stop

WOUNDS 273

the harassment of Julie. He went absolutely crazy at that, yelling and screaming that I hadn't taken it seriously enough, seeing as I hadn't been able to get the police to listen. He told me that he had moved back to Funen to make it clear to people that you don't treat his daughter like that. And that, unlike me, he would use any means necessary to get the police to listen."

*　*　*

The paramedic reappeared in the doorway, and Liam nodded that he was ready to see Annette out. He stood up and offered her a hand before accepting the blanket that was held out to her. She was barefoot and wearing only a short-sleeved T-shirt and a pair of light-colored leggings. She pulled the blanket around her as he wrapped it around her shoulders.

"What happened to the policewoman?" she asked as she hobbled off with him to the ambulance.

Liam paused. "The policewoman?"

"I thought she was dead. At first I didn't recognize her when I entered the room and saw her lying on the floor. But when he picked her up and carried her out, I could see that it was the same woman I spoke to at the police station. Has she been taken to the hospital? Is she going to be okay?"

CHAPTER

39

D EA WAS SURROUNDED by complete darkness. In flashes, she surfaced from the merciful sea of unconsciousness and could feel the very cramped and warm space she was in. Fear gripped her, and every muscle in her body quivered with tension. She gasped for air in the stifling heat and felt the intense high temperature tightening her skin all over her body.

Gradually she came to, and the first thing she realized was that a violent nausea was rippling through her body. She tried to turn her head, but a pain coursed through her in a fierce rush that made her eyes tear in the darkness. She tasted blood in her mouth. Cautiously, she tried to bring her hand up to her face, but she quickly withdrew her hand as her fingers hit the burning-hot iron that surrounded her on all sides.

Slowly, she realized she was in a hellishly hot and tiny room, barely big enough to hold a human. Panicked, she tried to remember what had happened. The air burned her nose and lungs, so she breathed in careful little gasps. Her

WOUNDS

275

open mouth felt parched all the way down her throat. She tried to moisten her lips, but her tongue was swollen and felt like a dry sponge in her mouth.

The courtyard and the stable door. Now she remembered the sounds she had heard. She had wanted to go out of the factory building to use another door. But then she remembered nothing more.

The nausea was unbearable now, but the pain in her head prevented her from turning her head to the side. Her body contracted in spasms, and her mouth filled with vomit, which she let seep out of both corners of her mouth. She kept her arms close to her body to get as far away from the burning walls of the small room as possible, but it didn't help. Her skin felt like it was bubbling, and she caught the smell of burning hair.

She thought of Katrine, picturing her adult daughter in front of her. They had argued the last time they spoke. About Rolf. Dea had gotten angry and accused her daughter of getting in the way of her happiness. She regretted it. Regretted every harsh word she had ever said to Katrine. The person who meant the most to her in the whole world.

CHAPTER

40

Dybbøl bent down and lifted the agonized Labrador into her arms. Her slippered feet slid in the mud as she staggered back to the car with the heavy dog, who wheezed loudly when she touched its large wounds. What the hell kind of sick person had subjected Lady to this treatment? And why did they do it? She spoke soothingly to the dog and gently set her down on the ground while she unlocked the car and spread the dog blanket over the front seat. She had just opened the trunk to grab the small box of treats when she saw the sign on the other side of the road.

Ebbe and Astrid's Tomatoes.

She had been so preoccupied with the old tomato nursery and Edna, her daughter's visiting friend, that she had barely noticed the almost surreal orange glow that lit up the rainy gray autumn sky from across the road. That could be where Zenia was, it occurred to her. It was not unlikely that Zenia also knew the people at the large nursery when she had come to stay with Edna.

WOUNDS 277

She hurriedly started the car and slowly rolled across the road, driving into the parking lot of the large tomato nursery.

Next to her in the front seat, Lady had curled up and lay with her head on her front paws. Every now and then, she would twitch and her fur would quiver as though electricity were coursing through her shaved body.

"There, there, old girl," Dybbøl whispered, and put her hand on the Labrador's head. They had had her since she was a puppy. Zenia had just started kindergarten when the three of them drove to North Jutland to pick her up. She and Zenia had to stop by the vet before they went home, she thought as she scratched the dog behind her ear and told her that she was just going to get Zenia.

She got out. The tomato nursery was deserted. There were no other cars in the parking lot and no lights in the windows of the main house or the other buildings.

She pulled her cardigan around her, although there was little the thin wool could do against the rain and the cold that swirled around her in strong gusts. She sent another message to Zenia. *I'm at the big tomato nursery now. Is this where you are? Come to the car.*

After a moment, Zenia replied that this was indeed where she was, and then she asked her to drive a little farther ahead. *Drive down to the end of the two greenhouses. It's raining and cold.* She then added a mischievous emoji. Dybbøl found herself smiling as she stood there shivering from the cold with soaked slippers and water running down her hair and face. Typical Zenia!

Slowly she drove down the length of the greenhouses. She passed several smaller buildings and a large heating

278   SARA BLÆDEL AND MADS PEDER NORDBO

plant. It seemed that the buildings at the back, farthest from the road, belonged to the old part of the nursery that was no longer in use, except for two modern silos that towered between the greenhouses and a run-down warehouse.

When she reached the end of the greenhouses, she honked a few times and stopped with the engine running. It was deserted; Zenia was nowhere to be seen. A murmur of irritation began to spread through her as she turned off the engine and got out. It was only now that she noticed a faint light emanating from the warehouse that she'd thought was abandoned.

Again, she wrapped her cardigan around her and made her way to the double doors. She had just entered the dimly lit, high-ceilinged room when a hand placed itself tightly over her mouth. A pungent smell of ether forced her head back.

CHAPTER

41

"WE HAVE TO go through everything. Search every inch of this place," Liam roared as the ambulance drove off with Annette Villadsen. He turned to Thorbjørn. "If he left Dea out here, we'll find her. But I think it's more likely that he took her with him. Have Piil put a roadblock on his car. Put an APB out on it, and put an APB out on him at the same time. Name and description, but we'll keep it internal. If Dea is with him, it could be extremely dangerous for her if he realizes we're after him."

Thorbjørn nodded in agreement and was about to walk toward the car to start it when Liam grabbed him and held him back.

"We need a guard posted outside Monika le Fevre's room at the hospital." The thought had struck him the moment Julie's mother started talking about the vendetta Rolf was on. Monika le Fevre was basically the cause of the whole thing, and there was a high probability she was in danger. Everything had started with her exhibition. He thought about the threat she had received when she got into

280   SARA BLÆDEL AND MADS PEDER NORDBO

her car on Sunday evening to drive to the police station. *The list is long and you are on it. Nothing stops until someone takes responsibility.*

Responsibility. Who did Rolf want to take responsibility? And what would the responsibility he wanted look like? Liam tried to clear his head and nodded as Thorbjørn walked back toward him and announced that police protection was being put in place for Monika le Fevre—an officer would be sent to N2 immediately. The hospital and the consultant had been informed and had offered to move the patient to the back ward, where a movable partition in the hospital corridor could be used to screen off the room so that it could only be accessed from one side.

"Dybbøl!" Liam exclaimed, and now his mind was racing. He thought about the envelope that had landed on her desk with the message *#thinkbeforeyoutype*. Zenia. "We need to get hold of Dybbøl. She had overall responsibility when Annette filed her reports. And she's Zenia's mother."

One by one, he thought, Rolf had narrowed down the responsibility. First the outer links—the weak ones, the ones who had persecuted his daughter with nasty messages and online hate. Then Annette, who had not lived up to her responsibilities as a mother. Liam had no doubts; he could see the case vividly now. Rolf wasn't finished, and Zenia was his next victim. She had been gone for a week. The question was whether he would go after Dybbøl next. And then finish with Monika le Fevre as the crowning glory.

His thoughts quickly worked their way back and forth. He couldn't figure out how Dea fit in, but he realized that maybe she didn't. The thought made him feel a little lighter.

WOUNDS

281

Four missed calls from Dybbøl. He tried returning her calls straightaway. The first two had arrived several hours ago. She didn't answer, but there was a connection. He let it ring out before calling Piil and asking her to trace Dybbøl's cell phone immediately. If that meant pulling all the employees from Dybbøl's telecom company out of their holes to get them to do an emergency mast search, then she had to do it. He didn't care as long as she found out where Dybbøl's cell phone was.

Thorbjørn approached him again. "The APB has gone out," he announced.

Liam nodded. If Rolf's Volvo passed one of the Road Directorate's highway surveillance cameras, they would be notified, just as they would be notified if a police patrol car was near the car, because the license plate would be picked up by the police car's ANPR camera and there would be an immediate ping. They would also be contacted the moment he crossed one of the bridges.

"We can't find Dea. She's not here," Thorbjørn continued. He was pale and composed and told Liam that a canine patrol unit was on its way.

Paradoxical, Liam thought. One of the police's best sniffer dogs was standing just on the other side of the door. Ask had stopped barking, but the moment someone approached the back door, there was a deep growl, and if someone went up the steps, the dog barked menacingly.

"Good," he exclaimed before crossing the courtyard to go back to the room where they had found Annette. At the same instant, he was interrupted by a loud shout.

CHAPTER

42

WHEN DYBBØL SLOWLY came to, she was lying on her stomach on the floor. She felt the moisture from the cold concrete seep through her clothes and settle like ice around her bones. She was dizzy and uncomfortable, and the sharp vapor of ether scratched her throat, making every intake of breath painful.

For a moment she just lay still and tried to get her bearings. Slowly, she blinked her eyes open. Her hands were tied together, and as she tried to push herself up a little so she could sit, she felt her feet were also held together by something sharp and hard. Cable ties, she thought, and registered how her panicked brain suddenly switched gear and became constructive. She moved silently as she lifted her head from the stone floor. The stench of ether still stuck in her nose and brought tears to her eyes, but she blinked them away and tried to focus. She needed to think. Someone had her daughter, and she had walked right into the trap, that much she knew. But who was it that had tricked her?

Then she heard it. The sound of someone breathing. Not close, but not far from her either. She wasn't alone—someone was watching her. Dybbøl felt her anger flaring up. She pulled herself together and dragged herself halfway to a sitting position so that her back rested against the wall. "Who are you?" she said into the darkness. "Where is my daughter?"

There was complete silence. Then she heard a scraping sound across the floor, as though a chair was being moved.

"I want to see my daughter!" she declared, this time louder and in a clear voice.

She had chills and realized she was shaking.

"I was wondering if you would really come out here. Alone, even," said a voice in the darkness. "But here you are! Welcome."

Dybbøl could hear the icy hostility in his voice. All her senses were on high alert. She wanted to catch every tone and remember every word. She wanted to etch everything he said into her memory so she could use it against him later.

"I want to see my daughter," she repeated in her most determined voice. She would not let him see her fear. She would keep her guard up and shut him out. Her keen intuitive sense told her that this was the only possible strategy to use with a person who could show so little emotion. If she let him see that she was afraid, she was lost.

"You'll get to see your daughter, but you have to be prepared that you won't take her home with you. It's not like the dog; you can take it. But Zenia stays here."

"Is she here?"

She could hear his soft laughter. The hairs on the back of her neck stood up. "You didn't think you were lured to this horrible place because it was time for a chat, did you?"

"What do you want?" Dybbøl asked as calmly as she could.

"We're way past the stage where talking to each other can help anything."

She heard him pull the chair across the floor again.

"No one had time to talk when my daughter needed help. No one would listen or come to her rescue. No one tried to stop your daughter from doing what she did to my girl. So, no, Dybbøl, let's not make small talk; it's far, far too late for that."

He laughed softly again, then there was silence. Dybbøl felt terror rush through her arms and legs. It was unsettling that he had used her name in that personal way.

"Who are you?"

She could hear him moving around. Then there was a click, and a fluorescent light began to flicker until it cast a bright, cold light down on them.

She sat for a moment, staring at him, trying to understand. Trying to remember if there was something she had missed. Should she have realized that Julie was his daughter? He had been hired sometime in the spring, as far as she remembered, but she knew nothing about his family circumstances other than that he was now dating Dea. Had he been hired before or after Julie took her life? She had no idea.

"Rolf," she said quietly. "I am truly sorry. I am terribly sorry for what happened to your daughter. And I can only apologize and regret my daughter's behavior."

He snorted and pulled his face into a hateful grimace.

"'I'm sorry and apologize,'" he snarled, mimicking her voice. "You ignored a cry for help. You caused my girl to throw herself in front of a train. And you 'apologize and regret'!" He laughed his cold laugh again, which made Dybbøl's blood freeze.

WOUNDS

"I didn't know Zenia was involved."

"Does that change anything?" His voice was hard as flint. "How does it feel to have raised your daughter to become someone who thinks it's okay to stalk and bully a girl her own age—a girl who has done nothing to her?" His face moved in involuntary tics. "So much so that my girl is driven to the point where suicide is the only way out. How do you feel about that, Dybbøl? Is that something we should talk about?" He smiled fiendishly and looked at her expectantly.

"No," Dybbøl whispered hoarsely. "We don't need to talk about it, but know that I feel terrible about it."

Dybbøl looked down at her clenched hands as she blinked hard to hold back tears.

"Is Zenia alive?" she asked, looking up.

He looked at her, and it was clear that he enjoyed watching her suffer. Then he nodded.

"She's alive." Again that soft laughter. He looked at her as though he was enjoying himself.

"You can't kill her!" Dybbøl shouted, and threw herself at him with a force that she could see surprised him. In a quick leap, Rolf was out of his chair and swung his fist at her head, causing her to black out and fall, hitting the floor hard.

She lay down for a while after coming to, trying to recover. Then she pulled herself back against the wall and sat up again.

"Take me instead! It was all my fault. I should have stopped Zenia, and I should have listened to your daughter's mother."

"Oh, so you admit it now?" Again, the involuntary tics pulled his face askew.

286   SARA BLÆDEL AND MADS PEDER NORDBO

"Yes, I admit I didn't take it seriously enough!"

"A bit late, isn't it?"

Dybbøl nodded and felt blood running down her cheek. There was silence for a long time.

"I didn't know anything about it," Rolf said. He suddenly spoke in a soft and vulnerable voice that sent a chill down Dybbøl's spine. "I haven't seen my daughter since she was three. I wasn't allowed to see her. Her mother and I had a hard time . . ."

He remained silent.

"We weren't good together," he continued. "I wasn't good with her. I tried to make a cohabitation agreement, but I was rejected." He smiled self-pityingly.

Violence, Dybbøl thought. It could only be violence or abuse. But it couldn't have been reported, because if he had been convicted of violence, he would never have been admitted to the police academy.

"I wasn't very good at handling that rejection." He continued. "But I stayed away. Until the day I got the message that Julie was dead. That she had committed suicide."

"Then you came back," said Dybbøl. "To Odense Police."

He nodded. He seemed content with his own appearance of vulnerability.

"Yes, then I came back." There was a cold gleam in his eyes.

"And Dea? Does she know anything about this?"

He looked away briefly before turning back to her. "I don't want to talk about Dea," he said shortly. "This is about you."

Dybbøl looked around the warehouse. It looked like an old packing hall. There were long tables on one side of the room, and in the middle there was a pit like those found in

WOUNDS   287

a car repair shop. From a skylight, she could see the orange glow of the surrounding greenhouses.

"I'm genuinely sorry for what happened," she tried again. She was about to say something more when he abruptly stood up and went to turn off the ceiling light, leaving the room in twilight, lit only by the dim light from a small lamp. He then came back and pulled her up from the floor with a hard shove. He pushed the chair he had been sitting on next to the hole in the floor. Before she could resist, he had forced her down onto the chair and was tying her up so tightly that the rope cut into her skin. She could feel the opening in the concrete floor right in front of her feet and instinctively pulled them back a little.

"'Genuinely sorry,'" he mimicked again, almost whimpering to himself as he went to turn on the lights. The sound of the switch sent a small hollow echo through the empty building, and after some flickering, the fluorescent lights once again bathed the room in a bright light.

Dybbøl screamed like she had never screamed before. In the hole right in front of her lay Zenia. She was naked, and her skin seemed blue in the cold concrete depression. She lay perfectly still, her eyes open and staring up at them. Her body was marred by the same kind of wounds that Dybbøl had just seen on Lady. But on Zenia, the wounds were not patched together with clumsy stitches. They were spread across her torso like gaping dark-red holes. Her daughter lay perfectly still, not reacting to Dybbøl's presence with so much as the slightest twitch. Only her eyelids moved when she blinked.

"What do you want?" Dybbøl didn't recognize her own voice.

"What do you want?" he sneered. "I'll tell you, Dybbøl." He twisted her name, too, in a voice so full of hatred that it sent chills down Dybbøl's spine. "I want you, Chief Constable Margrethe Dybbøl, to experience what it's like to see your own daughter die without being able to do anything to help her."

CHAPTER

43

"TURN THE POWER off!" The angry shout echoed across the courtyard. It came from the abandoned plastics factory and sent Liam running the last few meters to the door.

"What's going on?"

"There's someone inside the oven," the officer replied frantically. "Does anyone know where the main switch is?" he bellowed into the air. Liam quickly ran to the elongated oven. Just then the lights went out, the humming of the machines stopped with lazy sighs, and he stumbled over a box of molds as he continued around the large production oven and came to the narrow glass pane in the oven door.

He tried to push the handle down, but it remained closed. "How the hell do you get it open?"

He turned in frustration in the flickering light of the others' flashlights.

"Maybe there's a lock on the side of the handle," Thorbjørn suggested, and Liam fumbled until his fingers hit a small latch that could be pressed in. He burned himself on the hot metal of the oven. The glass in the window was smeared and brownish from the heat, but through the dark markings he could make out the outline of a body lying inside, its feet close to the glass.

There was a click, the door opened, and heat poured out toward them in a stifling blast. She was lying in there on her back.

"Dea!" he shouted loudly, and stuck his head close to the oven opening.

The heat tingled the skin on his cheeks. She did not move. "Ambulance!" He turned to the others. "We need something to put her on."

"Is she alive?" Thorbjørn asked. He looked scared. It was hard to see; she wasn't moving. Dea lay with her eyes closed and didn't respond to their shouts.

Liam stepped aside and asked two young officers standing close to him to lift her out of the oven. He couldn't, feeling powerless and dizzy. He tried to clear his mind to remember how much time had passed since they had arrived at the farm and the power in the factory had been turned on. Had there been a light over here when they'd found Annette Villadsen? He couldn't remember.

"It was me," Thorbjørn said behind him. "I was the one who turned on the power. I could clearly hear all the machines in here starting up. It was me who turned on that oven." He looked at Liam, deeply upset.

"He's expecting to come back," Liam said, deliberately avoiding commenting on the fact that it was indeed the police themselves who had turned on the oven and thus caused Dea to be roasted alive. Right now, they needed to stay focused—there was no time to deal with Thorbjørn's torment. "The dog is here. He's hidden Dea away, but he hasn't tried to hide the fact that Annette is out here. I think he's coming back for them."

"But until then?" Thorbjørn said.

Liam nodded. Until then, there was a risk that Rolf was with Dybbøl and Zenia.

"She's alive! Get a helicopter out here! Is it safe to take her out, or should we wait? Can the skin withstand the extreme temperature change?" Questions and commands flew through the air.

Liam had retreated a little. He stood listening to the agitated voices trying to figure out what would be best to do in the impossible situation they found themselves in.

"Water! She needs to be bathed in cool running water until the rescuers arrive." Suddenly Liam couldn't remember what they used to do when they were present after firefighters had rescued victims from a burning house. He could feel his eyes were fluttering and closed them to try to steady himself.

"Are you okay?" It was Thorbjørn who had put a hand on his arm. "Pull yourself together, for fuck's sake." Liam's head raged. But it was as if there was no longer a usable connection between his body and his brain.

He just nodded, gave Thorbjørn what he hoped could pass for a reassuring smile, and watched silently as Dea was carefully pulled out of the oven.

* * *

She was unconscious when she was placed on the rescuers' stretcher. Her skin was burned and glowed an unnatural pink color.

292   SARA BLÆDEL AND MADS PEDER NORDBO

"Yes, she's alive," the paramedic said, reading the measuring device she had placed on Dea's chest. "The epidermis is over fifty-three degrees . . . she's severely dehydrated." She looked around quickly. "Everyone out, please!"

Liam was the only one who stayed behind. He introduced himself and explained that Dea was his friend and colleague.

The paramedic nodded without looking at him. With efficient and quick hands, she was strapping Dea to the stretcher. "We'll start an IV once we're airborne. Prepare for burn treatment."

"Is she going to be okay?" Liam asked.

"I don't know the degree of dehydration yet, and she could still go into shock. In the coming hours she will be extremely prone to infections, but she is breathing and the internal body temperature is around forty degrees, so I would estimate that she will survive."

"Thank you!" Liam didn't know what else to say. He watched Dea as the stretcher disappeared into the helicopter, and he ducked as the rotor blades whipped the air around, whirling his hair back and forth. Slowly, the great machine took off. It made an arc in the air and then headed toward Odense.

Liam has been standing still for a while, trying to take everything in, when Piil called.

"Rolf Lundgren grew up on a farm in Bellinge," she announced, and gave him the address on Assensvej. "It's a big tomato nursery. His adoptive father still lives out there, and we've just traced Dybbøl's cell phone. It's at the same address."

CHAPTER

44

THE PARKING LOT in front of Ebbe and Astrid's Tomatoes was empty. The rain had formed large puddles in the gravel, and the light of day had all but disappeared when Liam and Thorbjørn arrived at Rolf's childhood home.

The only sign of life was the orange glow of the large greenhouse complex. There were no people in work clothes, as there had been a few days earlier when he had met Ole, Ebbe and Astrid's eldest child, who had been grumpy as hell.

Liam looked toward the house the Eastern European men had gone into the last time he was here. But the building was bathed in darkness. The parking lot was also empty, and neither Rolf's nor Dybbøl's car was anywhere to be seen.

Several patrol cars pulled into the parking lot, and Liam asked Thorbjørn to brief those who didn't already know about the case. They had to be made aware that it was one of their own who might have both Dybbøl and her daughter in his custody right now.

"He's dangerous and probably armed," he heard Thorbjørn say before heading to the main house to speak to Ole.

No one answered when he rang the doorbell, so Liam went inside. He found the old man on the sofa.

"Good evening, Ole! So, we meet again." Liam lifted an imaginary hat.

"Who let you in?" Ole straightened up and gave Liam a dirty look.

"I did, because you didn't open the door. And we need to talk."

"I have nothing to talk to the police about," Ole grumbled reluctantly.

"That might well be the case." Liam tried to control his irritation. "But I have something I want to talk to you about."

"No one asked you to come running back here. Just go back to whatever hellhole you've just come from and leave me the fuck alone," the old man continued.

"Do you really think your threats are going to help?" Liam said calmly, and sat down opposite him. "What's going to happen now is that I'm going to let some of my people into your house and ask them to search your home."

"Don't you fucking dare!" Ole exclaimed angrily. "You can't fucking do that."

"We can, and we will." Liam raised his eyebrows and signaled to Thorbjørn, who was now standing in the doorway, to send in the first teams. With protective suits, masks, and hairnets, four officers entered. Liam quickly stood up and pushed Ole back into the sofa as he furiously tried to struggle to his feet. "You can wait here while we search your property, or we can take you in to the police station." Liam spoke in a neutral voice to calm the agitated man.

"What the hell is going on?" Ole said, now sounding a bit more subdued.

WOUNDS 295

"I'd like to talk to you about Rolf."

"Rolf?" Ole repeated in surprise. "What's that clown got himself into now? Wasn't it Jørgen you wanted to talk about last time you were here?"

"Does Rolf often get into trouble?" Liam asked.

"That kid's always been a hothead."

"What makes you say that?"

"Yeah, it's just . . . well, you know . . ."

"No, I don't know, but I understand that he lived here as a child. That he grew up in this house?"

"Yeah, I let him stay when his mom wasn't able to take care of her own offspring."

"Are you related?"

"He called me uncle, if that means anything these days. His mom is my half sister. She was a wild one." Ole sniffled hard.

There were shouts from the courtyard. Liam looked out the window as Thorbjørn came rushing down the stairs. It was the dogs that had marked him. A police officer came rushing in. "They've found Dybbøl's car. It's parked next to a warehouse along with a Volvo station wagon."

CHAPTER

45

DYBBØL WAS COLD to the core. She wrapped her arms around herself and rocked back and forth in a futile attempt to calm herself down. Softly, she called her daughter's name. "Zenia, my little darling!"

She had screamed and begged when Rolf lifted Zenia's bloody body from the depression in the floor. She had asked that he take her instead. Abuse her. She had promised him money. She'd tried to convince him that killing her daughter would not change his grief. "Grief doesn't go away," she had desperately tried to explain.

"No," he had said, "but it feels better when someone is held accountable. And your daughter needs to be held accountable. You need to be held accountable. All of you need to be held accountable. All of you who hurt my girl."

"What is it you want from us?" she had shouted, and she had wept with despair when he had laughed his creepy little laugh and replied in an almost gentle voice that he wanted them to suffer. He wanted them to feel what it felt like to break into a thousand pieces and be pushed to the

WOUNDS 297

point where it felt like a liberation to throw themselves in front of a regional train.

Zenia would not survive. Dybbøl herself would not survive. She had no doubt for a moment that Rolf meant every word he said and would do whatever he could to see his plans through. She could see that he wasn't afraid, and she knew how dangerous he was.

She had pleaded with him as he carried Zenia across the room and threw her down hard on the floor by the door. She had pushed herself and the chair back across the concrete floor to follow her daughter with her eyes, but he had stomped angrily over to her and hit her so hard that, still strapped to the chair, she had toppled face-first onto the floor. Her lip was split, and she carefully placed her tongue behind her two front teeth, which had come loose.

"I will come back for you. Because I swear, I'll let you watch her die."

CHAPTER

46

D EA WAS SLIPPING in and out of unconsciousness. She had no idea where she was, but she was certain that her whole body hurt like hell. It stung when she tried to open her eyes, and it felt like her face was covered with a wet cloth. She was shivering with cold and felt confused. She couldn't remember what had happened, but she could recall the feeling of distress, isolation, and claustrophobia.

Her skin tightened and ached as the cold shivered through her. Her teeth chattered, and she gradually realized that the reason she was shaking so uncontrollably was because ice-cold water was slowly trickling down her body.

She tried to get up but was gently pushed back onto the bed she was lying on. The fabric over her face was carefully removed. She squeezed her eyes tightly shut to protect them from the bright light and tried to cover her face with one arm. Sweat was pouring out of her every pore.

"It's best if you lie still," said a voice.

"It's so cold in here," she croaked with stiff lips. Her throat burned when she spoke, and she couldn't help but

WOUNDS

whimper in pain when the stranger's hands gradually moved her around. Dea tried to focus. The lamps. The cold water. The blue suits. The face masks. "Hospital?" she asked hoarsely.

"You are in the hospital, yes. You have suffered from severe burns, which is why we are now cooling your body with cold water."

She nodded. "How long?"

"We've been at it for about an hour, and we'll keep going until you're not in so much pain anymore. Cold water is the best treatment for now. You've been unconscious, but now we've given you some painkillers."

Dea closed her eyes. She had never been so exhausted. "Rolf?"

"What?" the voice asked.

"What happened?"

"I'm afraid I don't know anything about that. I'm just looking after you."

CHAPTER

47

"DO YOU HAVE a car?" Liam asked. He had run back to the main house and stood breathlessly in front of Ole, who was still sitting on the sofa with one leg stretched out in front of him. He seemed both angry and confused, and he snorted in offense before answering.

"Yeah, but I don't use it anymore because of my leg. Now I use shuttles to the hospital twice a week. It's a hell of a firm with those shitty drivers . . . you can never count on them—you make an appointment and then . . ."

Liam interrupted him. "Do you remember your car's registration?"

Ole looked put out; he obviously didn't like being interrupted. He thought about it with a look of importance and shook his head. "Uh . . . YD 47 . . . no . . . 3 . . . No, it's gone, but it's an old jeep. One of those Land Cruisers. It's green with a white roof." He fell silent and tilted his head slightly. "Why do you ask? What do you need my car for? Is it the road tax?"

Liam held up a hand to stop him. "Where are the keys to the car?"

"The keys?"

Liam could see something happening in the old man's eyes. He had a wary and sly expression on his face, as if he was afraid of saying something that could get him in trouble.

"The keys," Ole repeated, shrugging slightly. "Well, they're in the workshop in the glass jar on the windowsill. Everyone here is allowed to use the car, so if the keys are in the jar, you can just help yourself," he explained reluctantly.

Thorbjørn had been listening from the door. He had disappeared without Liam noticing and reappeared shortly after, announcing that there were no car keys in any jars. "And we haven't found the car either."

Just then, a message appeared on Liam's cell phone. He read it and hurried to drag Thorbjørn out of the living room. "They've found Dybbøl and her daughter. They're down in the old tomato packing hall. We need two ambulances out there straightaway."

* * *

Liam and Thorbjørn ran along the lit greenhouses of the tomato nursery toward the far end of the grounds, past the tall silos and several smaller buildings until they reached the disused packing hall. Liam gasped as he entered the brightly lit room and saw his boss slumped on the concrete floor next to an overturned chair. A blanket was draped around Dybbøl's shoulders, and as he got closer, he could see Zenia lying on the floor in front of her.

He walked hesitantly toward them. A police officer came by with two blankets, which Dybbøl carefully spread over her daughter's naked and mutilated body while she spoke to her incessantly with love and reassurance. She told

302   SARA BLÆDEL AND MADS PEDER NORDBO

her that it was all over and that an ambulance was on its way. She repeatedly reassured her that she was safe and that Rolf could not hurt her any more.

"Where is he?" he asked.

Dybbøl didn't take her eyes off her daughter as she silently shook her head and said almost inaudibly that he had disappeared.

Zenia lay motionless, staring up into the bright fluorescent lights. Tears flowed freely from her eyes, and every now and then, she would grab her mother's hand and hold it tight.

Liam squatted down next to his boss and put a hand on her shoulder. Dybbøl turned her face toward him with a stiff movement and looked long and hard into his eyes with a broken expression. Then she slowly wrapped her arms around his neck in an embrace and clung to him as she sobbed. Liam waited and then gently asked if she could tell him what she had experienced.

Dybbøl pulled away and wiped her face with her sleeve. Then she pointed to the recess in the concrete floor and told him in a delicate voice that Liam had never heard her use before how her daughter had been lying there when she arrived. She told him about the message, about how she had thought it was from Zenia. "I should have known it was him," she said. "Not that it was Rolf—I would never have guessed that—but I should have been prepared that it could be a trap." She looked away for a moment. "I was so determined to get Zenia. I was so relieved. I was trying to reach you." She leaned her head heavily on his shoulder.

"If you hadn't driven out here, we might not have found her alive," Liam consoled her, listening as she explained what had happened.

"He wanted me to sit here and watch Zenia suffer and die. He's going after all of us. All of us who didn't help his daughter back then. And he's succeeded, Liam. He's almost there.

"He described it as 'a bonus' that Monika le Fevre crashed her car on her way to the police station to deliver the envelope with the threat he had left for her. He delivered it to her because he wanted to use her as a messenger. He wanted to make sure the message reached us. Me. It sounded like he was disappointed that it took so long to find Lise Bruun in our boathouse. He wanted to make sure we understood the message when he placed Jørgen Andersen at the inn in Verninge, but we didn't understand it because we hadn't received the envelope back then. We only got it when Dea went to the garage."

Liam nodded in understanding, even though Dybbøl's explanation seemed somewhat garbled. They would have plenty of time to talk things through; he didn't need to know all the details right now.

Dybbøl turned to her daughter again. She gently stroked Zenia's hand and sat like that for a while before continuing to speak. "I feel so sorry for Dea; she seemed so in love and happy, and then that bastard took advantage of her. I didn't think she'd find love again after what happened to her husband. How is she taking it?"

Only now did Liam realize that Dybbøl had no idea what had happened at Rolf's farm. He quickly told her about Annette Villadsen, whom they had found in the room with the disgusting couch, and about the oven that had been lit when they turned on the mains switch to search the abandoned factory.

"So, Dea . . ." he began, stopping to compose himself. "Dea is badly hurt. She was in the oven." He explained how she had been flown by helicopter to the burns unit at Odense University Hospital. "Luckily, plastic melts at low temperatures, so the heat in such an oven doesn't exceed a hundred degrees Celsius, but it's also a lot for a human body to stay in for a long time, and the heating elements in the oven gave her severe burns."

He remembered a time when Helene had lured him into a sauna. The temperature had reached 110 degrees Celsius, and after seven minutes he was ready to throw himself into an ice bath and stay there for the rest of his life. He didn't dare think about how unbearable it must have been for Dea to lie in the confined space and be cremated alive. Had it been twenty minutes? More than that? Less? He really didn't know.

"Oh," Dybbøl said quietly. "I thought she had gotten away."

"Rolf couldn't have known that the oven would be turned on. It happened when we started a search out there and wanted the lights on. I think it was more likely he wanted to make sure she was well hidden away while he came out here to meet you."

"Yes," said Dybbøl, and nodded. "Then he could go back and complete his mission. It was Dea who took the report when Julie's mother contacted the police. He told me he'd been reading the old reports. It was Dea who decided that the report should not be passed on to me, even though Annette Villadsen had explicitly asked for me by name."

CHAPTER

48

D EA HAD BEEN moved to a hospital room and had
dozed off. She had no sense of time, didn't know how
long she had been under the trickling water. The light hurt
her eyes; her body felt heavy, and her mouth was so dry it
hurt her throat.

She swallowed with difficulty. Her throat felt like
sandpaper.

She sensed someone sitting by her bed, but she couldn't
bring herself to open her stinging eyes to check.

"Dea!" A gentle voice called her name. "It's okay . . .
You're safe now . . . Look at me."

Dea concentrated on her voice. She carefully tried to
open her eyes in a way that hurt as little as possible. Next to
the bed sat a woman in blue clothes.

"Do you remember your name and social security
number?"

Dea looked around. There was an IV in her left arm.

She tried to focus.

306   SARA BLÆDEL AND MADS PEDER NORDBO

"Dea Torp," she said, and added her social security number.

"I'm Stine," the nurse said. "You were brought in to us about four hours ago with severe burns over large parts of your body. Mostly first- and second-degree burns, but in some places you have third-degree burns. You were and still are severely dehydrated, and that's the primary purpose of your IV."

Dea nodded and listened as the nurse told her that they would keep her topped up with painkillers for some time to come.

"I'd like to talk to my daughter," she said. "It's important that I get hold of her so she knows what happened." She missed Katrine like never before. The thought that she had been on the verge of losing her life without having reconciled with her daughter was unbearable. She longed to see her so they could agree that it wasn't worth falling out over something as trivial as the age difference between her and Rolf. Or anything else, for that matter, she thought. "Do I have my cell phone?"

"You didn't bring anything with you when you were brought in, but I can contact your daughter when I'm done fixing your burns."

Dea felt woozy. She wanted to close her eyes and fall back to sleep.

"I want to talk to her now," she said, struggling back to the surface. She gritted her teeth and tried to sit up. Her thoughts revolved around Rolf. The sudden change in his demeanor when he had told her to pack her things and leave. She remembered that she had been hit on the head

WOUNDS 307

but didn't understand the connection. "My daughter," she said again. "I need to talk to her."

"Shhh," the nurse reassured her, placing her hand on top of the sheet. "All this effort is not good for you."

Dea pushed the nurse away and struggled to sit up again. She watched the nurse attach a needle to the IV and felt a calming sensation spread through her body instantly. She closed her eyes and surrendered to sleep.

CHAPTER

49

THE JEEP WAS wanted everywhere. Patrols were sent out to Rolf's address, and a helicopter circled the area between the tomato nursery, Odense, and the highways. The message had gone out to all police districts. The intense police hunt was also shared in the media, which asked the public to come forward if they saw the green Land Cruiser. The call was followed by a recommendation not to contact the driver of the car, as he was considered extremely dangerous.

All resources were deployed, and they would keep looking until they found him, Liam assured Dybbøl. He was in the ambulance when Zenia was picked up. His boss still had the gray blanket wrapped around her shoulders. Liam had managed to get hold of Søren Dybbøl, who had driven directly to the Trauma Center, where he would be waiting when they arrived. Now Liam patiently tried to go through with Dybbøl what had happened in detail since she had arrived at Ebbe and Astrid's tomato nursery. They were both sitting up front with the driver, who was approaching Odense at full speed while the paramedic in the back took care of Zenia.

WOUNDS   309

"Did he say anything else?" Liam asked, hoping that Rolf had revealed something about his plans that would help them in their search. "Did he mention anything or anywhere in particular?" But Dybbøl just shook her head.

He kept reminding himself that Rolf didn't know what had happened at the farm since he left it to meet Dybbøl. He couldn't know that they had found Dea and Julie's mother out there and that they had both been taken to the hospital. He would be back; Liam had no doubt about that. Besides, Ask was still locked in the back hallway, so Liam had decided to postpone the forensic investigations and instead escape in an attempt to lure Rolf back.

He had coordinated with his people to get them to keep their distance while monitoring the residence and to call for backup as soon as Rolf showed up. No one was to go in alone. He would join them as soon as he had delivered Dybbøl and her daughter at the hospital and had checked on Dea.

Dybbøl was out of the ambulance the moment it stopped in front of the wide glass doors of the Trauma Center. Liam saw her husband running toward them. He stayed in the background as they embraced and Zenia's stretcher was lifted out. The parents walked on either side of their daughter as she was wheeled into reception. Liam stood and watched them disappear behind a sliding door that slowly closed behind them.

* * *

"She's sleeping, so you can't check on her right now," a nurse announced, and she was adamant, even when he pulled the investigation card and said it was imperative he see her. He also tried to say that he was one of her closest friends. But that didn't help either. He had to come back, she said.

Liam stood in the hospital corridor, wondering if anyone had even bothered to contact Annette Villadsen's relatives. He walked out to the elevator while he called Piil.

"Her brother is on his way," the IT investigator announced. "He lives in Nyborg. I got hold of him shortly after we sent the ambulance."

He was about to thank her when she continued: "I've taken the liberty of requesting police surveillance in front of Dea and Annette Villadsen's hospital rooms without discussing it with you first. I heard over the police radio that he had escaped from the farm, so . . ."

"Thank you," Liam said quickly, noting again that she was worth her weight in gold. "I'm going to head to Monika le Fevre's room now and agree with the officer sitting with her that they're going to run a four-hour shift rota. Can you get Lene Eriksen to coordinate that staffing is allocated for this?"

"Copy that," Piil replied, before explaining that she had started a trace on Rolf's phone. "I haven't gotten access to the mast information yet, but I wonder if it's turned off and left somewhere where it won't help us anyway?"

"Yes, it probably is," he admitted, studying the large information board to locate department N2. He stood for a moment, waiting for the elevator. Then he turned on his heel decisively and headed back to the burns ward. Even before the ward door had closed behind him, he had pulled out his badge and walked down the empty hospital corridor with it as a shield in front of him. He found her in ward eight.

Dea lay perfectly still, sunk deep into a white pillow. The skin on her face was deep red and shiny, and small blisters had formed on her forehead. She was asleep. Liam sat down in the chair by the headboard and watched as his colleague breathed in shallow little puffs. Her body was covered with a sheet, but her hands and arms were bound with gauze wraps.

He became heavyhearted and suddenly very aware of everything he had lost when Helene kicked him out. Life was so vulnerable, and what you thought would always be there, you suddenly risked losing. He stood up, walked over to the sink, and pulled a paper towel out of the holder. He thought for a moment, then drew a matchstick man and wrote: *See you later. L.*

He had just stepped out into the hallway when the nurse from earlier came out from another room. She was about to say something, but he raised his arms in surrender and, with an apologetic look on his face, ran down to the elevator.

Neurology ward N2 was on the tenth floor. Liam skipped the stairs and waited patiently for the elevator. He texted Thorbjørn to ask him to come by the hospital and pick him up when he drove back from the tomato farm. Liam would visit the ground floor store and buy them coffee and a couple of sandwiches. *Buy some chocolate too*, his colleague wrote back, announcing that he would be there in five minutes.

Up on the tenth floor, Liam immediately spotted the screen set up down the hospital corridor next to the back room where Monika le Fevre had been transferred. He greeted a nurse coming out of the kitchen with a pitcher of

312   SARA BLÆDEL AND MADS PEDER NORDBO

lemonade and a stack of clean glasses still steaming from the dishwasher.

He had previously wondered if one guard in front of the room was enough or if he should order two guards for each of the three guarded rooms for the duration of the intense police hunt. Conversely, it seemed that it was the abuse that Rolf was preoccupied with. The disfigurement and the pain. The suffering and fear. Death didn't seem to really interest him. One guard was enough, he decided. It was highly unlikely that Rolf would dare to show up at the hospital to further torment his victims.

Liam had made it all the way into the room before he realized there hadn't been a police officer behind the screen outside the door. He looked around in confusion, only to realize what he already knew deep down. The room was empty.

* * *

"Where is Monika le Fevre?" With quick steps he was at the nurses' station. Some gown-clad nurses and doctors sat on the other side of the glass around a table. There were thermos jugs on the table, and a peaceful Sunday atmosphere reigned.

The nurse at the desk looked up at him.

"I don't comment on our patients," she said dismissively. Liam pulled out his badge again and introduced himself. "Deputy chief inspector. I'm the one who initiated the police protection; she's not in the back room as agreed. Where is she?"

She studied the badge carefully and let her gaze slide up to his face inquisitively before nodding.

WOUNDS   313

"She was taken to safety," she said.

"Safety where?" Liam stared at her. "Where's the officer who was stationed by her room?"

She seemed confused.

"I don't know; I think he was relieved. I was just told that Monika had to leave the ward. He borrowed a wheelchair, and we showed him to the bed elevator."

Liam turned and started running down the hallway while calling Thorbjørn. "We have to go right now."

CHAPTER

50

DYBBØL CRIED AND leaned into Søren. "He wanted to kill her," she sobbed. "He wanted me to watch her die. And he wanted to enjoy it."

She was wearing white hospital clothes. Her soaked clothes had been put in a bag. She had told the young woman who had brought her clean clothes that she didn't want to take her old clothes home. She didn't want to take anything home that would remind her of what had happened. "Not even the car," she had said to her husband.

"We'll look into it," he replied, and pulled her closer to him. They had handed Lady over to a police officer who had taken her to the Odense Animal Hospital, where they promised to call as soon as they had examined her. Søren had already spoken to them once, but they'd just started cleaning the wounds.

Zenia had been taken directly to the examination room. Dybbøl had been told that right now they feared the wounds had become infected. Their daughter was dehydrated, she had been starved since her disappearance, and she was suffering from hypothermia. Dybbøl had also been told that a plastic surgeon was going to look at the wounds and decide whether skin grafts were needed.

The door opened, and a masked doctor in a white coat approached them. Both Dybbøl and Søren stood up quickly.

"Your daughter is asking for you," he said, and motioned for them to follow. They were both dressed in thin coveralls, hairnets, and face masks. "The operating room is being prepared. Her wounds are completely open, so we're protecting her from bacteria."

Dybbøl prayed her daughter would be okay as she thought about the dirty hole Zenia had been in. And of all the bacteria and filth that must have found its way into her body long ago.

She was lying with her hands folded on the cover, looking toward the door, when they entered. She looked so small, Dybbøl thought. She was her little child again.

"I'm sorry," she whispered quietly as Dybbøl leaned down and kissed her on the forehead. "I had no idea what I was doing. I didn't mean to hurt her; I just . . ." Her eyes were wide open, vulnerable and yearning for forgiveness.

"Shhh." Dybbøl hushed her and gently stroked her cheek. "Of course you didn't, my darling," she said as Søren agreed. "Of course you didn't!"

CHAPTER

51

LIAM RAN WITH long strides toward Thorbjørn as soon as he saw the patrol car. He ripped open the passenger side door. "Drive!" he shouted, prompting Thorbjørn to hit the accelerator.

"Where the hell do you want me to go?" Thorbjørn slammed on the brakes, throwing them both forward. He turned to Liam and put a hand on his arm. "What's going on?"

Liam closed his eyes for a moment, then pulled himself together. "Rolf has Monika le Fevre," he said. "It's possible he's taking her out to his own farm, but I think he's on his way to her house. If we try to think like him, it all started in Monika's workshop. My guess is that he wants it to end there too."

"How big is his lead?" Thorbjørn asked. The siren wailed as he swung into the sparse Sunday traffic and headed for the artist's workshop on the outskirts of the city.

"He probably drove straight from the nursery to the hospital. It didn't take him long to convince the staff there that he needed to take Monika to safety. He had his badge and probably sent the officer off with a message that there was a change of shift. He also had a police radio in his car. He must have been listening in to know where le Fevre was."

Thorbjørn nodded. "Then he also knows that we have people out at his house."

"No," Liam said. "I coordinated with Piil on the cell phone and asked her to send a message over the radio that we were done out there. But he can follow the search, and of course he'll avoid the routes where the road department has cameras up."

"Shit!" Thorbjørn hammered the steering wheel and swerved around two tourist buses while Liam called Piil.

"We need backup on standby at Monika le Fevre's farm." He briefly filled her in on the situation. "No communication via police radio. No information or comments to the press. We're going dark from here on in."

"How sure are you that he drove out there?" Thorbjørn asked, his eyes glued to the road.

"I'm not fucking sure," Liam admitted. "It's just a hunch. A logical assumption." Something struck him, and he grabbed his cell phone and called Piil again. "Send a patrol out to le Fevre's parents. Tell them what happened and have someone stay with them. We don't want to risk them hearing anything from the hospital and maybe showing up at Monika's workshop."

"Roger that," Piil replied, and then she was gone again.

* * *

There were no green Land Cruisers in Monika le Fevre's courtyard. Nor was there any sign that anyone had been in the house recently. A mound of brown autumnal leaves was piled in front of the front door. Again Liam called Piil, who was annoyed that they couldn't use the police radio. "Negative," he said. "We're going in. Have backup ready if we need it."

"Copy that."

Thorbjørn had pulled up behind the barn so that the patrol car wasn't visible from the road. The trees in the driveway blocked his car from view from the larger road leading toward Tommerup and Verninge. He got out of the car and stood for a moment, drawing air deep into his lungs. Then he remembered that Rolf could also have chosen the inn where he had placed the body of Jørgen Andersen. It was closed and abandoned and still cordoned off after the site investigation, and Rolf knew all about that.

"How far is the Verninge Inn from here?" Liam asked.

"About fifteen minutes by car." Thorbjørn pointed in the direction of the inn. "Do you want me to drive over there and look out for the car?"

"No," Liam said. "We're both staying here. You take the barn; I'll take the workshop. Once we make sure he hasn't left her here, we can drive over there."

They went around the back of the farmhouse. All the windows were dark, and there was no sign of life. Liam crossed the courtyard and pushed open the gate to le Fevre's workshop. He had seen pictures of the workroom after the search that had been conducted out here. He knew about the den and the extra room where the fur was dried before the animals were stuffed. He shined his cell phone flashlight around to avoid attracting attention if Rolf approached. No one was around. He moved a little farther into the workshop. For a moment he thought he could see a faint light at the far end of the room and cautiously crept closer. He turned off the cell phone light and kept his hand on his gun.

The first thing he saw when he entered the workshop was a wall with seven lights mounted on it. Six of them were switched off and pointed to the ground, while the seventh and middle one was switched on and pointed horizontally out into the room like an operating lamp. Liam followed the cone of light with his eyes, and then he saw it. Monika le Fevre lay motionless and stretched out on a metal table on wheels. Her wrists and ankles were tied to the table with zip ties, and her upper body was exposed.

Liam quickly drew his gun and spun around, but the room was empty. He walked sideways and slowly toward le Fevre, scanning the room with his eyes. She lay with her eyes closed. He leaned forward, placed two fingers on her neck, and was relieved to feel a faint pulse. He took out his phone to call Thorbjørn. "Catch!" a voice shouted behind him, and before he could turn around, he was hit by a hard blow to the back of the neck that threw him to the floor. The phone flew out of his hand and he lost his grip on the gun, which slid across the polished concrete workshop floor with a scraping metallic sound.

He tried to raise his head, but was struck again and momentarily lost his sense of vision. Liam fumbled for the gun and crumpled as a kick hit him clean in the stomach. He lay still for a moment, gathering his strength and trying to judge the distance before leaping off the floor. He stood facing the dark room, his eyes frantically scanning the space. Then he grabbed an awl from the workbench and began to move silently to a stack of tall crates for cover. Then the shot rang out.

It hit him in the right side of his chest, sending violent waves of pain through him. He sank to his knees, unable to see or hear Rolf, not knowing if he was still in the room. He pressed his left hand hard against the wound and felt the blood draining too quickly between his fingers. Then Rolf began to speak.

"Did you know that le Fevre refused to back up my daughter when she came to her for help? She let a sixteen-year-old girl take the blows while she herself cowered in hiding. Did you know that? Did you read the police report? Because it's all there."

He snorted.

"Now she gets to end up as one of her own works." His voice had suddenly taken on a bright, playful quality.

"There are police everywhere, Rolf! You won't get away from here."

"Let's see," he replied.

Liam had spotted some old garden tools on the other side of the crates. He cautiously walked farther forward.

"Why would I want to escape?" Rolf continued in the darkness. "I'll never be able to live with what happened to my daughter. And now I'm making sure that those who hurt her can never live with it either. And that's why it's all been worth it." He let out a small, unconvincing laugh. Liam shuddered.

There was a rustling at the back of the room, and Liam moved again to face the sounds. His chest burned, and he felt like he couldn't breathe properly. He gasped for air and began to speak with difficulty. "You weren't there for your

WOUNDS

daughter," he said tentatively, and waited, but nothing happened. He had to provoke Rolf so he could keep a conversation going with him until Thorbjørn hopefully came to his rescue soon. He must have heard the shot, he thought.

Liam cleared his throat and decided to walk the plank. "If you had been there for Julie, she might not have committed suicide. You could have looked after her. But where were you? Why weren't you there?"

The blow came out of nowhere. Liam was completely unprepared and was hit with such force that his head slammed straight into the wall. Rolf had been standing closer than he had expected.

"Shut the fuck up," Rolf snarled. "Don't you dare judge me. You don't know shit!"

"But apparently you have the right to judge others?" A new blow made him lose his vision once more.

"And Dea!" Liam continued, spitting blood on the floor. "You're a pathetic man."

"You know nothing!" Rolf shouted with madness in his voice. "She didn't even bother to pass on the police report to Dybbøl. It would have taken her five minutes, but it wasn't important enough, apparently."

Again, Liam picked up a faint rustle and hurried to continue talking.

"And now she's lying there with burns all over her body."

"What the hell are you talking about?" A tiny, puzzled crack into something human revealed itself in Rolf's tone of voice.

"I'm talking about her being badly burned after you left her in the workshop oven in the old plastics factory. She was flown to the hospital in a helicopter, and it's a miracle she's alive."

Liam felt the blood running from his chest and down his jacket. It had to stop now; he could feel he was close to losing consciousness. He saw a shadow slip past the window and mobilized the last of his strength to keep the conversation going.

"You knew we'd find her." He nodded toward the table where Monika still lay motionless. "Did you also know that we would find Annette in that room?" He paused for a moment. "Was it too hard for you to keep killing anyway, or were you just running out of time because you wanted to make sure you didn't miss your big finale with Dybbøl?"

He braced himself for another blow, but just then the door slammed open and a bright light flooded into the room. Liam hid his face in his hands and collapsed, exhausted, on the floor. Two shots rang out and Rolf fell forward, landing right in front of Liam. His eyes stared wide open and his mouth was twisted into an almost surprised smile.

CHAPTER

52

LIAM LAY WITH his eyes closed and felt the warmth of Helene's hand. He had a feeling that she had been sitting with him all night, but perhaps it was just his imagination. He knew he had had emergency surgery but had no idea how long he had been in recovery. What he did know was that she had been sitting by his bedside for a long time now. "His next of kin," as the doctor had called her before he was wheeled down to the operating room. The pain was constant and unbearable—he would soon have to ask for painkillers again.

He squeezed her hand and felt her stroke the back of his in the same way she used to stroke the children's when they were small. Laura and Andreas had been here; maybe they still were. He had been asleep and needed to sleep more but enjoyed them being here with him. He wanted to take it all in and not sleep until they left. But Helene hadn't left; she'd stayed.

There was a knock on the door to the small, single-occupancy room. "Come in!" He was delighted to hear Helene's bright voice.

He looked toward the door, expecting to see his parents, who must be worried, but to his surprise, Dybbøl walked through the door.

"Can I come in?"

He could sense Helene's reluctance, but she politely stood up and offered Dybbøl the chair she was sitting in.

"No, no," said Dybbøl. "I just wanted to pop in for a moment." She winked at Helene. "Dea says hi; I just came from her room. You guys have made this easy for me."

"What?" Liam said. His chest hurt when he spoke, and his mind was woolly and slow.

"Right now I have Zenia, you, and Dea on the same floor!" She brought a box of grapes and stepped up to his bed. Liam cracked a smile. The concern shone from her face, but she seemed like a completely different woman than the one he had followed in the ambulance when Zenia was brought in.

"How is your daughter doing?" he asked.

"Better. She spoke to a plastic surgeon today. They say you'll hardly notice it if she's careful to keep the scars out of the sun for the first few years."

"What about Rolf?"

Dybbøl handed the grapes to Helene. "He's dead," she said. "He died shortly after arriving at the hospital. It was a member of our task force who fired the shots. It was completely by the book. Several of the people who were there have already confirmed what happened."

Liam closed his eyes. He didn't want to think about what she called *by the book*.

"And Monika?" he asked, looking at her again. "How is she?"

WOUNDS   325

"Monika le Fevre is okay. Very shocked, of course. Both her parents are with her."

He heard her take a deep breath.

"Thank you, Liam!" she exclaimed. Dybbøl looked up at the ceiling and quickly blinked away a few tears. "I'll never be able to thank you enough, but I want you to know that Søren and I will always be deeply grateful to you for saving our daughter."

"I want to quit," Liam said without opening his eyes. It wasn't a sudden impulse; he had already made the decision as he lay on the floor of Monika's workshop and felt the blood seeping out of his body. He caught Helene's little gasp. He grabbed her hand and pulled her toward him.

"Quit?" Dybbøl repeated.

"The police," Liam continued, looking Dybbøl calmly in the eye. "I can't go on after this . . . I . . . I want to find a job where I can maybe do something preventive."

For a moment there was silence. He thought of Monika le Fevre. She had been rushed to the hospital in an ambulance right after him. Thorbjørn had gone with her, and in the ambulance she had told him that she would never make art again. She would close down her workshop and in the future only concentrate on things that brought joy to herself and her surroundings. Thorbjørn had smiled mockingly when he retold what Monika had said, but Liam understood her well. He felt the same way. He felt drained and just wanted to go home. Home to his family and to the life he had helped create. To the life that made him happy and really mattered.

"I had a feeling you might; it doesn't surprise me, Liam. But you can't quit," Dybbøl said, and the compassionate and vulnerable tone from before was gone. Now she was back to being Chief Constable Margrethe Dybbøl, who expected to have the last word. "The thing is," she continued, "I have resigned. I want you to apply for my job. Odense Police will need someone like you."

"I don't want your job!" Liam exclaimed vehemently, and turned to Dybbøl. "Yeah, sorry, I didn't mean it like that." He smiled wryly.

"I'm very sorry to hear that," she said. Liam felt Helene's warm hand in his.

"Then I would at least appreciate you staying in your position until my replacement is found and fully settled. They can't do without you."

"You have both Dea and Lene to hold the fort," he reminded her, still feeling a bit flattered.

"You are needed."

He ignored the last part and instead asked what she was going to do herself.

"First we'll have a big birthday party for Zenia. Then we'll buy a boat and sail out into the world for six months. Søren has taken a leave of absence. Zenia is taking a sabbatical. And then we'll see what happens after that."

She sounded excited and happy.

"I'll say," he said, smiling warmly at her. "But that doesn't change the fact that I've made up my mind. I'm not coming back! You'll have to find someone else to take your place."